"Some people float to the top and some sink to the bottom, but in the end we all get flushed."

D1737232

FLUSHY

Written by Lorenzo di Tonti

Disclaimer

This book is a pure work of fiction and not based on real life in anyway. None of the events in the book took place in real life. None of the characters in this book are based on real people. None of the ideas in this book are based on real ideas. Flushy is a complete work of fabrication and not based around or on a real company or real events in anyway. This book was written to be humorous, satirical and poke fun at some of the disruption in the insurance industry.

About The Author

When I was in second grade, I wrote a short story called "The Blob". The Blob was a simple story about my mother making me a school lunch and a young boy who forgot to take it out of his backpack. In fact, he forgot to take it out for the entire school year. There the lunch sat in the bottom of his backpack. While it sat there somehow the mold of the sandwich mutated the sandwich into an evil blood thirsty amorphous blob. After reading the Blob, my second-grade teacher called my mother and accused her of writing the story on my behalf. Apparently, a second grader at a public school couldn't use the word grotesque or amorphous. I mean, at the time I was rather insulted. But, that day, when my second-grade English teacher called me a liar. That is the day I fell in love with writing. I write for the passion of putting words on paper and bringing people a modicum of happiness in their day. I hope you enjoy my story.

Foreword

The Insure-tech industry has become an overnight sensation and darling of Wall Street. In the span of a decade the Insure-tech industry has become a Ten Billion Dollar behemoth. Leading the way is a fast up-start Insure-tech plainly named Flushy. In the blink of an eye, Flushy has become the most powerful Insure-Tech of them all. Flushy set out to up-end the entire insurance industry and become the world's first insurance carrier to be valued at One Trillion dollars. "<u>Flushy: A Tale of Corporate Satire in the Insurance Industry</u>" follows our main character Mike Allen through the ups and downs of his insurance career. Mike Allen gets easily wrapped up in the glitz and glamor of this niche, but booming industry. At Flushy, some people float to the top, some sink to the bottom, but in the end they all get flushed. Mike Allen tests that very proposition as a young money hungry insurance executive thrust into a prominent role in the corporate toilet bowl.

Table of Contents

Contents

Chapter 1: The Interview

Have you ever thought about what causes a train wreck? All man-made large-scale disasters have one thing in common, one singular thread that connects the sequence of events. One event, that if avoided, would prevent the entire accident from ever occurring. There is always that one decisive moment before every single disaster. There is always that one moment where someone had to make a decision. There is always that one moment that started it all. There is always that one moment that ultimately led to the disaster occurring. For me, I was starting to think that moment in my life was going to be the moment I met Bill Montrosian.

It's funny how opportunities in life kind of just spring up on you unexpectedly. For me, meeting Bill Montrosian was an opportunity of a life-time. When most people go to bed they dream of all sorts of things. When I go to bed, I dream of one thing. I dream of being rich. Go ahead and call it a lifelong obsession. Go ahead and call it greed. Go ahead and call it ambition. Go ahead and call it whatever you want. Because, for me, I call it my dream. I didn't have grand ideals, I didn't want to save the whales, I just wanted to be filthy stinking rich.

This was an opportunity for me to start my career off on the right footing. It was Monday morning and I found myself sitting in the lobby of small insurance agency. Mind you, at the age of Twenty-Two my experience with insurance agencies was rather limited. My experience with insurance was limited to overhearing my parents bicker at the dinner table. Believe it or not, at this point in my life, I can't say that I've ever even stepped into an agency before.

The agency was located smack-dab in the middle of the exotic and luxurious *West San Fernando Valley*. *Tap. Tap. Tap.* If it weren't for the loud thuds that followed my dress shoes, I probably wouldn't have even noticed the noise. I tapped my feet nervously waiting for the inevitably of those five words that typically prompted every interview, 'Mike, he'll see you now'. Monday was turning out to be just like any other typical Monday in the *SFV*, it was ten minutes past 9:00 a.m. and the thermometer inside the lobby was approaching 110 degrees. Part of the charm of the living in the *SFV* was waking up to the very familiar aroma of heat melting the asphalt. It was an acquired odor that only the locals could appreciate.

To offset my nervousness, I perused the various magazines scattered around the lobby. The kind of obligatory browsing that goes on in lobbies as people wait for an appointment. I couldn't help but be a little anxious. This would be my first interview as a post grad. In fact, this would be my first 'real' job and I didn't want to screw it up before it even began. I found myself looking down at my watch every 30 seconds or so. Aside from my normal neuroticism, I guess I thought that by constantly looking down it would somehow make the time go by faster. I showed up about 15 minutes early to the interview. Showing up early was one of my trademarks, people either appreciated that or hated it. 'Early is on time and on time is late', as my grandfather always used to say. I walked around the parking lot trying to convince myself not to back out. I think part of me was afraid. Mostly I was afraid that I'd end up being successful and not know how to handle it. The walking helped bring me back down to reality, I mean, I had to get the job first. See, for the last four years I'd been waiting tables to pay my way through an overpriced private college education. As luck would have it, waiting tables is how I landed this interview in the first place.

At this point time in my life, I've only known one thing and that was being a server. For the past three years I waited tables at an up-scale steakhouse in the *San Fernando Valley.* It wasn't glamorous, but it paid the bills. About two weeks ago, a group of business men walked in and sat down at a booth in my section. Through some minor observations and cross-selling I was able to impress them. Tools of the trade for someone who earned a living based on the generosity of others. It was abundantly clear to me that none of the men 'worked' for a living. They had the telltale signs of high privilege and high society. The mirror like polish on their dress shoes gave it away. Shoes don't tend to get scuffed unless you find yourself pounding the pavement. In my mind, that immediately ruled them out of being 'road warriors'. Which meant that most likely, they sat behind a desk all day making the big bucks. Part of me envied that about those guys, you know, the good life.

Turns out one of them ran a local insurance agency here in the *Valley*. I'm a people pleaser by my nature and that faithful night was no different. My goal wasn't to get a big tip, I played the long game. I looked at this gig as my ticket to the big leagues. My goal was to leave such a good impression that I wanted the guest to think, 'Man I gotta hire that kid.' Throughout the course of the evening I began to strike up some conversation. It started off with some rather innocuous table side conversation. You know how it goes, the monotonous kind of small talk you would expect from an upscale restaurant server. As the night progressed and more importantly the drinks refreshed, one of the patrons took the bait and asked me how a 'sharp' kid like me ended up waiting tables.

I explained my situation, which was to say that at the moment, I was 'vetting' my options prior to graduating. I was 'interviewing' with some of the most notable names in high finance, banking, etc.

Now, did they have to know that I struck out at every firm in town? Heck no! Okay, so maybe I was bluffing a bit. What did I have to lose? It was always a dream of mine to go into the world of finance. Who wouldn't want to be in the world of Finance? Who wouldn't want to make a *Six-figure* payday? Who wouldn't want their own slice of the *American Dream*? You get your name on a parking spot, a secretary and even a corner office with your own private bathroom. The only thing more exciting to me than gambling, was gambling with other people's money. I had to say that I was rather infatuated with the idea of success and success looked like a pin-striped suit with a corner office.

Turns out this guy ran one of the most lucrative and successful insurance practices in the *San Fernando Valley*, self-proclaimed of course. I was intrigued and he knew that my interest was piqued. I might as well of had a bummer sticker on my forehead that read, "Desperate Broke College Student". At the very least he was decent enough to invite a follow up meeting. So, he left me his business card and said, "Call me."

And that's how I met Bill Montrosian. I took his

business card and placed it in the stack of cards that I'd been collecting for the last six months. I didn't want to call him the next day and make it abundantly clear that I was desperate to find a job. The truth of the matter was, even though I had been working full-time to pay off school, I may have accumulated a small amount of student loan debt. I racked up somewhere in the neighborhood of $100,000 or so in student debt.

After six grueling months of attending job fairs, networking and interviewing, I found myself with one viable option on the table. I found myself here, in a rundown strip mall, staring at a door-knob, waiting for someone to open it. My anxiety was at a peak state. Mind you, it wasn't interviewing that gave me anxiety, not at all. Interviewing is easy. Anyone can fake being competent for Fifteen to Twenty minutes. It wasn't even waiting for the interview that gave me anxiety. What gave me anxiety was the idea of being successful. Success wasn't just a goal in life. Success was everything to me. Success was part of my identity.

The waiting room was quiet and small, not much

bigger than a prison cell. "What was behind that door? What waited for me beyond that door?", I thought to myself as I stared at the door. Somehow I thought aimlessly staring into the abyss of the door would produce some kind of magical insight. Just as I began to space out the phone rang at the receptionist's desk.

Ring, Ring, Ring!

At the same time the receptionist was equally entranced on her cellphone. Lost down an endless rabbit-hole of swipes and clicks, slipping away into the endless void of social media. The ringing barely phased her at all. She was staring down at her lap where she kept her phone. I imagine that's how she spent the better part of her day. She woke from her trance and jolted up from her phone. She sprang into action and answered the phone. "Yeah boss?", she asked in an uninterested tone.

"Uh-huh...", she responded.

I turned to her with my eyebrows raised in anticipation. I hadn't even realized it, but I rose out of my chair while staring at the door. Sweat dripped down my hands, I quickly wiped them off on my pants and hid them behind my back.

"He's sitting here in the lobby. Uh-huh... Yeah, uh-huh...", she said while hanging up the receiver.

The receptionist looked over at me and calmly said, "Mike, he'll see you now."

Just the five magical words I'd been waiting for. Butterflies swarmed my stomach with the prospect of landing this job. The receptionist flashed me a big smile and went back to trolling on her cellphone. Seconds later, the door swung open and this giant of a man stuck his head through the doorway. It was just the man I was waiting for; it was Bill.

He smiled and said, "Mike, nice to see you again!"

As soon as Bill opened the door, he was followed by a flurry of noise on the salesfloor. The salesfloor was a bustle of activity. The phones were ringing off the hook. People were clamoring on as if it were the last day to Earth.

"Great seeing you...", I replied sheepishly.

Before I could finish my response he interrupted and said, "Right this way Mike."

He held the door open with his left hand and motioned me over to enter with his right. As I walked through the door I was hit with the aroma of four decades of scarcely washed commercial carpet. I walked through the door and began following Bill to his private corner office. As we walked back, I was stunned by the condition of salesfloor. To be kind, it was far from what I had envisioned in my mind.

"What was I signing up for?", I asked myself.

On the journey through the salesfloor we traversed past about a dozen or so bedraggled salespeople. The salesfloor was dimly lit. Aside for the occasional desk lamp most of the room was supported by the resplendent glow of the computer monitors sparsely scattered around the salesfloor. As we passed each desk, I noticed that they were covered with sticky notes and mounds of paperwork. These desks were mostly held together with particle board, wads of duct tape and hope. As we passed the salespeople, there were about another dozen or so empty desks leading up to Bill's office door. The desks looked baron, nothing but disconnected phones, scraps of paper and seemingly wasted potential. It was like the elephant boneyard of former salespeople.

What caught my eye immediately were the over-sized, almost gag-gift sized whiteboards situated behind each desk. We were walking too fast for me to make any sense of the whiteboards, but I assume it was for tracking leads or sales. What really struck my eye was the jumbo old-fashioned *Sea Captain's* Bell next to his office door. The bell was mounted on the wall between Bill's office door and the breakroom. As we approached the back of the salesfloor, there was Bill's office. A substantial private office and on the door it read "The Boss" in a big bold letterhead. I was following Bill, more like acting as his shadow. He must've been *Six-Feet-Four* or *Six-Feet-Five* easy. If I were to guess, he probably weighed-in around *three hundred* pounds. Bill opened the door and said, "Come on in and take a seat."

"Thanks!", I said.

As I entered his corner office, I was a little taken a back. Bill's office was a throwback, an homage to the 1980's. It was like the land time had forgotten. The walls were covered with family photos, awards and almost endless insurance degrees. The walls were lined with 30-year-old wood-paneling, black marble floors and forest green wallpaper.

I started scoping out the room for some ice breakers. There's a lot for me to work with in here. I mean, maybe I could brush up some small talk by noticing one or two of the jazzy trophies in the trophy case. I've always thought that the best salespeople are kind of like detectives. They have to notice things other people don't and use deductive reasoning to connect the dots. What stuck out to me the most was the fact that Bill had all these old movie posters on the wall; Scarface, The Godfather, Goodfellas, etc. After standing in the middle of his office, I quickly grabbed a seat and sat down.

"I already made a good impression at the restaurant, just hear him out and hope for the best.", I thought to myself.

As I sat down, the chair wobbled to the right. I had to brace myself by grabbing the armrest. When Bill sat down, it was more of a crashing thud rather than a delicate placement. I could tell Bill was probably somewhat of a brute. He carried himself more like an ex-Navy Seal rather than an insurance agent. As he got situated in his seat, he immediately started looking at one of his computer monitors. Bill slowly rolled up his sleeves and started vigorously clicking on his mouse and pounding on his keyboard. I did a little double-take, I was expecting more of a captive audience for an interview.

"I just need to finish *this* up really quick. Give me a second or two.", he said dismissively.

He typed a couple of words and clicked a few buttons. I could tell that he was probably faking work to look important.

"*O-kay* all done.", he said.

It's not like he gave much of a choice. I think he was feeling me out to see how desperate I really was. Maybe he was trying to establish his perceived level of superiority. Or maybe he just had some work to finish up. Either way I was probably reading into the situation a little too much.

Luckily for me, I came prepared. I made sure to do extensive research on his company. I looked at online reviews, job boards, hiring sites, consumer sites and anything I could get my eyes on. Even after that level of preparation, nothing could've prepared me for what was about to come next. Bill clasped his fingers and looked over at me with a subtle intensity. He leaned forward in his chair and what he said next I will never forget.

"Let's say you're meeting with a client at their kitchen table. Our typical client is in their mid to late 50's, owns a house and has 2.5 kids. Odds are one of those kids is probably right around your age. What is some kid right out of college going to tell me about Life Insurance? What are you *Mike Allen* supposed to tell that client of any possible value? You're going to come into my house and tell me what exactly? You're practically just coming out of wearing diapers. What are you going to tell someone like that? Why should they listen to you? Why should they give you the time of day? What're you going to say that prevents them from just slamming the door right in your face?"

Bill sat back in his chair with the most self-congratulatory smirk I've ever seen. Clearly he'd practiced this speech before. Obviously he was thinking that I'd be stumped by his line of questioning. In all fairness to Bill, I was genuinely stumped. I've been on dozens of interviews at this point, but nothing compared to this one. I took a deep breath and leaned forward in my chair.

"What's stopping the client from protecting his family?", I asked.

Bill appeared irked by my answer. I wasn't quite sure how to take it. I mean, was that a good thing or a bad thing?

"You serious? That's your answer? You're going to walk into someone's home and tell them they don't care about their family? That's what you're going with?", he asked.

His tone noticeably shifted down, I figured he was stalling for time. It was clear to me that most people

Bill interviewed probably stumbled their way through his question. I decided to press forward, it was becoming more obvious that was unusual territory for Bill. Bill was selling insurance long before I was born, a fact I was trying to be well aware of during our interview.

"Well Bill...", I said an in irreverent tone. Bill crossed his legs and adjusted his lapel. He ever so slightly smirked which was laced with a hint of 'Gotcha!'.

"Is that a picture of you in Italy?", I asked with an inquisitive and inviting tone. I sheepishly pointed over to a photograph behind his shoulder. Bill turned his head and said, "It is."

"Ah. I've never been. Is it nice?", I asked.

"Let's put it this way. We like it so much that we spend two weeks of ever year there.", he said.

"Well Bill, I guess I just have one question.", I said while scratching my head.

Bill started tapping his fingers on his desk. He was becoming increasingly fed up with me stalling to answer his question.

"It seems like you enjoy traveling to exotic places, and based on your Trophy collection spend a considerable amount of time on Golf courses. What's getting in your way from protecting your family with life insurance?", I asked in a cagey tone.

My strategy was rather simple in theory. I probably wasn't going to win this battle, but that didn't mean Bill had to win either. He raised his eyebrows and clasped his hands together. Bill was noticeably perturbed and decided to take some time to mull over his response. He shook his head and unpredictably surrendered.

"Okay... I'm impressed. You're more clever than you look Mike Allen. I give you that. But, that sure doesn't mean you can sell life insurance. Life insurance isn't something you just go around and buy like a sandwich or shampoo. You don't just go to the store and buy it."

Bill paused again, but this time it was a longer more intentional pause.

"Do you understand what I'm trying to get at Mike?"

"I think so…", I responded.

"Mike, everyone who walks through that door has enthusiasm and thinks enthusiasm alone entitles them to sell insurance. That somehow passing an exam gives them the right to sell insurance. As if somehow just getting an insurance license and having a good attitude was enough to make it in this industry."

At this point Bill was monopolizing the entire conversation and I dare say starting to project a bit. It was clear by the wall of sales trophies and accolades that Bill had a distinguished track record. It was clear this was the horse to park my wagon behind. It was clear I had no clue what I was getting myself into.

"Do you understand? Get what I'm saying?"

"I understand.", I said followed by welcoming nod of acknowledgment. I couldn't help but just shake my head in agreement, like a trained seal waiting for someone to throw him a fresh fish.

Bill asked in a deflecting and slightly dismissive tone,

"Why should I hire you?"

I've always found it annoying to answer a question with a question, but found it useful during interviews.

"That's a good question. Let me ask you something Bill, what would you say got me to this point? Why am I sitting here?"

"You're quick on your feet, you're good with numbers and good with people. Those aren't easy qualities to find in someone from your generation."

Bill developed large overlapping circles of sweat under his arm pits. I wouldn't have noticed it, but he kept stretching his arms in the air.

"What kind of people tend to succeed in this position?"

Bill shot me this little grin and readjusted himself in his chair. He faintly started swaying back and forth in his all-black executive leather chair.

"What kind of people? People who tend to succeed in this position are people who don't bother me. People who tend to succeed in this position are people who don't give up. People who tend to succeed in this position learn to get things done. I hire people assuming that they know what they're doing."

I nodded my head in agreement. I've always followed a pretty simple rule for success in sales, and in life, open my mouth half as much as I listen. Bill paused and waited for me to say something.

"What do you think this is? What do you think we're doing here?"

What an odd question to ask someone during an interview. I wasn't really sure how to answer something like that. I was in uncharted waters and decided to proceed with a healthy amount of trepidation.

"This is all part of your selection process? Isn't it?"

Honestly I was a bit confused by the question. What was I supposed to say?

"*No. No. No. Mike, this* is the *de*-selection process. This is the part of the process that I use to weed out all of the qualified yet destined to fail candidates.

This is where I thin out the herd.", he said while making quotations marks with his fingers.

"Hmm..."

I was still grappling with his question.

"I get a lot of people with fancy college degrees, obnoxiously high Grade-Point-Averages, internships from fortune 500 companies, and all sorts of active collegiate experience. I get a lot of people that on paper are better than you."

"Oh..."

Bill was certainly expeditious with his critiques and generous with sharing his opinions. There are two ways to pull off a band aide, fast or slow. Clearly Bill's preference was to rip it off as fast as possible.

"*But*, and there is a but to that proclamation. What I've found, from my years of experience, is that none of that stuff means anything in the *real world*. What matters in sales, particularly in life insurance sales are the intangibles. The things you cannot measure easily. The things that tell me who you are as a person."

"The intangibles?"

"That's right!"

Bill took a brief pause to drink some coffee, out of what seemed to be a late 90's porcelain coffee mug. He clutched that coffee mug, almost like a Boa Constrictor latching on to an elk. Bill started this annoyingly loud slurp at the end of his sips. I wasn't really sure what to say, so I started looking around the room. He had half-empty coffee mugs littered all across his office. As he slowly lifted the cup, I noticed he had three distinctive gold rings on. His right-hand adorned a class ring, along with a pinky ring and a wedding band.

Bill slowly finished drinking his coffee and said, "Numbers on a spread sheet are just that, numbers. Data is just data. Any corporate moron can read a report and regurgitate the numbers on it. Ultimately, all that data stuff is completely meaningless without knowing the intangibles."

Bill commenced drinking his coffee a lot like he spoke, very meticulously and deliberately.

"Does that make sense?", he asked.

"It does", I replied in a dastardly tone of voice. In all reality, I had no clue what he was talking about. I was trying to retain my composure, but didn't have the slightest clue what he was talking about.

"What I'd like to know Mike is... What I'd really like to know from you is simple."

He slammed down the coffee mug on his desk. Bill started looking for something, I couldn't tell what. His inquisition completely hindered the conversation. I noticed he didn't have a coaster under his mug, so I started looking around for one. There was a stack of them hidden under a ream of papers on the corner of Bill's desk. I carefully sifted through the paper and grabbed one of the coasters. I dusted it off a bit, and handed it to Bill.

"Thanks kid. You're alight."

"No problem."

"Like I was saying. Wait, what was I saying?"

"You wanted to know something about me."

"Ah, yes! What do you think your biggest weakness is?"

"My… my biggest weakness…"

I can't say that I've ever given that question a lot of thought before. Bill went back to drinking his coffee, so I took some time to think about. One thing I hated was not having the answer right on the top of my head. Being quick witted always seemed to be my meal ticket in life. Naturally, I blurted out the first thing that popped in to my head.

"My greatest weakness is that I don't have much of a dimmer switch. I've got an on switch and an off switch."

Retrospectively, that sounded a lot better in my head.

"Yeah… I kind of picked up on that."

Bill chuckled a bit and slowly put down his coffee mug. He grabbed the top of the mug with his fingers and spun the mug around.

"Okay… *so*, here's the process in a nutshell. You're

going to go and get licensed, that way I know you're serious about working here. A license by itself has almost nothing to do with selling insurance", he said. Over the next few months I'd come to find out just how true that was.

"Sounds *easy* enough."

I mean, it's just insurance, it's not like we're talking about chemical engineering.

"Don't get *too* cocky kid."

Bill shook his head at me. I think he saw a lot of me in him. I don't know if that was a good thing or a bad thing. At least I had something going for me.

"At that point, if you get licensed, you can apply for the open position. Go on the website and apply like everyone else. If you can do all of that, then you're going to have to compete for the job. Obviously, the sooner you get licensed the better chances you have of getting the job. We're looking to hire someone within the next 30 to 45 days."

Bill extended his fingers and started spinning the brim of his coffee mug. He twirled the mug for a few seconds. I wasn't sure if it was a nervous tick or just his way of killing time.

"Just so you know, we've posted this position on your University's job board. So the people you might even know the other candidates."

Bill put down his coffee mug and started checking his gold plated wrist watch.

"Assuming I get past the other candidates, what then?"

"Great question! I like that you're thinking long-term, but you're getting way too far ahead of yourself. Once you've done *that,* then you'll need to take an online sales test."

"A... sales test?"

"Don't worry. It's probably not nearly as bad as you think. Plan on it being *much, much, much* worse."

Bill starting waning in and out of his dry humor. Bill had a certain way of making you feel right at home when he spoke. I mean, aside from the sinister overtones and the gaudy jewelry.

"The test is going to be approximately 200 questions. You'll have up to three hours to complete it. The test is mostly a combination of word, logic and math problems. Okay... that's it. If I never hear from you again, great. But, if I do hear back from you, I'll know. I'll know that you're serious about making something out of your life."

Bill stood up abruptly out of his chair. He towered over me from behind his desk. He offered his hand to me. We shook hands and he rushed me out of his office. That was it, that was my first interview.

Chapter 2: Accept, Reject, or Counter

About two weeks later I found myself sitting in that same lobby. There I was sitting on that same pleated couch. There I was sitting in the lobby waiting for a follow up interview with Bill. There I was gushing over the aroma of burnt asphalt and triple-digit temperatures. There I was pacifying that same feeling of anxiety churning away in my gut. There I was waiting to hear those same five magical words. Believe it or not, I crammed for eight-hours a day for that insurance exam. For two weeks straight, I ate, slept and dreamt insurance. In just shy of three weeks, I went from sniveling broke college student to an elite fraternity of licensed insurance agents. What I wasn't prepared for was that absurd 'sales' competency test Bill made me take.

"Bill will be with you shortly. He's just in the middle of wrapping some things up with an important client.", the receptionist said.

I shot her a quick thumbs up and went back to counting the dots on the ceiling tiles.

The receptionist giggled and asked, "Nervous much?"

I smiled and gave her another quick thumbs up. In all fairness to myself, this was only my first soiree in the working world.

"Well, don't be. Bill… Well, Bill can be a little intimidating at first. But, he's a real sweetheart once you get to know him."

"Really?"

"Really, really.", he responded in a bubbly yet somewhat dismissive tone.

She smiled and went back to trolling on her phone. I realized she was trying to put my nerves at ease, but the anticipation was really starting to eat at me. Did I get the job? Did I fail the test? What in the world happened? Bill left a lot for the imagine in his email.

"Do you enjoy working here?", I asked in a sheepish tone.

"Well, I've been here for almost *Thirty* years now."

"Thirty-Years!?!? That's some job security.", I thought to myself.

The receptionist was a tall slender woman with a smile a yard long and not one wrinkle on her face. Maybe smiling all the time was how she refreshed her youthful appearance.

"I've seen quite a few people come and go. I've seen quite a few people sit right there on that very couch. I've seen quite a few things in my time here."

Her face was buried in her phone. She was bewitched by the blue phosphorescent glow from a six-inch screen.

"What could be so entrancing? What captivated her attention in such a way?", I thought to myself.

Small talk aside, I needed a real distraction. So, I decided to really take in my surroundings. The lobby wasn't much larger than a standard eight by ten prison cell. Every time I squirmed, even a little bit on this pleather couch, it made a loud squeaking sound. It was the only thing that was able to draw the attention of the receptionist.

"This couch has seen some better days. It's got some miles on it, huh?"

"Oh, does it ever. That couch has some stories to tell."

"I can imagine. It must be at least ten years old?"

"Try *twenty-five*. Trust me, I still remember the store where I bought it."

Almost instinctively, she went back to trolling on her phone, almost like an ostrich sticking its head in the sand. All of a sudden the door swung open and Bill stepped into the lobby with his chest bowed out. He seemed to be in a good mood, at least he looked like he was in a good mood.

"Come on back Mike."

Bill paraded me through the salesfloor, like a child walking around the sandbox with his favorite toy. Occasionally patting people on the back as we headed over to his private office. As we walked back to his office, the mood on the salesfloor suddenly shifted. Something was clearly different, this time the salesfloor was quiet. I could hear the old commercial carpet crunching as I walked through the salesfloor.

As we walked through his office door Bill whispered, "Well Mike, I'm not going to sugar coat this for you…"

With one statement the entire life drained out of my body. The anticipation was really making me squirm. Bill pulled out a chair for me to sit in. I unassumingly plopped myself down in the chair across from Bill.

Bill seemingly noticed my squeamish demeanor and asked, "Are you okay? You seem to be sweating a lot…"

My face was flush and I could only respond by murmuring out, "Yup. Sure am!"

"Okay, well. Let's get down to business. We need to wrap this up a-s-a-p. I booked you back-to-back with the other candidate."

Bill gazed into my eyes and started slowly patting the tips of his fingers together. His composure was still and silent. Meanwhile, I was sweating bullets under and over my three-piece suit. Bill was steadfast in his commitment to make this meeting as awkward as possible.

"You know how important that test was right? I did stress to you, how important that sales test was, didn't I?", he asked me in a sultry tone. I couldn't even respond I just shook my head and anticipated the worst.

"Everything came down to you and this other candidate. Turns out you both attended the same university. His name is Lars. Know him?"

"Oh, yeah. I know Lars, we had a finance course together. He's a pretty smart guy."

I paused for a second. The one thing I knew about Lars was that he was super smart and I was, less than super smart.

"Are you curious about how you scored on the sales assessment?"

"Very…"

To say I was curious was somewhat of an understatement. I was chomping at the bit to hear the outcome. I pinned all my hopes on that stupid test.

"You scored... Well, you scored in the top *1 percent percentile.*"

"I did?"

"You did. Trust me, I'm *just* as shocked as you are Mike."

"So... that means... I get the job, right?"

"The test, the licensing, those are all really just formalities..."

"So... that means I get the job, right?"

"That's what I like about you Mike Allen, you don't waste any time. You get right to the point. Now, let's not get a head of ourselves quite just yet."

"Fair enough."

"Let's talk logistics."

Bill took a protracted and slow sip of his coffee.

"You'd start off as a Trainee. The Trainee program is about six months long, the time of the program depends on your performance. It's kind of a pass or fail program. You have six months to sell at least 10 life insurance policies in a 30-day period. If you can do that, then you can cut it."

"Okay, assume I make it past the Trainee program. Then what?"

"*Good question.* When you make it past the Trainee program, that's when the fun really begins. You have the chance of build-up your cash flow. You'll effectively be working for me, but really, in reality you're working for yourself. Technically as a "consultant", you make your own hours, all that matters is your quota."

"*Okay...* What happens if I don't make my quota...?"

Bill picked up his coffee mug and swirled it around a bit.

"Don't let that happen and you won't have to find out."

"Okay... Well, what kind of salary are we talking about?"

Bill leaned forward in his chair with his forearms implanted on the arm rests.

"I like that. Right to the point. When I built this business, just 35 short years ago, I had to do so purely on commission and sweat. No salary, no benefits, no nothing."

He took a second to adjust his wrist watch. Normally I wouldn't notice something so innocuous, but he had a giant gold wrist watch.

"What *we* like to do here is empower you to be your own boss. Think of this less like a job and more like a business opportunity."

I didn't know Bill well enough to know if he was being truthful or pulling my leg. Bill didn't strike me as the egalitarian type, so I took him at his word. For whatever that was worth, I had no clue.

"Be my own boss, I like it.", I thought to myself.

"Sounds good to me. Where do we go from here?"

"It's all rather simple actually. We start every Trainee off with a generous Base Hourly Wage plus a Bonus and a Commission."

"And after the Trainee Program? What happens

then?"

"The fixed part of your earnings, the minimum wage, becomes a draw."

"*A draw?* What's a draw?"

"A *draw* is a guaranteed amount of money that I'll pay you each month. Think of it this way. I'll pay you $1000 a month no matter what you sell. Whether you sell $1 or $1000, you'll get make at least $1000. The commissions that you earn you will keep once you exceed the $1000 per month in sales. Simple enough?"

"Sort of. I've never worked on commission before. How does it work exactly?"

"Every time I sell an insurance policy, I make around 100% in commission. That is to say, 100% of the first-year premium goes into my pocket."

"So, if I sell a $1000 policy, then I'll make $1000 in commission?"

"Slow down there Mikey. I said that when *I* sell a policy *I* make a 100% commission. When you sell a policy I get a cut of that. You know, for expenses, training costs and overhead."

Bill paused for a moment to assess my interest. He tilted his head to the side and raised his eyebrow.

"That way I protect my investment. My money, that is. I'm training you, putting a roof over your head and paying a guaranteed salary for a certain amount of time. That ain't cheap!"

"So... what happens if I don't sell at least $1000 a month? Would I have to pay back the difference?"

"Don't let that happen and you won't have to find out."

Bill started twirling his pen, it was a gold-plated Monte Blanco. The thing probably cost more than my car, more than my parent's first house. To be honest, this all sounded pretty good. To be honest, I didn't comprehend most of what he was saying. To be honest, I didn't care all that much. I just wanted a j-o-b.

"Mike, Mike, Mike. Let's not get buried in all the details. There's a lot of moving parts to this thing.

What I need to know is what kind of person you are. If you're in, then you start bright and early on Monday."

Bill stopped twirling his pen, he put it to the side of his desk. He treated that pen with gentility, probably a rare event from what I knew about Bill. I imagined he probably only took it out to impress interviewees.

"If you're not in, then you're just hogging up space and you need to leave."

Bill paused and waited for an answer. I mean, it's not like I had much of a choice here. I had *zero* other job prospects lined up. I took a few seconds to think it over, which turned into a few minutes. The silence must've been aggravating to Bill. He was beginning to fidget in his chair. His leather chair made this distinctive crackling sound every time he squired in his chair.

Crackle... Crackle... Crackle...

Bill stood up abruptly and stuck out his hand. I snapped out of my trance and stood up. Reflexively, without even thinking, I anxiously stuck my hand out. It's not like he left me with much of a choice, or I had a plethora of options waiting for me once I walked outside this office.

As I stood up, I said, "Glad to be on the team."

"Just remember one thing Mike.", he said as he grabbed my hand.

"What's that?"

"Chance only favors the prepared mind."

I slowly shook my head up and down in agreement. It sounded a lot like Bill listened to motivational speech at the airport this weekend and wanted to opine some of his wisdom on me.

"Remember that, and remember that well. If you show up to work unprepared, you will get fired. If you show up to a sales appointment unprepared, you won't get the sale. If you show up to an interview unprepared, you won't get the job. Show up prepared and your odds of success will exponentially increase."

"Sounds good to me Bill."

To be honest, I wasn't quite sure what to make of all that. Was that some kind of weird veiled threat? Was it his attempt at humor? Either way, I'd chalk it up to just good life advice. So, we shook hands. In retrospect it was more like a Boa Constrictor latching on to his next meal. Bill motioned me to the doorway that led back to the sales floor. I turned around and scurried to the door. As I opened the door Bill yelled at me.

"Don't forget to introduce yourself to the team on the way out!"

It was one of those yells that was kind of a suggestion, but really it was more of a demand. I turned around and shot him a thumbs up. He somewhat dismissively waved me away. I began walking past row after row of empty desks, one after another. Each desk was a relic of the past, kind of like a time capsule. To put it nicely, the office was decorated in a more rustic décor. It was clear to me that some of the furniture was probably purchased during the Carter administration.

"*Hey… hey you!*", someone shouted from the

salesfloor.

I stopped dead in my tracks and began to slowly look around the room. One of my biggest pet peeves was being called 'hey you', but I was new here, so I didn't mind it.

Standing directly behind me was Robert O'day. Robert was towering over me, probably standing close to seven-feet tall.

"Do you mind?"

I shrugged my shoulders a bit. I had no clue what he was talking about.

"You're standing in front of my desk. Come on kid time is money on this job."

I could tell he was kind of joking, but I acquiesced and moved out of his way. Robert swiftly jumped back into his seat, spun around in his chair and grabbed the phone. He rested the phone on his right shoulder and started drumming on the desk with his hands. Robert looked up at me from his tattered and decrepit desk chair with a somewhat curious gaze. He slowly put down the phone. I could see the wheels turning in his head. Or maybe he was just confused why I was still standing around like a lost kid at an amusement park.

"Ah. You must be the new guy!?"

Robert was thoroughly impressed with himself, almost as if he just found the missing piece of a jigsaw puzzle.

"Mike Allen, nice to meet you."

I always found the longest lasting friendships started off with an awkward beginning. The best way to make a buck is to make a friend.

"And you… are?", I asked.

"Robert is the name and sales is my game."

For some reason, I got the distinct feeling that Robert was a used car salesman. You know the kind, the kind of guy who smiled ear to ear with pearly white teeth.

"Nice to meet you."

Robert upsprung from his chair to greet me. He enthusiastically pointed over to one of the empty desks and asked, "See that Mike?"

"The desk? Yeah. What about it?"

"No, no, no. That's not just a desk. That is the 'elephant graveyard' of life insurance brokers. That is the 'Trainee' program. That is where dreams go to die."

"Ah…"

"A lot of great salespeople have started right over there and a lot of not so-great salespeople failed right over there."

Robert pointed with his thumb, kind of like he was gesturing to hitch a ride on the side of the road.

"Everyone starts off right over there, but eventually you work your way closer to the exit. See, the most senior life brokers get to sit closest to the escape route."

I could tell we would get along great. We both shared the same sense of dry humor.

"Ah… makes sense to me."

"I mean, at this point in the game everything better

make sense to you, because you don't know nothing yet."

"So… are you my manager? Or…?"

Robert tilted his head to the left and his expression turned to rage.

"Don't ever call me a manager, I actually have to work for a living."

I could tell that the abounding years as a crusty salesperson had thoroughly beaten the spirit out of Robert. To say the least, Robert was quite rough around the edges. Robert was an affable kind of person, but clearly he didn't pride himself in his appearance. He was wearing a tattered sports coat, blue jeans and a polo shirt. No of which at all resembled a matching outfit. The only thing more distracting than his outfit was his mangy facial hair. To be honest I didn't think much of Robert at the time.

"On Monday, you'll be sitting right over there next to me. I'm your upline. I'll be your trainer. *Assuming* you make it past day one, I'll be your trainer for the remainder of your Trainee program."

"Sounds good to me."

Robert grabbed the cup of coffee off of his desk and took started to chug what was left in the mug.

After he finished swallowing his Luke warm he asked, "By the way Bill wanted me to ask you, did you have a chance to wrap up your old job?"

"Wrap-up? I don't follow."

"What's the deal with that? You gonna quit or what?"

"I'll probably put my notice in over the weekend."

The truth is that I hadn't given it a second thought or even a first thought for that matter.

"I mean, aren't *you* millennial types all about that hashtag side hustle?"

"Respectfully, if I'm going to do this right. I should really just only focus on *this* and only *this*."

Robert didn't know this, but I tended to get distracted pretty easily. The last thing I wanted to juggle was managing two work schedules.

"*You* sure? Aren't you millennial types all about that side hustle?"

"Yeah, I'm sure..."

I felt this awkward pause in the conversation, neither one of us was fully committed to making eye contact. So, I decided to change the subject.

"What should I bring on Monday?"

"Just show up and I'll take care of the rest."

"Great. I'll see you next week."

I stuck my hand out for Robert to shake. We shook hands and he waddled back to his desk. I stood around for a second taking in my surroundings one last time. Robert made a loud coughing sound and cleared his throat.

"Kid, do I look like a GPS?"

"GPS?"

"Clearly, you're looking for directions. Well, the exit is right over there. You're taking up space. Get on out of here."

I guess that was my cue to exit. I hightailed it towards the main exit. This was the next big step in my life. This was my chance to prove myself. This was my big break into the world of finance. Maybe it wasn't 'high' finance. Maybe it was glamorous. Maybe it wasn't a hedge-fund. Maybe it wasn't an investment firm. Maybe, just maybe it was my chance to see what I was really made of.

Chapter 3: First Day of Training

Once again I found myself eagerly tapping my feet in anticipation, waiting for someone to let me into the office.

Tap... Tap... Tap...

This time was quite a bit different than the last time I found myself sitting on this super comfy pleather couch. The decades of worn-in pleather created a marshmallow like scaffolding to the couch. Today was my training day and I was determined to make a good impression. I once read that there are *Twenty-One* things a person should do on their first day of work.

There was a large black and white wall clock staring me right in the face. I was told to report into work at 9:00 AM on the dot. I didn't get the impression people around here showed up early to work. It was a quarter till nine and not a soul in sight, not even the receptionist. I prided myself in being the first person on a job-site and last person to leave.

To kill some time I decided to flush out some of the magazines. On the lobby coffee table there was a wide variety of magazines to choose from. Right as I was about to grab one, the door swung open. The door slammed against the wall, which was accompanied by a loud *thud.* Robert leaned in and peered over at the chairs, I had met him the week before, yet he didn't seem recognize me at all.

"Mike?"

Robert had an almost inquisitive tone. Had he forgotten me already? Little did I know he was blind as a bat without his glasses.

"Robert! Nice to see you again."

As I stood up from the chair, he motioned me over to come on back. I eagerly followed him back onto the salesfloor.

"Here's your desk. It isn't luxurious, but it's yours. For now at least."

On the desk there sat; a phonebook, a notepad, a ruler, and a telephone. He pulled the chair out for me.

"Here, grab a seat."

He made sure to pat the seat down to get some of the dust off. I clutched onto the chair and sat down, like a kid getting onto a rollercoaster for the first time. Robert grabbed the adjacent desk chair and pulled it over. Is there anything in this world more awkward than your boss sitting next to you while you work?

"Like I said last week, you'll be sitting next to me."

"Perfect. I've got a ton of questions for you Bob."

"*Woah!* Let's pump the brakes right there. You're way too new here to be having questions and don't call me Bob. My name is Robert."

He quickly stood up out of his chair and hovered over my desk. He planted his hands down on my desk and leaned in. His breath was arthrosis. I made a concerted effort to subtly hint to that effect.

Robert whispered quietly, "The only question you need to be asking yourself is how much money you want to make over the next 30 days."

I got the feeling he had a certain way of handling people like me, which was probably the same way he put out camp fires. Which is to say, to stomp them out. I couldn't blame him. Here I am asking questions when I should just shut up and listen.

"Roger that."

For a brief moment Robert expressed some tenderness with a feint smirk of acceptance.

"Every new Trainee here at Montrosian Insurance Partners gets a robust hands-on training experience."

What Robert was basically trying to say, is that you get your hands on a phone book and a telephone. Robert O'Day was my direct supervisor, but in reality, he was just another broker who had the misfortune of training a newbie. Robert had all the telltale signs of a grizzled veteran of the insurance industry. This guy had bags under his eyes that had bags under them. Robert had on all the gaudy jewelry, he really walked the walk and he talked the talk. This guy lived, breathed and dreamt of insurance.

I took a second to take in the room and see what my new place of employment had to offer. Looking around I could tell that most of these brokers were just one cup of coffee away from a panic attack. I glanced around to do a mental intake of my colleagues. No one had bothered go out of their way and introduce themselves, aside from Robert that is. I deduced that was probably due to the high employee turnover. What's the point of introducing yourself to someone who ends up leaving in two days?

After a thorough amount of voyeurism, Robert wrangled my attention back to the training discussion. He had been droning on for a few minutes while I was spacing out. Luckily enough for me, he didn't notice, or did and just didn't care enough to say anything.

"Day One of Training is rather simple. Today we're going to get you familiar with the phone. This phone is going to be your best friend for the next six-months. Our entire business revolves around your ability to contact as many people as humanly possible. Contacting them is the hard part, convincing them to buy life insurance is the easy part."

"Okay, great. So… I'm doing what exactly? Calling a bunch of people and asking them to buy life insurance?"

"*Woah! Look* at this guy! What a genius we got over here! Did you hear that fellas? This guy got licensed two weeks ago and now he's crushing deals."

Robert made sure to broadcast his sarcasm to the room. The rest of the brokers started golf clapping and howling like a bunch of hyenas. Robert wasn't shy and clearly found enjoyment in making a small spectacle of the training process.

"I'm glad that college degree really paid off your you Mike. I mean your powers of deduction are quite impressive. No, seriously. Have you ever heard the term dial for dollars? Smile and dial?"

"Smile and dial? Nope. Can't say that I have."

"The more calls you can make, the more money you can make. There are some Trainees who start here and somehow think that every call will mean they sell a policy. Somehow that every phone call they make, people are going to all of sudden be enlightened enough to buy 100% of the time."

He paused for a second, leaned back in his chair and stretched out. Robert took a big yawn and asked, "Does that make sense?"

"It does." I nodded in agreement. This was all par for the course, but I reminded myself it was just part of the training process.

"Today we want to introduce you to the concept of rejection. Rejection is the cornerstone of our industry. Think of this initial part of the training period as the feeling out period. While we're not going to talk about sales, we're going to stress test your resilience. Today we're going to see what kind of person you're made of."

Robert didn't have much of a bedside manner about him, but I could tell that his candidness came from a good place. Robert's clearly felt the need to be circumspect with building rapport.

I interrupted him and asked, "When will I learn about

the products?"

Robert was baffled by my question. A discernable look of concern coated his face.

"As we go through the training process, we aren't going to spend much time talking about the products. The life insurance process is tedious, time consuming and exclusive in nature."

"Exclusive? Meaning, what exactly?"

"Meaning that everyone can apply, but not everyone can qualify. It also takes a lot of time to figure that out. Really the best salespeople at the firm know the least about the products. What they know the most about is how people make purchasing decisions and what motivates people to buy. You can know next to nothing about the products and still be wildly successful, and to be honest the firm encourages that. I'd go as far to say that not knowing the products is a best practice at this firm."

Robert took a break from speaking to crack his knuckles. He outstretched his arms and let out a loud *CRACK*!

"You still with me Mike?"

"Yes, sir."

"Mike, you see that guy over there?"

Robert discretely pointed to one of the other brokers across the room. He didn't seem like much from the looks of it.

"Yeah... what about him?", I replied with some hesitation.

Aside from being a pocket protector on steroids, he seemed like the run of the mill insurance bro.

"That's Jacob. Today, Jacob is going to be your first lesson."

"First lesson?", I asked sheepishly.

"He's a walking-talking insurance policy encyclopedia. Look up the definition of thorough in the dictionary and they got a picture of that guy's face on it.

"Wow. He must be a great salesperson, right?"

Robert shook his head unamused.

"I think the last time he sold a life policy President Truman was in the Whitehouse. I mean, the guy couldn't stumble and fall into a sale if his life depended on it."

There was this subtle intensity about Robert, I wondered what about Jacob irked him. Before I could utter a word, he started up again, "Let me ask you something. Do you like talking to telemarketers?"

I spontaneously busted out laughing. What kind of absurd question was that? What in the world was I supposed to make of that?

"No, I can't say that I do. I mean, who likes talking to telemarketers?"

"No one does, but why do people do it?"

"I... I... have no clue."

"Newsflash kid, because it works."

Robert looked at me and repeated, "*Because it works.* You're going to be expected for first couple of weeks to make anywhere between 400 to 500 phone calls..."

"That doesn't sound too hard.", I interrupted.

In reality, I had no concept of how hard that would actually be.

"Four to Five hundred calls, per day."

"Oh…"

"Yeah, *oh* is right. Not per month, per day. Four-to-Five Hundred calls per day."

Robert took a second and gestured over to the phone on my desk. It wasn't fancy, but it would get the job done. The phone was a black touch tone corded phone, the kind you'd see in an old movie or at your grandparent's house. I could tell this phone, like this entire office, had probably seen better days. He paused and stared at the phone for a second, it was almost like he was having some kind of traumatic flashback. I started looking around the room for some kind of que. Robert was lost deep in thought, so I interjected myself back into the conversation.

"The phone…"

"The phone, *yes*, the phone! Today we're going to role-play some typical situations you might encounter while cold calling. The last thing I want, is for you to call people and make me look bad."

Robert stood up and stretched his arms out like a cat waking up from a nap. He took his hands and cracked his neck, and then proceeded to crack each finger individually.

"Let's pretend for a second. I'll be me and you be you. Call me up and ask me for life insurance."

"When, now?"

Role-playing was not my strong suit. I may have had a lot of tools in my tool belt, but role-playing was not one of them. I might have been quick on my feet, but I really didn't care for role-playing. In fact, the whole thought of role-playing left a queasy feeling in my stomach.

"No Mike, I want you to come back in two-weeks and then we'll role-play! What's the matter with you? Of course right now."

Robert was doing his best to suppress his laughter. I

wanted to make a good impression on my first day, but at this point I'd settle for not making an abject fool out of myself. It was trial by fire time and I had nothing to lose. What did I have to lose? I mean, besides my job. Robert picked up the phone and handed it to me.

"Well? What're you waiting for? Let's get going kid."

"So, did you want me to actually call you or...?"

"No, genius. Just pick up the phone and pretend with me."

Well, no time like the present.

Ring... Ring... Ring...

"Hello?"

"Hi. This is Mike Allen from---"

"*I don't care. Click.* Hang up. You fail."

Robert slammed the imaginary phone down and started laughed.

"What'd I do wrong?"

"That was truly awful, I mean just terrible. If you

hesitate in this business you die. Even for one moment."

"Thanks, I really appreciate your words of encouragement."

I smiled, shook my head and looked down at the desk. I wasn't used to failing so miserably and I didn't want to make a habit of it.

"No problem, that's what I'm here for. That's my job."

It seemed Robert was oblivious to my sarcasm or maybe he was now being sarcastic himself. Either way, I was off to a rough start.

"Start again."

"Robert I really don't see the point in all of this."

"Sweat saves blood. That's why."

"Sweat saves blood?"

"Yeah, it means if you don't practice for battle you end up getting slaughtered. Now, start again."

The way I looked at it, I was about to swim. Enough

dipping my toe in the pool it was time to jump in head first. Robert was trying to take me into deep waters and drown me, but I don't give up easy.

I decided to skip the ringing process and said, "Hi is Robert home?"

"No! Click! Try again."

"Hi, is Robert available?"

"I'm Robert, who are you?"

"Robert, my name is Mike Allen and... I sell insurance."

"Good for you. *CLICK!* Start again."

Robert was clearly attempting to teach me a lesson, in what, I had no idea. What was I doing wrong? Maybe I needed to mix up my approach.

I asked again, "Hi, is Robert available?"

That seemed to work better than the previous two attempts.

"Depends, what do you want?"

Robert had begun to pace back and forth as we

spoke. He was fidgeting with his hands and twirling a bright red ball point pen.

"Is this a good time to speak?"

I paused and looked around, but to my surprise Robert started slowly clapping.

"Good job kid. It takes some trainees two or three weeks to learn that."

"Learn what?"

"Don't open someone's refrigerator without asking for permission. Most trainees get so eager to start rattling off life insurance factoids that they forget the basics. Ask for permission to have a conversation and people will open up."

He motioned me back toward my phone. Robert was incessant about practicing, almost like a drill instructor demanding orders.

"Let's keep going. No time like the present."

I stood upright in my chair and thought how hard could this be? Heck if enduring four years of an overpriced college education couldn't break me, then cold-calling sure wouldn't.

"Is this a good time to talk?"

"No, my hamster just died. *CLICK!* Let's start again from that point."

He took all the wind out of my sails with one breath. I'd imagine that was by design. I never knew what to expect next with this guy.

"Is this a good time to talk?"

"It depends, why are you calling? What'd you want?"

Robert had paused and looked me dead in my eyes. His look was an infusion of curiosity and annoyance.

"I---I don't really know what to say after that."

"That's fine, you don't need to know at this point. Here's what you do need to know. Do you know what makes a business great?"

"What?"

"What's, what? You speak English, right? You went to college, right? What do you think makes a business great?"

"I have no clue.", I said with a disappointed and submissive tone. It seemed Robert was starting to get irritated, maybe it was something I said or maybe he just needed another cup of coffee.

"Process and Principles. Every great business relies on scalable processes and strong principles. Here's what we're going to do today. Today is the day I teach you some of those scalable processes."

"Sounds good to me."

"Here is a simple recipe for success when it comes to cold calling. Step one is you gotta ask if the person is home. Step two is to ask if the person has time to talk. Step 3 is to ask how the person is doing. The final step is to just explain who you are, what you do and why you're calling. It's all really all that simple."

"Sounds good to me."

I was more interested in getting a cup of coffee than listening to Robert filibuster all day about these processes. I started looking for the breakroom, when all of a sudden Robert started his diatribe back up.

"Insurance is a relationship business and to that end,

you must be able to cultivate relationships."

"Yeah? How am I supposed to do that exactly?"

"How are you supposed to build relationships? What, are you serious?"

"What I meant was, how am I supposed to do that over the phone?"

"Ah. Well, let me ask you a question. Can you hold a conversation?"

"Yeah? I suppose so... I mean, we've been talking for some time now."

Robert's demeanor turned from loquacious to sagacious in the blink of an eye. Robert's sagaciousness was overshadowed by his loathing. I took it he had given this speech one too many times in his life.

"Your success in this business is entirely contingent on your ability to do just that, to be able to hold a conversation. Conversation is the bedrock of all relationships. Conversation is the cornerstone of sales."

Evidently Robert was a lot smarter than I initially gave him credit for. He wore glasses, but upon closer examination he didn't have lenses in the frame. That was fitting, because Robert was the kind of guy who wore suspenders and a belt.

"Okay, so... What if I get someone on the phone and they want to buy right then and there? What if I stumble my way through the conversation and they're ready to buy?"

"You want to go in to every single call with that kind of PMA."

"PMA? What's that?"

"Positive Mental Attitude. Try to keep up with the TSAs."

"TSA?"

"Three Letter Acronyms. You're too much kid."

"Ah. Yeah, I knew that."

"Okay, so. If you find someone interested enough to buy on the first call, then you need to close them right there. Get a commitment, send an online application and get them to sign the dotted line."

"One more question.", I asked tenaciously.

"What is it?"

"What's an App?"

"You know, an app. An application, you schmuck."

He took a long pause and out stretched his arms again. Robert was starting to become slightly irritated and I picked up just a splash defensiveness in his tone.

"You mentioned something about principles earlier? What'd you mean by all that?"

Robert stuck up his hand, sprung up three fingers and placed it in front of my face.

"There are really only three rules to selling life insurance. And three rules only."

Robert closed his fist and stuck up his index fingers, again in my face.

"The first rule is don't accept a "No" for the first and final answer."

"Don't accept a no? Is that ethical?"

"Woah. Woah. Woah. Ethics police pull over. Slow down there kid. What I meant was, don't give up at the first sign of conflict. Sometimes people mean no, sometimes they mean yes, sometimes they mean maybe and sometimes they mean *NO!*"

"Yeah, that makes sense."

In reality, his speech was the verbal equivalent of sucking up noxious gases after an oil spill. Robert was unfazed, and a bit jaded. He stuck up his middle finger waving his two fingers in front of my face.

"The second rule to selling life insurance, whether on the phone, in-person, through text messages, or whatever, this has been and always will be a relationship business."

Robert closed his fist again and pounded his knuckles on the desk three times in a row.

Knock. Knock. Knock.

Robert put up three fingers and waged them in my face.

"The third and final rule is to never spend the client's money for them. Don't assume the person knows what they don't know. The quicker you can accept these three rules, the quicker you can start making money. Does that make sense?"

"Yeah, makes sense."

"Do you think you're ready to handle some calls or we gonna sit here all day and stare at each other?"

Such an exquisitely simple question, propositioned like a dead fish wrapped in a newspaper. What could I say?

"Sure thing! Sounds good to me."

Robert placed a few items on my desk; a phone script, a black marker and a lead sheet. The lead sheet was just a glorified bunch of pages ripped out of the phone book. He picked up my phone and handed it to me.

"Let's make some money. I want you to call the first 50 people on that list. Maybe then we can see what you're actually made of."

"Who are *they*?"

"There you go asking questions again. Who are they? It doesn't matter, that's who *they* are. Mike, Just make the calls."

Figuring I had nothing to lose, I looked down at the list and started making calls. Robert smiled, pointed over to his desk and whispered to me, "I'll be right over there in case you run into any trouble."

He pointed at his desk, gave me a thumbs up and casually walked away. And that's what it was to Robert, all just a very casual occurrence. Just another walk in the park for Robert. Regardless of my feelings, I started making those *50* phone calls. Regardless of my anxiety, I was started making those 50 phone calls. Regardless of my fear, I started making those 60 phone calls.

The first 10 phone numbers either went dead or didn't answer. Before I knew it *ten* minutes had passed me right on by. When I looked up again, Robert pulled his magician act, in that he vanished before my very eyes. This wasn't so bad. So, I kept calling. Only forty more numbers to get through and then on to the next task. I dragged my finger down the list and murmured aloud, "Okay... John Cane... 294-555-3020..."

The phone began to ring. *Ring... Ring.... Ring...*

Well, that's a good sign. I mean, at least its ringing this time. To be honest, I wasn't even sure how many times a phone could ring before going to voicemail. So, I decided to give it about 7 or 8 rings before pulling the plug.

Ring (4) ... Ring (5) ... Ring (6) ... Ring (7) ...

Just as I was about to hang up the receiver someone answered, "Hello?"

Taken by complete surprise, I stumbled into my opening part of my script.

"Hi, is Mike Allen home?"

Followed by the palm of my left hand smacking the upside of my head. I was so nervous I completely flopped my first phone call. The bright side, if there was a bright side, was that it couldn't get any worse. At least, that was until I looked up from my desk.

Robert was standing over by his desk looking at me with his jaw practically on the floor. Turns out he went to go grab some coffee. The man on the other line responded befuddled by my question.

"Mike Allen? Nobody lives here by that name. Who's this?"

I could tell this guy was just as surprised as I was to be talking to someone. So, I tried to recover the call. I fumbled the ball, what did I have to lose by trying to pick it up and run?

"Hi, I'm Mike Allen. Is John Cane home?"

My question was redressed with a gargled response. The kind of grumpy-old-man response you might expect in the morning.

"Yeah, that's me. What do you want?"

My brain froze, again. Okay, *Step One* complete. Step two... step two... ah!

"Is this a good time to talk?"

"No. It's not a great time to talk. I've got to go. *Goodbye!*", John said followed by an audible *CLICK!*

I held the phone next to my face and pretended that I didn't just get hung up on. I slowly looked back up and Robert was hovering right over my desk. He sipped his coffee and presumably was waiting for me to say something. Yet, I had nothing to say. What could I say? I couldn't even remember my own name. Robert stopped sipping his coffee and clasped his coffee mug with both hands.

"What happened? What'd he say? How'd it go?"

I paused briefly to think about his question. My gut was wrought with anguish, but I couldn't let him know that. So, I said the first thing that popped into my mind, the truth.

"He told me he didn't have time to talk..."

"What was the first lesson of the day? What was the first thing I taught you?"

Before I could respond Robert pulled a chair up to my desk and took a seat. He put down his coffee, which is how I could tell he was serious. He looked at me and titled his head slightly off to the left. He looked at me with intent, like he actually had some kind of vested interest in my success.

"Don't accept a single No as a first and final answer. The thing about sales is that people often use No as a defensive mechanism against salespeople. No is not absolutely used as an indication of intent. In some Native American languages, there are 32 words to express the word love. In the English language we just have one, it's love. Maybe the person is saying No and maybe the person is saying *NO!*', or perhaps the person is saying 'I don't know'."

"So, you're saying... what?"

"I'm saying just ask in a different way to discover the intent of the person. Are they intending on hearing you out or have they heard enough?"

Robert sipped down the rest of his coffee and slammed the cup on my desk. The desk reverberated and some dust came flying up.

"The next time someone says I don't have time or I got to go or some other lame excuse like that, I want you to pretend that you're looking them right in the eyes. I want you to say 'It'll only take about sixty-seconds or so...' Then shut up and see what they have to say."

I nodded my head in agreement. Robert cross his arms and implanted his hands under his arm pits.

"Yeah, no, that makes a lot of sense."

"Have you ever heard the phrase that 'haste makes waste'?"

"Nope. Can't say that I have."

"The biggest mistake most trainees make, is that they get *so* excited on the phone, just to talk with someone, that they forget the entire purpose of the call. All they want to do is rush people through the script as fast as possible. Selling isn't a sprint, it's a marathon. It's a conversation, not an interrogation."

"That makes sense."

I nodded in affirmation. Robert tended to let off a bit when I noticeably acquiesced with my body language.

"You need to trust the process, but not be a slave to the process. The difference between a robot and a person, the best part about being human is that you have this little thing in between your ears, it's called your brain. Never let someone or something use your brain for you."

Robert had stood back up and started meandering back towards the breakroom, presumably to get some more coffee.

"Want a cup?", he asked as he was walking away. Lord knows I could use one.

"Sure thing!", I responded with an exuberant tone of voice.

"Well, get up off your butt and follow me."

I couldn't help but laugh a bit. I got up out of my chair, it was the first time all day and boy did I need to loosen up. I stretched out a bit and then proceeded to follow Robert to the break room. It was an arduous journey, maybe a good twenty feet from my desk.

As I walked back to the break room, I noticed that there were stacks of phone books just kind of lying all over the place. There were whiteboards hanging on the walls, clearly, they hadn't been used in a while. I could tell because they had these feint remnants of words imprinted on them, as if the previous marker ink had faded away years ago.

The breakroom itself wasn't much to look at, but it had a comfortable feeling to it. The room was painted sky blue with old ceiling tiles and what appeared to be some glow in the dark stickers on them. The breakroom was the only room with actual windows in it, aside from the lobby that is. There was a single round table and five old plastic chairs surrounding it from all sides. Robert walked me over to the coffee machine and pointed with his pinky.

"This is the one nice thing in the whole office, so treat it well. Treat it with respect and it will pour out mana from heaven."

He opened up the adjacent cupboard and grabbed two mugs. The cupboards were painted in a glossy white paint and had these interesting oval shaped knobs on them. Robert clearly took a lot of pride in showing me the inner workings of the coffee machine, more so than even my training.

"This is the Espresso Taleggio 5000, a masterclass in coffee making technology. It was imported about 10 years ago from a small town in Italy and hasn't stopped working since."

We poured our coffee and headed back to the salesfloor. On our way back, I was hit with this treacherous odor. Probably, the amalgamation of decades of uncleaned commercial grade carpet. The aroma of the coffee did little to dampen the smell of the carpet.

Robert grabbed his chair and sat back down. Every time he sat down it made a large 'PLUMP' sound. He looked at his watch a few times and then back at me. He motioned over at the phone, pointing at it with the same hand he was holding his coffee mug. Maybe it was a bit taboo to take a break, but I really wanted to get a good idea of my environment.

"We gonna do this or what? Time is money on this job."

"What about our break?"

"C'mon Mike. Breaks are for school kids and

athletes."

I scurried back to my desk and joined Robert.

"Sounds good."

Robert pulled out a white piece of paper and a ball point pen. He placed it on my desk and started drawing. I couldn't quite figure out what he was drawing.

"What we use here is called the *Yes Sales Method*."

He drew two equal sized boxes on the paper and a line down the middle of the paper separating the two boxes. He stopped drawing for a second to admire his work.

"It's as simple as getting the prospect to say yes as many times as possible during the sale."

Robert drew ten small vertical lines connected to the top of the right box and one thick vertical line connected to the top of the left box.

"Think of it kind of like an elevator. Do you want the elevator to have one support cable or ten support cables?"

He paused and pointed down at the drawing. He tapped on the box with his pen. Tap. Tap. Tap. I wasn't quite sure what this had to do with sales, but I didn't have much of a choice. I mean, at this point anything was better than hopping back on the phone.

"Well, uh, I'd rather have ten, right?"

"Exactly! Because what's gonna happen when that one-line breaks? The elevator plummets to the ground, but if you have ten cables, then your elevator is fine."

"Mm-hmm."

"The idea is to get small commitments along the way, instead of just ambushing the prospect with a major decision at the end of the sale. See, you want to get the person to say yes enough times so that the last yes becomes a lot easier to say yes to."

"And, that really works?"

"Mike, the thing about sales is that it's not an exact science. It's more of an art form."

That was probably the best non-answer I was going to get out of him. What else was I expecting from a sleezy insurance salesman?

"Okay, it's just about eleven-thirty. Which means we have about an hour or so until lunch. I want you to make 100 phone calls in the next hour. I'm going to be right over there at my desk. Someone around here has to actually make some money for this place. If you need something, just, I don't know, waive your hand or throw something at me."

Those were my marching orders and I was bent on getting the job done. I gave Robert a thumbs up. I took a deep breath and pulled the lead sheet in nice and close. I did quick once over on the list, it seemed like a bunch of pages pulled right out of the phone book. The next name on the list seemed as ordinary as the rest, a Rachel Maloney. I dialed her phone number and waited for the inevitable.

Ring... Ring... Ring...

"Hello?"

"Hi, is Rachel Maloney home?"

I planted my feet up on the desk, might as well relax a bit and get comfortable. If Robert could do this, why couldn't I? He didn't even go to college. How hard could this insurance thing really be?

"*Rachel?* Who's this? Who's calling?"

The voice on the other line responded in a frantic tone. I mean, was my voice that irritable to hear this early in the morning?

"My name is Mike Allen with Montrosian Insurance Partners, LLP."

"Insurance... why do you want to talk to Rachel?"

The volume of his voice dampened and shifted from startled to a more somber tone.

"Is this a good time to talk?"

I asked and somewhat bumbled through the script. This script was a lot like this office, dated.

"No, no it's not. Why do you want to talk with Rachel?"

It was clear he started to become somewhat fed up with the questions and was more interested in answers. If anything else, I was persistent. So, I asked again in a slightly more affirmative tone of voice.

"*Sir*, Is Rachel available?"

The other line went silent, I figured he just hung up. Something was wrong, something was off. I couldn't tell what, but I felt I just stepped in *it*. The man on the other line started to clear his throat and what followed was a long-winded sigh.

"Ra-Rachel-is-is... Rachel passed away two months ago..."

"...Sir, I-I-I-... I'm so sorry to hear that. I had *absolutely* no idea."

I had kicked my feet off the desk and buried my head into the bottom part of my desk.

"What did you need to talk to her about? Why did you call?"

Then I quite possibly said the stupidest thing that had ever been said in the history of the sales.

"I was handed a list and she was a name on that

list."

I had to hold the phone away from my ear as the person on the other line had begun shouting belligerently. I shook my head and as I looked away from the phone Robert had been looking right at me with his eyebrows comically raised. He stood up and walked over to my desk, probably to intervene or do some kind of damage control. All I could possibly think about was the fact I had just shattered this persons' entire world and probably lost my job in the process. As soon as Robert walked over and the line went dead.

"What was that all about?"

"One of the people on the list was, dead."

"Oh. Well, did you at least try to sell them?"

Robert patted me on the back and shrugged his shoulders.

"I know. I know. I picked up on the end of that conversation. That was just dreadful, but unavoidable in our business. The faster you get used to it, the better off you'll be. People die, it happens.

We're in the business of profiting from people's death. It's that simple."

"I... uh..."

"Why don't we take a step back? Where do you figure that train wreck started? Where did it go wrong?"

"I-I-... uh... I have no idea."

"The mistake you made was saying she was just a number or just a name on a list. I mean, that's just cold, even for you."

"I wasn't thinking..."

"Clearly..."

I couldn't help but yelp out this awkward chuckle. What else could I do? I stumbled and fumbled that call into oblivion.

"This might be the most important lesson you learn today. Everyone is just a name on a list to us. Everyone is just a number to us. Everyone is just no-one to us, but to someone else, that person is a loved one, a spouse, a relative and that person on a list has a story. Behind every number and behind every name on this list, there is a compelling story and a reason for buying life insurance."

Robert was personally vested in my success at this point. He snatched up the script from my desk and started holding it up as a prop. I could tell he genuinely cared about helping me make it through the Trainee program. He slid the list back over to me, unknowingly I had pushed it almost completely off my desk.

"Some people will want to buy life insurance and some people will not, but in the end, there is always someone out there looking to buy some life insurance."

He picked up the receiver on the phone and held it out for me to grab. I grabbed the receiver from Robert, almost instinctively and looked up at the clock. It was 11:45 and I had forty-five minutes to call forty-nine people. I pulled up the lead sheet and searched for the next name on my list. I dialed and smiled for the next thirty minutes straight, nearly setting my fingers on fire in the process. Not a single person picked up the phone. Maybe it was a blessing in disguise. I'd worked my way about halfway down the lead sheet. I scrolled down the list skipping names in the hope I would find that one magical person who had some interest in buying life insurance.

"Let's try... Douglas Boccali", I mumbled under my breath. I'm not sure why but I had a good feeling about this one.

Ring... Ring... Ring...

"Hello? Doug speaking."

"Hi, is Doug there?"

"Like I said, this is Doug speaking. What's up?"

"I'm Mike Allen with Montrosian Insurance Partners. How are you today?"

"I was doing a lot better before you called. What'd you want?"

Okay, this guy blew through the process. What was *Step 4* again...? *Oh yeah*, explain who I was, what I do and why I was calling.

"Like I said earlier, I'm Mike Allen..."

"But *Of* course you are, *And* you're here to sell me what exactly?"

"I'm a life insurance agent with Montrosian Insurance Partners. I'm calling today to see if you'd be interested in buying life insurance."

"I really don't think I have the time right now kid. Thanks anyways."

"Do you have about two minutes?"

"Two minutes? *Uhhhhh...* Sure, go ahead."

Douglas was opening the door for me, now all I had to do was walk through it. The only problem was, I'd never gotten this far before. What in the world was I supposed to say next?

"Great! Umm... Do you currently have life insurance?"

"Uh... Currently? No, no I don't."

"Have you ever had life insurance in the past?"

"I used to have some through my old job."

"Huh. If you don't mind me asking, why don't you have it now?"

I wasn't really sure what kind of questions to ask, so I just started blurting them out one by one. I guess you could say I was in a test and learn environment.

"Wait a minute... Do I even know you? Why am I even talking to you?"

"I don't think we know each other..."

"Well, then how'd you get my number?"

"Uh. Well, I pulled your number from the phone book, but..."

Douglas interrupted me just as I was about to pull out some epic excuse.

"Look kid, your two minutes are up. I have to go."

His indignation was followed by a loud *CLICK!* I got hung up on mid-sentence, but you know what? I actually felt pretty good. I was making progress, or so I thought. Robert walked over from his desk, more of a lazy stroll than a walk. He was taking his time and clearly had something on his mind. Robert looked at me with a puzzled gaze, somewhere between bewilderment and befuddlement.

"What happened with that one?"

"I almost got one!"

"Almost did *what-now-huh-what*? Tell me more. What does almost mean?"

"Well, I got to the fourth step in the process and... and... I didn't really know where to go. But I managed to ask a lot of questions and he seemed interested."

"Why do you think that was?"

"Why do I think... what *was*?"

"Sorry, why do you think that the process fell apart?"

"I honestly couldn't tell you."

"Yeah, that's my point. You don't know what you don't know. Trust the process Mike. This is all part of the process. You got to learn to walk before you learn to sprint."

"Uh-huh. So, the process is to set me up to fail?"

"No. I didn't give you any questions yet, so that you would understand."

"Understand? Understand what?"

"That way you could understand from firsthand experience, that there has to be a compelling reason for someone to speak with you. Overtime we're going to help you develop that compelling reason."

"What if that guy really wanted to buy!?!?"

"Call him back in six months and try again."

Robert shrugged his shoulders and brushed off my question.

"Why should this guy even listen to you in the first place? There are over one million licensed insurance pros in America, there are billion-dollar *Insuretechs*, there are thousands of brokerages, why shouldn't a person just go there? What makes you so important?"

Robert asked me a rather pedestrian question, but how could he expect me to muster a coherent response. My breathing became increasingly heavier and more deliberate. Robert picked up on my uneasy feeling and laughed it off.

"C'mon man, this isn't funny. I could've made a sale."

"I'm laughing because I felt the same exact way you did. I learned this lesson two years ago, and it hurt. I was sitting in that same chair. I was sitting there with that same stupid look on my face. I was sitting there flustered. I was sitting there ready to storm out of the office and call it quits."

Robert walked back to his desk and started rummaging through his desk drawer.

"It's... *in* here... somewhere. Where in the heck did...?"

Robert began indiscriminately mumbling, as if he was scavenging for something. I really couldn't tell what he was going to pull out of that drawer.

"Ah-ha! Here it is."

Robert pulled out a large white sheet of paper. I stared over at him from my desk. I was slightly confused, but he definitely had my attention. He brought it back over to my desk and slammed it down in front of me.

"Take a look at this!"

I quickly grabbed the sheet of paper from him and started reading intently. It was a piece of paper titled 'SALES QUESTIONS' and had about 10 poorly worded open-ended questions on it. I had my reservations, but it was worth a try.

"Now, mind the grammar, because these are sales questions. Take a look at these and let me know what you think."

"Robert, what kind of salesperson complains about grammar?"

"Mike, you'd be surprised. They're out there."

I inspected the questions in further detail, maybe the spark of genius was lost on me.

"Sure, I guess these could help..."

By the time I looked up again and it was already 1:00 PM. I had completely forgotten about lunch, apparently the entire office did as well. I briefly scanned the room and not a single person had left the office. I stood up for a second and walked over to Robert's desk.

"What's up, people don't eat lunch around here?"

Robert tilted his head back and looked at me, with this kind of jaunted expression.

"Lunch? What's *that*? Better yet, did you sell anything today?"

Robert made a pawning motion over to the breakroom.

"If you get hungry, we have coffee and snacks in the breakroom. If you have time for lunch then you have time to make calls."

I hadn't missed a meal in quite some time, but I wanted to fit in and if that meant skipping lunch then I was going to skip lunch.

"Mike, you may not have realized this about me. I'm not a very book learn-ed kind of person. I'm a man of the people. And my business, is the people business. I know a little something-something about people."

"Pray tell. What do you know about me then?"

Robert smiled. I could tell that he was excited to accept my challenge.

"You Mike, you're a brain."

"What's that supposed to mean?"

"What I mean is... The problem most people have is that they use their brain. They use their brain too much and not their heart. Mike, you my friend, you use your brain far too much."

"How do you figure?"

"You're using your brain *way* too much. Let me ask you something. Why do you figure that is?"

"Because, I like to think? Really, I have no clue."

"It's *because* you're afraid to use your instincts. You gotta trust your gut. Processes are like training wheels. Don't second guess your gut. If your gut tells you to deviate from the process, do it. See what happens. Experiment a little bit."

"Ah..."

"How old are you?"

"How old am I? I'm 24... why? What does that have to do with anything?", I said with a slightly defensive tone. One of my pet peeves in life was someone judging me based on the misfortune of being attached to a do-nothing generation.

"Your brain is 24 years old. It's not even fully formed yet. The average male brain fully develops in the mid to late twenties."

"Thanks, I really appreciate your kind words there Robert."

"It's not a dig kid. I'm trying to teach you something. You millennials are so sensitive."

Robert took a second to catch his breath. Apparently monologuing was a rather taxing activity for Robert. Nonetheless, he proceeded to opine.

"Let me put it this way. How old are your instincts?"

"What do you mean by that?"

"Your instincts Mike. How old are your instincts?"

I wasn't really sure where he was going, so I just shook my head.

"Your DNA is over 200,000 years old. Your instincts have been crafted through hundreds of thousands of years of evolution. So, the question is. What do you trust more? Do you trust your 24-year-old brain or the 200,000 years of instincts that have literally resulted in the perpetuation of our entire species?"

I felt Robert enjoyed grandstanding and maybe even got off on it a bit. Either way, I was game for wasting time if he was.

"Mike... what is it that you think we actually do here?"

"We sell life insurance, right?"

I mean, on its face that seemed to be a softball question. Robert took a deep breath and sighed heavily. His forehead was dripping sweat, but he didn't seem to pay it any mind. A large droplet of sweat rolled down the left side of Robert's forehead and dangled ever so slightly on his chin. He was clueless, lost in his own mind.

"Mike, we don't just sell life insurance. We are the creators of dreams. We are the architects of feelings. We are the difference makers. I am the difference between financial ruin for your wife or her having a happy in the event of you dying prematurely. We sell life insurance, sure. What we really are in the business of selling is peace of mind. We are in the peace of mind business. People can choose to buy life insurance anywhere. They come to us, this brokerage in particular, for three reasons. I call them the 3 E's; experience, expertise and education."

"The Three E's... I like it."

I took a second to think about it. It was a simple enough proposition. I always figured insurance companies profited off the fear of others, but I guess I was mistaken. Insurance is actually a compelling social good, at least, in theory.

"Tell me more."

"How much do you weigh?"

"How much do I weigh? I'm about 185 or so. Why?"

"Do you know what it costs to bury a guy like you?

Ever think about it?"

"No... Uh, I can't say that I've ever thought about it before..."

"*Exactly!* Nobody ever does. That is, until it's too late to think about. And then *BOOM*. Guess what? You're a friggin' one-hundred-eighty-five-pound paperweight."

"That's pretty morbid..."

"That's the business. Seriously though, how much do you think it would cost?"

Robert was relentless in his pursuit for an answer. He was dead set on making a point. I was eager to learn, so I decided to play along.

"Really. I have no idea."

"Put a number on it."

"I don't know... How about *Two-thousand* dollars?"

"Only Two-thousand? For a stud like you?"

We both chuckled a bit, but I could tell by his stare, Robert wasn't nearly as amused as I was.

"Three-thousand?"

"If you were to drop dead today, in the San Fernando Valley area, it would run you about... $100 per pound. More or less."

"Robert, that's like $20,000!"

"It's that or for $100 I could bury you somewhere out in the desert. I'll even throw in the shovel. No charge."

Robert smiled and laughed out loud, not a ha-ha laugh, but the kind of laugh that reeked of self-congratulations. I was taken back a bit, because I'd never thought about the cost of my own funeral before. Before I knew it, it was only 15 minutes to closing time.

"Look at the time!", I said exuberantly.

Not a single person looked up from their desk. It was business as usual. Robert looked back down at his watch.

"You're right. Look at that."

Robert took a second, stretched out his arms and

brought his hands together. In one fell swoop he cracked all of his knuckles, his neck and began cracking his fingers. He leaned back in his chair and then jolted forward. He grasped the arms of his late 90's black pleather executive chair. His knuckles were turning white he was grasping so hard. I didn't notice it before, but Robert had neatly trimmed and manicured finger nails.

"How do you think you did today? Give yourself a grade."

His tone was deep, methodical and collected. He began to speak to me like a late-night radio Disc Jockey. The kind that played *smooth* jazz. I mean, what could I say? If you ask me, I think I did a bang-up job.

"Good. I hope? I mean it was only my first day. So..."

Robert sat there in complete silence. He had his legs gingerly crossed and his hands in his lap. Why he didn't answer me, I had no idea. He stared at me with these unconvinced eyebrows, with a look of quiet desperation and fleeting confusion. He appeared conflicted. He was grappling with my question. I could tell that part of him approved, but I had this feeling that he wasn't 100% sold.

"I've seen a lot of people come and go. A lot of people Mike…"

Robert just slightly tilted his head up, just enough to stare at the ceiling tiles. He leaned in and whispered to me.

"I've seen a lot of people come and go. The people who choose to go, go right away."

He paused, probably for dramatic effect.

"Mike, it's the people who choose stay that I worry about the most."

"What? What'd you mean?"

What would there be to worry about? It's just a job.

"There are two kinds of people who stay. There are people who stay for the right reasons, they tend to do well here. Then there are those other kinds of people, those who stick around for the wrong reasons. Some people are only in it for the quick buck, the easy dollar and they chase it all the way out the door."

Robert grabbed a napkin from his desk. He slowly wiped the sweat from his brow. Robert's forehead glistened under the incandescence of the ceiling lights.

"The real question is, which kind of person are you?"

Robert sat back in his chair and looked back at me intently. The look of a greasy war-torn insurance salesman.

"I'm... uh... I..."

"It doesn't matter! It was a rhetorical question, genius."

"Oh."

"What matters is, that *I* think you can do this job. That's all that matters."

I smiled while biting down on my lip. All I could do is nod like a trained sea lion at the zoo. Apparently, I had made a good impression. It was just the kind of validation I needed. Considering the day I just went through; his feedback was well received.

"Thanks. I appreciate it."

"I wasn't finished. I think you can do this job. I'm just not sure you should do this job."

In the span of two seconds, I went from being elated to deflated. Robert sure had a way with words.

"Should do this job? What's that supposed to mean?"

I couldn't help but object. I mean, the way I figured it; this was a pretty successful day.

"Mike, don't get me wrong. I think you might be too smart to do this job."

"Too smart? How do you figure?"

"Hang on there buckaroo. I said, I think. I just don't know yet."

"Uh. So, where do we go from here?"

"Ultimately, that is up to you my friend. Tomorrow we're going put you back on the phone and see what you can really do. That is if you show back up to work. The rest of the week we'll have you call the 'No-Sale' list."

"What's the 'No-Sale' list?"

Robert let out a big sigh and smirked.

"Are you not playing with a full deck of cards or what? These are people who we previously quoted but the agent did not make a sale, thus the name 'No-Sale'."

Robert took a second and swirled his empty coffee mug. He gazed at the mug with a look of complete bemusement.

"I want you to. No, I need you to go home and think this over. The last thing I want is for you to drag this out. Saying no tomorrow, is better than lying to yourself for two weeks and saying no then."

I nodded my head and clocked out for the day. I headed on out the door, I had a lot of thinking to do. That was my first day, that was what easily could have been my last day.

Chapter 4: On the Second Day of Training my employer gave to me...

The next day I found myself sitting in that same strip mall, sitting in that same insurance agency, sitting in that same lobby, sitting on that same pleather couch. Predictably, I showed up fifteen minutes early. I figured it would give me some time to ponder Robert's question. I wasn't the kind guy that placed a significant amount of value on self-reflection, honestly I kind of despised it thinking for the sake of thinking. I never really thought about it too much, but maybe it had something to do with the fact I had an incredibly short attention span. The receptionist walked into the lobby. She looked at me with a puzzled expression on her face. She trotted over to her desk, put down her purse and asked, "What happened? Did you get fired already?"

"Uh... I don't think so... I hope not."

I was a bit taken back by her question. What kind of greeting was that?

"Sorry. I didn't mean to be so blunt. I'm just curious

why you're waiting in the lobby, that's all."

She spoke with a hint southern drawl. I didn't pick up on it before, but she was clearly not from California.

"I'm just early... You know early to rise, early to work, etc, etc. Is it that taboo?"

"No, no, no. Of course not. That still doesn't explain why you're waiting in the lobby."

I could tell she wasn't trying to be rude, but then it hit me. Why am I waiting in the lobby?

"You do know that the door to the salesfloor opened about an hour ago, right?"

"Ah. Yeah. I really appreciate it."

I said as I got up out of my chair and slowly began walking towards the door. As I opened the door and began to walk through, I realized something. I didn't even bother to catch her name. That wasn't very characteristic of me, to forgo an introduction.

"By the way, I'm Mike Allen. It's nice to meet you. What's your name?"

"Tracey Jones, it's nice to meet you as well Mike Allen."

Tracey had probably seen hundreds, if not thousands of people like me walk through that door over the years.

"Have fun with the Trainee program."

She waved me off and I walked back to my desk. I still hadn't really branched out to meet the other sales people yet. I figured that over time I would meet most of them and hopefully even pick up a few friends along the way. After trudging around for a few minutes, I found my way over to my desk. Most of the salespeople had messy and unkempt work spaces. It was like a landfill of paperwork and sticky notes. How did they get anything done around here? I sat down and organized the few things I had on my desk. It wasn't much, but it was mine to work with.

"What's up?"

I looked up and Robert was standing over me with a confused look on his face.

"Well, I'm organizing my work space."

I didn't realize how absurd that might have looked to someone else. I mean, yeah, what's the point?

"Mike you have a whopping three things on your desk. What possible difference does it make moving your note pad from one side of the desk to the other?"

I stared at him for a second, and realized just how right he was.

"It's like re-arranging deck chairs on the Titanic."

"Fair enough... Good morning by the way."

No better way to start my day than making a complete fool of myself. Granted Robert had a flare for theatrics and making a small spectacle out of every little thing. It was one of his more charming qualities.

"Yeah. Good morning to you to.", He said as he shook his head and laughed.

Robert strolled on over to his desk and put his stuff down. Robert opened the desk drawer of one of his filing cabinets and started rummaging around for something.

"Where-oh-where did I leave it?"

I couldn't help but stare, it's not like I had anything else to do. What was he looking for? What was so important?

"Ah-ha! *There* it is. Right where I left it.", Robert said as he tugged on the end of an extension cord. He pulled out what looked to be some kind of headset.

"What's that?"

"This, this is a phone 'splitter', it's basically just a headset. I can listen to your calls in real time and coach you as you begin to screw them up."

"Robert, as always, your vote of confidence is greatly appreciated."

"I'm not here to puff your ego kid. I'm here to teach you how to make money."

He said as he plugged in his headset. Robert grabbed a few sheets of paper, presumably the 'No-Sale' list he was talking about yesterday. He gently placed the list down in front of me on my desk and pointed.

"This is a pot of gold. These are high intent leads that the company has purchased for you. Well, maybe not for you specifically, so you don't have to purchase leads on your own."

"So, who are these people?"

I was waiting for him to step in and say, 'but wait, there's more!'

"They're people who at one point wanted to buy insurance and made the unfortunate mistake of clicking on an online advertisement. At some point in time they gave us their personal information."

"Ah."

Part of me was fairly skeptical. I mean, if these leads were so good, then why in the world was he giving them to me? I'm two days on the job. I pulled the list away from Robert. I intently studied the list, like a superstitious old woman combing through the daily horoscope. At first glance, it didn't look like anything special.

As I began looking over the list Robert said, "Don't overthink it. Just call them."

"What should I say?"

"Don't overthink it..."

He repeated his ultimatum in a firmer tone of voice, like a decree made from behind a podium.

"So, you want me to just call them up and say... the same thing as yesterday? Or...?"

"Mike, get out of your own way. Pick up the phone. Pick a name on the list. Give them a call and read the script."

So, I did just that. I picked the first name off the list, Jeff Palooza. I picked up the phone, dialed the number and went back to work.

Ring... Ring... Ring...

"Uh... Hello?", the caller on the other line said.

"Hi, is Jeff Palooza there?"

"Yes, speaking."

"Hi Jeff, this is Mike Allen. I'm insurance agent with

Montrosian Partners... How are you today?"

"I was doing fine before you called. What'd you want?"

Robert snickered in the background. I made an intentional effort to not let it perturb me.

"Well, the reason for the call today, is that I'm following up on some information you submitted about getting a life insurance policy."

I looked over at Robert and he was perusing through a copy of *Solider of Fortune* magazine. The kind of magazine that you pick up at a mini-mart rack. He looked up long enough to make eye contact and give me a quick thumbs up.

"Ah. The thing is Mark... I... I was looking and realized that it was really just too expensive."

"It's actually a lot cheaper than you might think."

Robert started laughing, a bit louder than last time. Apparently, he found my performance rather comical. I covered the receiver with my hand, so the prospect couldn't pick up on Robert's peanut gallery commentary.

"I'm sorry. I just can't afford it right now."

Which was followed by a loud *CLICK!* And the phone went dead. I slowly put down the receiver and looked over at Robert.

"What happened there?"

"He said that he couldn't afford it and hung up."

"Couldn't afford what? Did you pitch him something?"

"I... He said he couldn't afford it."

"I heard what you said the first time. I'm asking you what happened. Do you know what happened?"

What was I supposed to say? I sat there stewing in my own pity-party. Robert couldn't help but insert himself back into the conversation. He preferred the driver's seat, which was fine by me.

"Here's the thing Mike. Eighty Percent of all people think life insurance is just too expensive. That's a fact jack. It's a fact that means absolutely nothing to nobody.", Robert explained.

"Uh-huh."

Honestly, I didn't have much to say. It wasn't for lack of trying. I just ran out of things to say.

"What happened? What happened was that you didn't ask the right questions…"

Robert's tone began to diverge into a more assertive and aggressive approach.

"For instance…?"

"He realized it was too expensive. Why? How did he come to that conclusion? What did you say about price?"

"Uh. I'm not sure…"

"That's exactly my point. You know his destination, but you don't know his journey. Do you even know why he was shopping in the first place? Why did he need life insurance and then all of a sudden not need it? How does he know it's too expensive?"

"Yeah, that makes sense."

"People often say one thing, but have underlying concerns. Maybe the price was too high, because the quote was too high. Maybe he went through a medical exam and found out he was seriously ill and couldn't qualify for a good rate. Maybe the agent was trying to pitch a pricey policy. You can't understand the destination without understanding the journey."

"Yeah, no, that makes sense."

"Let's try it again. Who's next on your list?"

I scanned my finger across the list until I found the next name, the name read Jared Pointdexter.

"So, what're you waiting for? We're burning daylight here kid."

Robert picked up the receiver and handed it back to me. I grabbed the receiver from him and started calling away.

Ring... Ring... Ring... Ring...

"Hello?"

"Hi, is Jared home?"

"This is him... Whose this?"

"My name is Mike Allen with Montrosian Insurance

Partners. Is this a bad time to talk?"

I was met with a long-winded pause and a heavy sigh on the other end of the phone.

"Are you calling about life insurance?"

"Yes I am! I'm following up on your recent request for an insurance quote."

"Ha! My *recent* request? If you call six months ago recent. Then yes, it was recent."

I paused and Robert pushed a note across my desk. I read the note and I looked back at him like he was crazy. Robert made a nudging motion with his hand.

"Six months is quite some time to be looking for life insurance. Have you given up on getting the right policy in place?"

"Given up? No! I'm still looking, just not looking that urgently."

I've never gotten this far before. I really had no idea what to do. I looked over at Robert for some guidance. Robert was entranced in his magazine.

"What's holding you back from getting a policy?"

Robert peered up from his magazine, apparently he was impressed, I guess he figured I was doing a pretty good job. There was another pause on the other end of the phone.

"Uh. Look, here's the thing. I'm young and healthy. I'm pretty much a stud. I really don't feel the need to buy life insurance.", he said with a jocular tone of voice.

"It's a lot cheaper than you might think. Especially for someone young and healthy."

"That makes sense. But, I still don't think I need it."

I had a serious case of mental blockage. I looked up and over at Robert for some kind of lifeline.

Robert whispered, "C'mon you've got a couple of minutes, right?"

"Jared, just a couple of minutes of your time. What do you say?"

"I've really gotta go. But, call me in a few days and we can talk."

CLICK! The phone went silent.

"Not too bad Mikey! I mean it wasn't good. But, not bad at all."

Robert smiled and put his fist out for me to bump. We bumped fists for a brief moment of celebration.

"Thanks. Yeah, that wasn't too bad."

"The quality of your questions has gotten infinitely better since yesterday. It's almost like you're reading a script..."

I chuckled a bit. Robert was right, I needed to trust the process and stop trying to fight it.

"Mike, ever hear of the Framing Effect?"

"Nope. Can't say that I have."

"It's a rather simple principal of psychology. The framing effect basically states that people are biased. As biased people, our choices can be manipulated by merely the way in which information is presented to us."

"Mm-hmm. For instance...?"

"For instance, this airbag has a 95% success rate can be re-worded to say this airbag only fails 5% of the time. You see?"

"Uh-huh. Can you give me another example? Like one for me to use during a call."

I know I was asking a lot, for the trainer to actually train me. But, what could I say? I had high expectations for people and was eager to learn.

"I sure can. You said something to the effect of life insurance is a lot cheaper when you buy young. Or some non-sense like that. Why not try it this way?"

Robert paused for a second and cleared this throat. He was re-adjusting himself in his chair.

"Mike, do you know the best part about buying life insurance when you're young? It's cheap."

"Okay, I'll give it a try. What else did you notice?"

"Besides you floundering around like a fish out of water?"

"Yeah, aside from me floundering around like a fish out of water..."

"You ever hear the phrase that telling isn't selling?"

"Nope."

"Mike, that was rhetorical question. How much do you like people bossing you around? Do you like people telling you what to do or how to think?"

"I mean, does anyone enjoy getting bossed around?"

"That's my point. When you just tell people what to do all the time, they hate it and by proxy hate you. When you ask them what they would like to do it becomes easier to build trust."

I hadn't even noticed it but the noise level had increased sharply as the other brokers filled out the office. The salesfloor was humming with excitement.

"Okay. Lessons over. Let's keep going. We're burning daylight kid! We gotta pick up the pace. You're starting to make me look bad."

I cracked my knuckles and picked up the phone. I slid my finger down the list. This time around, I called halfway through the list before a single person picked up the phone. I ran into a string of disconnected phone numbers and answering machines. So, I decided to take a breather and letup. I still wasn't accustomed to sitting all day, my lower back was killing me.

"You giving up on me or what?"

Robert didn't miss a thing, that is to say when he found time away from reading his magazine. Robert had started reading another magazine to pass the time by. This time he was reading some kind of sports magazine.

"I just need a quick break."

I rolled my shoulders out and sat back down in my seat. As I sat back down, the chair made a loud *thud* sound. I looked down the list and started back at it. This was the exact mindless kind of drudgery that I always envisioned people did at an office job. I convinced myself this is what I wanted. I convinced myself this is what I needed. I convinced myself to dial and smile.

Ring... Ring... Ring...

"Hello?"

The noise jolted me back into action. I quickly sat

upright in my seat. I wasn't expecting someone to pick up right away. After randomly shuffling the papers on my desk and blurted out, "Hello! Is... is Mr. Vega available?"

"That's me... How can I help you today?"

He responded with a little bit of intrigue, maybe just enough to keep this going a few minutes.

"The reason for the call today, is that I'm following up on your recent interest in life insurance. Is this a good time to talk?"

Robert started snapping his fingers to get my attention. I wasn't following the script and we both knew it.

"Actually, this is a pretty good time to talk. But... I'm not really in the market for life insurance. You see my wife filled out a form online and she put my information down because she thought I should get life insurance."

"Ah... Well Mr. Vega, why do you think she did that?"

"Because she wants a huge paycheck when I croak!

Why else would she do that?"

I blurted out in spontaneous laughter. I took a deep breath to regain my composure.

"No, no, no. Why do you think she put down your information and not her information?"

"Uh. Well, we've been talking about it for a while now and she wants me to get insured."

"Huh. That's interesting, tell me more."

"There's not much to tell. We have kids and I'm the bread winner for the family. I get it. I just don't think I want it."

"Really? Why don't you want it?"

I could hear a deep breath of on the other line. I could tell he was starting to think. I could tell this conversation was taking a turn.

"Why should I buy life insurance? I'm the one that will be dead!"

"Mr. Vega that is a coherent and logical way to think about life insurance."

"Yeah? Try telling my wife that!"

"Let me ask you something though."

"Sure kid. Go ahead."

"What happens to your wife if you die?"

"I'd imagine she would just shack up with my no-good best friend and they would live happily ever after."

I took a second to think about his response. He wasn't following me, or maybe he was and I didn't like the answer. I looked at Robert in a desperate plea for help and he whispered to me, "Kids, Mike. Kids."

I covered the end of my receiver and asked Robert, "Kids?"

"His Kids you dummy. Ask about his kids."

I asked in a soft whisper, "Mr. Vega, what about your kids?"

"What about them?"

"What happens to them? Sir, what I am asking is,

how do you want them to remember you? What kind of quality of life do you want them to have?"

The phone went silent, dead silent. That was my cue to do just one thing and that was to shut my mouth. So, I did just that. I shut up and I waited. A few seconds went by, all I could hear was a heavy breathing on the other end of the phone. Not a pleasant experience by any stretch of the imagination. A minute went by, then two and then three. I knew the awkwardness would break one of us.

"Like any parent I want the absolute best for my kids. In this life or the next, I want to make sure they have the best in life."

It was all going so great and then I decided to stick my foot right into my mouth. I saw that as an opportunity, so I pounced on his statement.

"Actions speak louder than words. Why don't we..."

And at that moment, I realized my temperance wrote a check my butt couldn't cash. It was at that very moment; I had stepped in a heaping pile of excrement.

"You think so? How about this action? How about I come on down to where you work and we meet in the parking lot? How about I come on down there and I break your legs? Who do you think you are talking to me like that?"

His rage filled diatribe was followed by a loud *CLICK!* I started sweating bullets and covered my mouth to mask the shocked look stamped across my face. I didn't want to make eye contact with Robert. I turned slowly over to his direction and his jaw was almost on the floor. His mouth was gaping open in utter disbelief. Some of the other brokers were looking over at me for the first time, and not in a good way. The entire salesfloor dropped what they were doing and burst out laughing at my expense.

Honestly, I couldn't realize it at the time, but the ridicule was their way of welcoming me to the club. Someone yelled from the peanut gallery, "Come on kid, stand up and take a bow!"

Why not? I stood up and took a bow. From across the room I heard someone start a slow loud clap.

Clap... Clap... Clap...

The room fell silent, but I didn't really know why. I turned around and Bill was standing right behind me. Clearly, based on his facial expression he was not amused by my performance.

"Are you going to make me regret hiring you?", he whispered just loud enough for everyone on the salesfloor to hear.

My face turned completely pale, my heart began to race and my palms awkwardly began to sweat. The mood in the room became overwhelmingly reticent. That was the power of Bill. That was the power of being the boss. Bill stared down the room and began to shout out sarcastic orders.

"How many other people in this room get paid to stand around? Please raise your hand. Raise your hand if you get paid to do nothing. If not, then *get back to work!*"

I immediately sat down and grabbed my phone. Bill slammed his office door behind him. I took that as my que to get back to work. Robert and I looked up for a second at each other and smiled.

"Whose next on your list?"

I looked down at the list and the next name on the list was Bob Reduka.

"His name is Bob."

"Well, what're you waiting for? It's time to sell Bob some Life Insurance."

I picked up the phone and started dialing.

Ring... Ring... Ring...

"Bob speaking."

"Hi Bob. My name is Mike Allen from Montrosian Insurance Partners. How are you today?"

"I'm good... What's up?"

Bob seemed to be in a jovial mood and surprisingly happy to talk to me. What an unexpected and frankly pleasant change in pace, I thought.

"The reason I'm calling is to see if you ended up getting your life insurance policy squared away."

"Life insurance? Uh. Turns out that I don't qualify for life insurance."

"Bob, can I ask you something? Why were you looking in the first place?"

"Doesn't really matter now, does it?"

Bob scoffed at me. His mood noticeably dampened as the conversation progressed. I looked over at Robert, I wasn't quite sure what to say. So, I took a leap of faith and just blurted out something.

"What if I told you... what if I told you that I could get you a life insurance policy?"

"Mike, it is Mike, right?"

His tone shifted from distain to indignation like the flip of a switch.

"Yes sir. Mike Allen."

"You seem like a nice enough kid, but it ain't gonna happen. I've got stacks of medical claims that put phone books to shame. It'd be a waste of time."

"Bob... What do you have to lose?"

"That's… You know, that's fair. Go ahead. I'll give you a shot. If you're okay wasting your time, so am I."

"Give me one second to just jot down some information…"

I grabbed the end of my receiver and looked over at Robert.

"What the heck do I say?"

Robert put down his magazine, waved me off and said, "Just go with it."

I couldn't believe this guy. What kind of advice was that? Just go with it? What a putz, but nonetheless I had to figure something out.

"Let's start with the basics Bob. Why are you looking for life insurance?"

"Let's get this straight, I *was* looking for a burial policy and nothing more."

"Ah. That makes sense. How much coverage were you looking for?"

"$11,000. That's all. I'm not looking for $100K, I'm

not looking for some glamorous expensive policy. I want eleven thousand dollars of coverage, no more and no less."

"Interesting. Why $11,000?"

I mean, it was an oddly specific number and he was adamant on that amount. I felt a certain level of entitlement to at least figure that out.

"What do you mean? That's just how much I need."

His voice became slightly more agitated. Apparently, I had struck a nerve. So, I decided to run it back a bit. I kept reminding myself to understand the journey, not just the destination.

"Sorry for the confusion. What I'm curious about is how you arrived at $11,000..."

"I figure that's what I'll need to bury myself."

Robert had slid a piece of paper across my desk. I read the note and nodded. The note simply said 'move on'. Just when I thought he had some kind of vest interest in my success, turns out that couldn't be any further from the truth. Robert was making a mockery of this entire excursion. Like any good foot solider I carried on with my marching orders and didn't let it phase me.

"Got it... $11,000. Who would be the beneficiary?"

"That's the problem..."

Bob abruptly cleared this throat and coughed. It was a splintery type of cough, like hearing static on the radio.

"Tell me more."

"I'm not married and I don't have kids."

"I see... Yeah, I could see how that would be an issue."

I looked over at Robert for some guidance, all I got in return was him shrugging his shoulders. Shoulder shrugs, what's that supposed to mean? So, I decided to just free style the rest of the conversation.

"What about a close family member? Do you have any siblings?"

"Ha! Oh, I've got a brother. I've got a brother that I can trust about as far as I can throw him."

"Stuck between a rock and a hard place… hmm…"

I looked over at Robert again, pleading for him to step in. Robert looked up from his magazine and shot me a thumbs up. He licked the tip of his thumb and turned the page of his magazine.

"Even if I could qualify, which is doubtful to begin with, I don't know who I could trust to give the money to."

"Let's not put the apple cart before the horse. Let's start with the basics. What kind of health issues do you have?"

"Where do I begin? Let's see…"

Bob began droning on about his various medial woes. Robert laughed out loud and slowly flipped through the pages of his magazine. He looked at me and tapped on his watch. I looked down at my watch and I had spent nearly 30 minutes talking to this guy. As he began telling me his entire medical history, I had started jotting down things on some scratch paper. I wasn't sure why, but I was taking notes. I didn't know what was useful and what wasn't, but regardless, if he spoke it then I wrote it.

"Let's see... I take Insulin for my Diabetes, I take super concentrated doses of Vitamin A for my Liver spots, I take..."

He continued on for several more minutes of expounding his medical history. I didn't have the nerve to interrupt him, nor the experience to know how. Bob took a breath and I realized that slight pause was the only chance I had to interject myself back into the driver's seat of the conversation.

"Bob I think I have all the information I need to run you a quote."

Robert had covered my microphone with his hand, leaned over to me and quietly whispered, "Let's wrap this up."

Before I could take a half second to think Bob was back at it.

"Oh yeah... I take a medication for my..."

As you could imagine this conversation was going nowhere fast. I didn't know a heck of a lot about insurance, but this guy definitely sounded uninsurable. Robert slid another piece of paper across my desk and whispered something to me.

"Read it. Say it. Repeat it."

I looked down at the paper, analyzed it, and took a shot.

"Bob, sorry to interrupt you. Let's do this. As your insurance agent, I recommend we submit an application and see what kind of policy we can qualify you for."

I put a lot of faith in Robert, maybe even a little too much faith. I just met this guy like three days ago and I'm hanging on his every word. Then again, it's not like a had much of a choice.

"It depends… How long would something like that take?"

I cleared my throat and then read directly from one of the scripts Robert provided me earlier in the day.

"It's a rather short process as far as the actual paperwork is concerned. I just need to collect some basic information from you. You know things like your Social Security Number, Date of Birth, Address, etc... Then I submit the paperwork to the insurance company. At that point they send out a nurse to your home or place of work to collect a blood, urine and saliva sample. They take all that information and figure out if they want to make you an offer for insurance."

It was a mouthful so I wanted to give him a second to digest it all. Bob's silence was noticeable, not even a cough. This was one of those times that I knew to shut up and wait. The question was, wait for how long? Bob made some inaudible noises on the other end of the line. I took that as my cue to jump back in.

"Does that, does that all make sense? The way I explained it?"

My question was followed by a long pause. Some uncomfortable sighs and some feint sounds of Bob moving around in his chair. He was mulling it over in his mind, weighing the pros and cons of jumping back down this rabbit hole with me.

"Okay. Let's do it. What do you need from me?"

We talked for another twenty minutes or so and Bob provided me with just about all the information I needed. At least, enough info to get the ball rolling. Robert was genuinely impressed with me. Some of the other Agents had gathered around my desk to listen in. All I had to do was wrap up the conversation and then set up a follow up appointment with Bob.

"So, Bob, any other questions before we submit the application?"

"Nope. That should do it."

"Oh... There is one thing. Who should we list as the beneficiary for the life insurance policy?"

I looked over to Robert and he whispered to me, "Leave it blank."

"Bob, why don't we leave it blank for now until we hear back from the insurance company?"

"That works for me. How long should this all take?"

"It could take anywhere from 3 to 5 days to set up

the medical exam, from there it could take anywhere from 1 to 5 weeks to get an offer."

"Wow! I didn't realize it would take that long...", he said almost like someone in one of those cheesy informercials you see on late night TV.

Robert grabbed my arm and whispered, "Don't worry Bob, I'll hold your hand every step of the way."

I nodded back at Robert.

"Bob, I completely understand how you feel. Don't worry though, I'll hold your hand every step of the way."

"I appreciate it Mike. So, is that it?"

"That's it. I'll follow up with soon Bob."

CLICK!

The other agents congratulated me with some well-orchestrated golf claps. I could tell right away that this was the place for me. The office wasn't very glamorous, but this is the place where I could make a name for myself.

"Alright! Alright... Alright. Everybody calm down.

Keep your skirts on. Good job kid. Walk with me. I need a re-fill."

Robert slowly got up from his chair and motioned over to the breakroom.

"Sure thing!", I shouted eagerly as I stood up out of my chair.

We walked over towards the breakroom. Robert was a step or two ahead of me and he stopped at the pot of coffee and stared at it for a second. As I approached he shouted something at the top of his lungs.

"*No!* It can't be. Is, is, is that? Is that decaf coffee in the coffee maker?!"

He grabbed the pot of coffee in his hands and swung back towards the salesfloor. Robert started belligerently berating the salesfloor. He held the pot of coffee up in the air.

"Which one of you morons made decaf? Whose responsible for this!?!"

The room was silent for a second, and then everyone

went back to making their sales calls. Nobody cared. As Robert turned his back to the salesfloor, someone yelled, "Your mother made it!"

Robert dumped the pot down the sink drain and started rummaging through cabinet drawers. Robert was determined, a man on a quest. A quest for what, I had no idea.

"Ha-Ha. Real funny. Laugh it up. Jerks."

He murmured indiscriminately to himself for a couple minutes. Robert was unusually irritated and I couldn't tell why. Who gets that mad over decaf coffee? I thought he would be elated after my call. I guess I was wrong. Robert was a hard man to please, and harder to understand. My grandfather would say he was a tough nut to crack.

"What's up?", I asked with compassion marred by curiosity.

He was standing up against the refrigerator with his head down trolling on his phone. He looked up for a second and said, "Decaf." Like I was supposed to know what that meant somehow. Robert didn't think that statement warranted a follow up question, but I had no clue why he was throwing such a temper tantrum over Decaf coffee.

"Okay... what about Decaf?"

"What kind of self-respecting salesperson drinks decaf? It makes our whole industry look bad, like a bunch of shmucks. This isn't some fly-by-night operation. This isn't a used car lot."

I wasn't sure where to go with that. So, I didn't. We both stood there with an awkward silent anticipation for the coffee pot to finish brewing. Five minutes or so passed by. I was fixated on the slow drip of the caffeinated coffee Robert loaded into the machine. Once the pot was finished it made a loud BING!

"Perfecto! That's the good stuff. Fully leaded baby."

He handed me a mug and we both walked back to our desks. We both sat down and got re-situated for another exhilarating round of sales calls. I'd finally gotten a base hit, and man it felt great. I took a big sip of that coffee and stared up at the old ceiling tiles. Maybe I didn't work in the most glamorous place, but why should that matter? I'd been given a chance, a chance to make something out of myself and I didn't intend on squandering that opportunity. I put my mug down and pulled in the lead list.

Robert looked at me, he raised up his coffee mug and said, "Let's get on it."

"What do we do about that last guy?", I asked with a supreme audacity.

Robert smiled at my youthful exuberance, or maybe my naivety. He slowly raised his coffee mug towards his mouth. Before drinking he said, "What do we do about the last guy? Nothing. He's uninsurable...."

It felt like someone hit me with a garbage truck, then for good measure slowly reversed over my dead corpse. You know, to make sure he finished the job. I clenched onto the handle of my coffee mug and contemplated my options. On one hand, I could shout it out with Robert on the salesfloor. On the other hand, I could throw this boiling hot coffee in his face.

I pondered my options and took a sip of coffee.

Robert had broken eye contact and went back to reading his magazine. I looked down at the lead sheet with an utterly deflated expression on my face. I shook my head and decided to take the high road. I decided to focus on the journey, not the destination. Begrudgingly, I shook it off, shrugged my shoulders and went back to calling. The next name on the list was a Geoff Wood. He sounded like a real winner. I took a deep breath and started dialing.

Ring... Ring... Ring...

"Hello?"

"Hi, is Geoff there? Err, Mr. Wood."

"This is him... How can I help? Wait... Who is this?"

"My name is Mike Allen, I'm a local insurance broker.", I said with fleeting luster.

"Okay... Good for you. what do you want?"

"Well Geoff, you recently submitted a request for a life insurance quote. Are you still in the market for a policy?"

"I was just curious. I'm not really in the market

anymore."

Robert looked at me and whispered, "Why not?"

I shot him back a thumbs up, his message was received loud and clear.

"That's interesting. Uh... If you don't mind me asking. What made you change your mind?"

A loud groan came over the receiver. I mean, at least he didn't instantly hang-up on me. That was a pretty good sign.

"After talking it over with my neighbor he said that I should just put money aside in my savings account instead of getting a policy. He actually made some good points."

"Geoff, that's interesting. Can you tell me more?"

"Well, he said that most insurance companies never pay out on term insurance policies. He said something like 95-97% of people outlive their term insurance policies, which to me seems like a big waste of money."

Geoff had a rational, logical and even dare I say

compelling explanation for why he thought life insurance was a waste of money. I sat quietly for a second to mull over his proposition. Should I quit or press forward? I decided to not let it deter me and press on. The way I looked at it, I really had nothing to lose.

"Geoff. Can I ask you something?"

"Sure thing."

"Do you normally take financial advice from your neighbor? I'm just curious."

I was riding a fine line, between overtly offending him and questioning his motives.

"Uh. Well, that all depends…"

"On?"

"It would depend on the advice."

"Yeah, that makes sense. Do you mind if I ask you another question?"

"Well, that all depends…"

"On?"

"That all depends on the question you want to ask."

"Fair enough."

We both took a second to chuckle. We clearly had a good rapport going. You know the kind, where you just instantly click with someone. That's the thing about being sarcastic, it either brings you together or separates you.

"Why did you want life insurance in the first place? What piqued your interest? I mean, it looks like something clearly got your attention. Why'd you fill out the request?"

"My wife and I are starting a family, or at least planning on it soon. We'd like to have kids."

"That's great! Starting a family is the fun part. You know the key to having kids?"

"What?"

"The more you 'practice' the faster it tends to happen."

"Yeah, the 'practice' is the fun part of the process."

I could tell that small overture was going to go a

long way with Geoff. Robert went back to reading his magazine. Not so much of a peep came out of Robert.

"Look, that's fine. Saving money is always a great thing to do. I'm not going to say that's a bad idea or that life insurance is a better idea."

I paused to see if he would immediately jump back in the conversation.

"So... you're saying I shouldn't buy life insurance? No offense Mike, but what kind of salesperson tries to unsell his product?"

"Well. Well, hold on. Let me qualify that. That depends on one thing."

"What's that?"

"Let's say you go to the gym tomorrow. Do you work out? Are you a pretty active person?"

"Uhh... I probably get to the gym about two or three times a week. What does that have to do with anything?"

"Let's say you and me hang up the phone right now.

And you decide that it's time to hit the gym. Let's say you go to the gym and have a great workout. Let's say as you walk out of the gym, you trip over your shoe laces and as you fall into the street you get hit by a bus. Let me ask you something... Is your neighbor going to step up and take care of your mortgage?"

I didn't know a lot of about selling life insurance, but I knew if I was going to ask a question like that, that I needed to shut up and wait for him to respond.

I waited and about 30 seconds later he said, "Uh. I don't think so. No... He wouldn't. That's a good point."

"Is he going to pay for your funeral?"

"No..."

"Is he going to pay for your wife's grocery bills?"

"No... I don't think he would."

"Then who will?"

Robert looked over and gave me a thumbs up. One minute he seemed overjoyed and the next Robert seemed to be almost jealous. Either way after this call I needed to confront him about the lack of actual training going on in the Trainee program. The other end of the phone was dead silent. There was an eerier comfortability in the silence. All I heard was heavy breathing and then a loud moan.

"I-I-I don't know. I guess my savings should cover it?"

"Do you mind if we explore that for a second?"

"Sure."

"How much do you have saved up, ballpark?"

"Uhh... In my savings, I think it's something like $25,000 and in our checking account we float probably, I don't know around $2,000 or so."

"If you're saving $2,000 per month, then we should hang up the phone right now."

I waited for a second to let Geoff mull that over.

"No... Uh... Not $2,000 per month... What I meant to say was that we try to have $2,00 in our checking account, $2000 total. You know, for emergencies.

That way we don't have to tap into our savings."

"Oh. Well, let me ask you something then Geoff. What do you think a life insurance policy cost? Roughly speaking of course."

"I have no idea."

"Take a guess."

"Like $500 a month?"

"For someone your age, in your area, like $50 to $100 per month."

In reality, the truth was I had no idea. I had no idea if this guy would even qualify for life insurance. I glanced over at Robert to get some kind of indication. He looked up and shook his head in disappointment. For the life of me I had no idea why it was so hard to please this guy.

"One-Hundred dollars a month... That's all? That's less than my cable bill."

"Believe it or not, most people tend to think it's much more expensive than it really is. Why don't we get you a quote?"

"Umm. I don't know about that Mike."

I pictured Geoff in my head with this beguiled almost grimaced expression. His voice was bellowing with a childlike timidness.

"C'mon Geoff. What'd you have to lose?"

"Eh. Err. How would something like that work?"

"I'm not going to bore you too much with the details. What I would like to do is just gather some basic information. With that info I will go out and shop the insurance market. When I find a carrier that looks like the best fit, then I can submit an application for you. How does that sound?"

"What's the catch? Do I have to give you my credit card info? Do I have to sign anything?"

"Absolutely not. Once we submit the application the life insurance company will do one of two things, offer to insure you or decline to offer. You get a take it or leave it offer. Until then, until you get an offer back, forget about it. For now let me just gather the basic info."

"Okay. Sure. Let's do it. What do you need from me?"

We spoke for another ten minutes or so. I gathered all the necessary info to get a quote going. I made sure to do a little dance in my seat. I was starting to get good at this.

"Great. That'll do it. I'll call you in about a week to cover the next steps in the process. How does that sound?"

"Sure. Evenings work best for me."

And that was that. I was struck with a sudden sense of appreciation for this whole cold calling thing and there was a certain level of satisfaction that came along with that appreciation. I slowly hung up the phone and looked over at Robert. This isn't so hard after all I thought.

"How was that?"

"It was great. You dared to be great. A valiant effort indeed. You're running on 110% enthusiasm and 0% brains. Kid, you still have no idea what you're talking about though. You have one clear flaw, one clear weakness, one clear *Achilles Heel*."

"Yeah. What's that Robert?"

I asked as I shook my head in dishevelment. What was with this guy? I mean, how much can someone put you down? I'm all for constructive criticism, but this was more like just criticism for the sake of criticism.

"You're a born winner, a cesspool of talent and good genetics. Your arrogance has arrogance."

"Yeah, no, I get that a lot. I really appreciate it."

It was mind boggling that a salesperson could be such a hater, especially considering he was my trainer.

"Watch the attitude, kid. My job is to tell you what to do. You need to lean into the process, stop fighting it. You broke the golden rule of sales."

"Golden rule?"

"You gave him a price."

"That price is about right, isn't it?"

"Are you that dense? Being right is not the point. That's not the point at all."

"*Okay*... What is the point?"

"How much does this guy know about insurance?"

"Uhh..."

"Don't answer that! It's a rhetorical question you moron. He knew nothing before speaking with you and now only knows one thing after speaking with you."

Robert shook his head and started laughing, but not in a funny way. Not in a Ha-Ha kind of way, it was more maniacal.

"All he knows *now*, is that number you put in his head. All he knows is $100 per month."

"Well, *I just*..."

"What happens when you get an offer from the life insurance company, after a month of work and the premium is *Two* or *Three Hundred Dollars* a month? How do you plan on explaining that in a way that doesn't make you look like a crook?"

"Well, I guess I just..."

"No. There is no *I guess*! You need to do what you're told."

Robert took a deep breath and collected himself. His face was becoming increasingly redder as the conversation progressed. It was becoming apparent that my self-proclaimed success was rather short-lived.

"Here's what just happened; you wasted the firm's time, your time and the prospect's time. Then guess what, he goes online and roasts this firm for misrepresentation and a *Bait N' Switch* style tactics. Every time you open your mouth you represent this firm. Got it?"

"I got it."

"Do you? Or are you just saying that you got it?"

"I got it. Don't give a price over the phone. Don't break the *Golden Rule*."

I never considered myself to be a quitter, but this wasn't quite what I expected. To say it lightly, this might just not be for me. Honestly, at this point, I just needed a breather to clear my head.

"Can we take a 15-minute break? Would you mind?"

Robert leaned over a bit and had this strange look on his face. I imagined he had some deep seeded reservations.

"Sure thing. I could use another cup of coffee. Let's meet back here at your desk in 15 minutes."

I slowly got up out of my chair and headed for the door. Suddenly, my legs were corrupted by a wobbly-debilitating feeling shivering down to my toes. The room and my head began spiraling. All I could see was the bright red florescent exit sign. I made a studder step to the door and thrust it open. Just as I opened the door the bright white sun hit me and I shoved my forearm over my brow. At the same time, I was scrambling for my car keys in my pocket. I pulled them out of my pocket and dropped them like a buffoon right Infront of my car. I squatted down, which was no easy task due to the Three-Digit temperature outside. The heat barreling over me and the sweat was dripping down my arm as I grabbed the keys off the ground. I shoved them into the key hole and opened the driver side door. What a day this was turning out to be. I jumped in the driver's seat and hit the ignition switch. As far as I was concerned, I couldn't leave this place fast enough. As I was shifting the car into reverse, I took a deep purposeful breath. The tunnel vision began to fade away and my head began to clear. The cloudiness that was cluttering my mind slowly subsided. What was I doing? Was that all it took for me to break? Was I having a panic attack? Maybe I was just over-thinking the whole situation and being a little dramatic. Either way, I needed a second to collect myself. Either way, I needed time to think. Before I knew it, ten minutes passed me by. I was sweating profusely so I turned up the air conditioning. I could feel my heart racing, like the beat of a drum. I could feel my heart pounding through my chest. I could feel my heart thumping.

I was stuck at a crossroads; some might call it an inflexion point. On the one hand, I could put this car into reverse and head on home. On the other hand, I could collect myself and go back to work. I had nothing to lose by walking away, but at the same time I had everything to lose by walking away. I tapped my fingers on my steering wheel for about five more minutes. I found myself with one hand on the wheel and the other fondling the tip of my car key.

That was it. I made a decision. I turned off the car and slowly made my way back to the office. I've haven't gone this far to only go this far. I wasn't going to give up for the sake of just giving up. I grabbed a crumpled-up wad of napkins to wipe the sweat off my forehead. As I walked towards the door, just as I was about to grab the handle, it swung open towards me. Bill walked out of the building like a man on a mission. We started passing each other, me on the way in and him on the way out. Presumably on his way to a client lunch or some important meeting.

"I'm hearing good things about you. Keep it up Mike."

He did kind of an awkward pat on the shoulder as he walked to his car. I stood there for a second and went back to my desk. That was all the encouragement I needed to keep on trucking. I think I made the right decision.

As I walked back to my desk, I noticed Robert was still absent. I sat down and took a long deep breath. I counted slowly to seven as I inhaled, held for a second and counted down from seven as I exhaled. I did this for a minute or so to get my rhythm back to normal. If calling dead people wasn't going to break me then nothing would. I was supremely confident. Nothing was going to stop me but me. I was going to see this through until the end. These were the cards I was dealt and I was going to play them out. Robert walked back over to my desk. That was my que to start back up. I picked up the phone and without provocation just started dialing. The next name on my list read Janis Dickey.

Ring... Ring... Ring...

"This is Janis Dickey speaking."

Ah, success! She picked up. Time to shine. Robert started drumming on his thighs to pass the time.

"Janis, this is Mike Allen with Montrosian Insurance Partners. I'm following up on your recent request for some information about life insurance. Did I catch you at a good time?"

"Yes, you did in fact, but I'm too old to get life insurance."

I was surprised by her level candor and found myself curtailing my own spontaneous laughter. At least she didn't hang up on me right away. That was a good sign as far as I was concerned.

"C'mon. Janis. You're never too old to get life insurance. Trust me."

I looked over at Robert for an assist. How do I ask someone how old they are without actually asking them how old they are? It was quite the dilemma.

"That's not what the last guy told me."

"The last guy?"

"Someone else called me, I think he was from your firm. He said I probably couldn't qualify based on my age, so I stopped looking."

"Believe it or not, even if you're over 70. Generally speaking, you can still qualify for some kind of life insurance."

I was met with a long pause on the other line.

 "At this point in my life, my time, the time I have left is valuable to me. I don't want to lose more of it talking to salespeople. You sound nice, but I'm just not interested anymore."

I blurted out the first thing that came into my head. I was barely scratching the surface of my right hemisphere. I was grasping at straws searching the furthest abscesses of my mind for some kind of intelligent retort. I blurted out what I could.

"Are you sure?!?"

"Thank you. You sound very sweet. I am sure. Have a nice day."

"You to Janis."

CLICK.

The line went dead. Once again, I found myself sitting in a chair holding a dead receiver next to my ear. Robert knocked on my desk with his right middle knuckle and pointed at the phone.

"Look at the bright side. She picked up the phone, right?"

"That's fair."

"It's all part of the game Mike. It's all part of the game. Most people end up going out to lunch and never end up returning. The rejection is rough, it breaks most people. A piece of advice, don't take it personally."

I looked at Robert and said, "I appreciate it the overture."

"Just make one more call and then we can wrap it up."

I didn't realize it, but it was almost 6:30 PM. Time sure does fly when you're having fun. I'd been smiling and dialing hours. I guess the day just passed me right no by.

"Sure thing."

One more call to end the day. That was fine by me.

Fine just fine. Maybe if I'm lucky they won't even pick up.

Ring... Ring... Ring...

"Hello?"

"Hello, is Craig Jones available?"

I could feel that my process was slowly slipping away from me, like sand pouring through your fingertips at the beach. I chalked it up to a minor dose of *Battle Fatigue*.

"I'm Craig. How can I help?"

"Craig, my name is Mike Allen with Montrosian Insurance Partners. Is this a good time to talk?"

"No, not really. I'm just about to sit down for dinner. Why, what's up?"

"Well, what's up *is*... I'm following up on your recent request for life insurance. Are you still in the market for a life policy?"

"Nooo. I'm good. I've got it through work."

Which was predictably followed by a loud *CLICK!*

Who said a career in life insurance couldn't be fun? Who said a career in life insurance couldn't be exciting? It's not a job, it's an adventure, right? I knew one thing. I knew that I wanted to be a millionaire and I sure wasn't going to accomplish that goal waiting tables. I slowly put the phone back down. As I began packing up for the day Robert slid his chair in nice and close.

"Don't take it personally, it's just business. Let's call it a day."

"Sounds good to me."

Robert disconnected his splitter connection from my phone and started packing up his stuff for the day.

"Look at it this way, it can't possibly get any worse. It can only get better from here."

I started cleaning up my desk space and stood up to leave. I stretched my arms out, yawned and headed home for the evening.

Chapter 5: Fake it Till you Make it

"How about cutting me some slack? I'm doing my best here Robert."

"What did you just say to me? Doing your best? I don't need you to do your best, I need you to do my best."

Another predicable workday at Montrosian Insurance Partners, just sitting at my desk on the receiving end of a barrage insults masquerading as "Constructive Criticism". Just as I was about to really hit my stride, Robert was waiting in the wings to pop my balloon. I wasn't the fastest starter, but once I got off the line I sure was able to pick up some real momentum. Robert and I had a certain way of communicating. In that, he would yell at me and I would do my best to completely ignore him. We made a good team in that regard.

"Mike, these are *Warm Transfer* leads. These people have already gone through the hoopla and now want to buy insurance. Every time I pass you the ball, you need to dunk it. Every time you drop that ball you lose me money. Not to mention you make me look bad."

"Mm-hmm."

All I could do was reluctantly sigh and do my best to placate him. Just when I thought I was starting to progress, Robert pulled me back down to reality.

"Let's cut out all the whiney pity-me-pretty non-sense. I'm here to help you get through the Trainee program, I'm not here to cut you some slack."

The typical Trainee was able to complete the program within about Five to Six months. I'd come close to hitting the Ten policies needed over 30 days. But, close only counts in horse shoes and hand grenades.

"Look these Warm Transfer leads are served up to you like pizza, Hot and Ready to eat! All you have to do is close them. Just think, 2 more policies and you'll graduate from the Trainee Program. On to bigger and better things. Best of all on to be someone else's problem."

"Oh joy, I cannot wait!"

Robert clearly came in to work today much like how he preferred his morning coffee, that is to say extra hot.

"What'd you think we expect from you at this point in the game?"

"I-I don't know. You want me to sell insurance policies."

"Exactly. We *don't* expect you to be some kind insurance savant. We expect you to show up and work your butt off. We expect you to put in the hours, whatever it takes to be successful here. We are not expecting you to be some insurance guru right now. Put your nose to the grindstone and get the job done."

"Want to get a re-fill?", Robert said as he pointed over to my empty mug.

"I thought you'd never ask!"

We both did this little laugh and headed back to the breakroom. The breakroom was really starting to grow on me. It was the one area in the office that I felt completely safe from ridicule. Our coffee routine was a rather predictable early morning outing. We'd throw out the Decaf, which turned out to be someone's idea of trolling Robert. What a sick joke to play on someone that was wound up so tight. Then we'd chit-chat for a little bit and drum up the usual watercooler type small talk. This time Robert chose to disband with any of our normal pleasantries. He didn't even check the filter to see what was on the pot. Something was impinging his regular routine. Something was amiss, but I couldn't quite put my finger on it. Robert had a knack for being habitual. Naturally, this salient change in behavior caught my curiosity. I decided the most prudent course of action was to take the roundabout approach.

"How's everything going?"

"Aside from you turning out to be a complete flop?"

"Well, yeah. Aside from that. What's good?"

Robert beamed me this big smile. I knew that a little small talk would cheer him right up.

"There's been quite a bit of rumbling lately."

"What about?"

"About? About these new "insurance" companies that are popping up like a bad case of athlete's foot."

"I mean, aren't there like thousands of insurance companies already?"

"Well, yeah. It's just that..."

Robert began to trail off and fixating on the coffee pot. The coffeemaker finished brewing and pinched out a few loud droplets of coffee.

Drip... Drip... Drip...

The sound of the drips had totally captivated my attention and monopolized Robert's eye. He wasn't the most stable individual, but we had a good working relationship.

Drip... Drip... Drip...

"Mike, do you ever kind of feel like we're just spinning our wheels?"

"What do you mean?"

"Do you ever get the feeling that we're just bringing

one policy in the front door only to lose two out the back door?"

"Robert, when I sell a policy. I'm just happy to sell a policy. I mean, we all got bills to pay, right?"

"Yeah, that's fair."

"Is it fair? Or are you just saying that?", Robert asked in a smarmily tone of voice.

"To be honest, I don't know anymore. I just don't know."

We grabbed our mugs and tiptoed back to the salesfloor. The office was reverberating with generic sales lingo. It was the sound of business. It was the sound of commerce. It was the sound that struck a chord in my heart. We touched down in our seats and got back to work. There was a brief respite in the conversation. Robert still had something on his mind, so I decided to throw him a curveball.

"Why don't we go for a walk?"

"A walk?"

"Yeah, let's get some fresh air."

"HA! Fresh air? In the San Fernando Valley? Is that a joke? It's like *Five Hundred* degrees outside."

"So… yes?"

"Sure."

We put our coffee down and headed for the nearest exit. As we approached the exit Robert drummed up some chit-chat with the other brokers.

"Hold all of my calls boys. I'll be back."

Robert put on his aviators and dodged a bunch of crumped up wads of paper that were tossed at him. The peanut gallery here was rather unforgiving. As we exited the building it was like stepping into a microwave. The scent of the burning asphalt really deepened my appreciation for the *San Fernando Valley*.

"What's going on?"

"What's going on? What'd you mean?"

"Well Mike, I'm assuming it was important because you wanted to take the conversation outside of the office."

"No. No. Nothing like that. It just seemed like you had something on your mind. That's all."

"I sold over $100,000 in insurance last month..."

"Good for you?"

"I wasn't finished. I sold over $100,000 last month, but do you know how many clients I lost?"

"No clue."

"You better get a clue real fast kid. In the last month alone I lost over $10,000 in cash flow."

"That's quite a bit of scratch."

"No kidding. And for the life of me I have no idea why."

"Really. You have no idea?"

"Well, I have my suspicions. They're just unconfirmed."

"Such as?"

"Such as, some of these new fly-by-night insurance carriers offering dirt cheap policies."

"Ah. That's where your clients are going?"

"Well, I don't know, yet."

"What do you mean? Are they telling you that when you call or what?"

"I haven't been calling."

"Why in the world not?"

"What's the point? They already left me for a cheaper company."

"Uh-huh. That's fair."

In reality, that had to be the sorriest excuse for an argument, maybe of all time. How could you assume that people were leaving because of price and then not try to verify it? I couldn't help but laugh out loud. The conversation was becoming rather circular so we mutually decided to head back to the office. Robert's problems seemed more or less self-inflicted in nature. At the end of the day though, Robert's problems were just that. They were Robert's problems. I couldn't afford to take my eye off the prize. I was too close to fail now. I invested way too much time to fail here.

It started out just like any other day. I found myself sifting through the seemingly endless mound of paperwork that covered what used to be my desk. Don't get me wrong, the office wasn't the Taj Mahal, but for strip malls in the *San Fernando Valley*, it wasn't really all that bad. The agency still had a very comfortable feeling to it all. At least, that is what I convinced myself to think in order to endure this long. The foot traffic at the strip mall had been rather tame the past few years. The lead flow, much like the atmosphere was baron. It's hard to believe it now, but this office was once booming with excitement and activity. Look at me, talking all nostalgic and what not. The last three years of my life here felt like an eternity. Robert didn't make the Trainee program easy, but I can't argue with the results. I'd come a long way from that know-nothing kid, to a pretty successful insurance agent. It's funny how in just the blink of an eye three years could pass a person by.

Late last night a potential customer sent me an email

and was curious about getting a quote. So, in accordance with the laws of proper insurance etiquette, we scheduled an early morning meeting, bright and early at *Eleven Thirty*. At first glance it seemed to be a rather mondain request. On the face of it, just another run of the mill insurance quote. To be honest, it was just the kind of break I needed. The phone hadn't been ringing much lately and for some reason people have been hesitant to come by the office. There was a noticeable shift in how people wanted to do business. I didn't care for it one bit. Just as I began to re-arrange the stack of papers on my desk, the door swung open. The secretary popped her head onto the salesfloor.

"Uh... Mike your appointment is here."

I peeked over the mounds of paperwork on my desk to see who it was. I was shocked the prospect arrived so early. To my noticeable confusion and dismay, there was the client sitting in the lobby. He showed up about three hours early.

"John, good morning!"

I was off kilter and it was transparent to everyone on

the salesfloor. Luckily, it just was myself, Robert and the client.

"Mike? Nice to meet you."

As if he thought I would forget the appointment time or just go with the flow. He was right. That's sales and I was desperate.

"Did... did you have time to talk now? I know I'm a bit early. But, I was in the area."

John knew I wasn't in a position to turn him away. He had all the leverage and worst of all, it was abundantly clear to both of us. Sales had started to slow down across the entire office and nobody could really figure out exactly why. Don't get me wrong, we all had our separate theories. I went from lighting up the score board to barely scratching out a living.

"John that's not a problem at all. Luckily, my *Eight* o'clock appointment was re-scheduled..."

I said with a resounding sense of fake bravado. John didn't have to know that was a creative truth. In sales, sometimes you have to be creative with how you phrase things. Lawyers call it 'salesman talk', but in reality it's just part of the vocabulary of sales. I stood up and gestured over to an empty chair with my hand.

"Grab a seat John, let's chat."

John casually strolled over to the empty chair and took a seat. I made sure to let him sit down first. It wasn't a power move or anything like that, I just thought it was the courteous thing to do. A little bit of San Fernando hospitality goes along way.

"So, you're interested in getting some life insurance?"

"I... I was thinking about getting some life insurance. Yes, that's correct."

"That's great! Firstly, let me say congratulations on making a responsible and selfless decision. The only question I have is, why?"

"Why... Why what? What'd you mean?"

His tone shifted dramatically. The thing about having a sales conversation is that once it shifts to an interrogation you have to immediately re-establish rapport or you risk losing the sale completely.

"Ah! What I meant was, why are you looking for life insurance John? Why now? Why not tomorrow? Why not last week? Why today?"

"I've... I've just put it off for a while now. And decided that I should finally just get it over with."

I made sure John saw me nodding in agreement, almost like a bobble-head doll. You know the kind, the commemorative kind you get when you go to *Dodger Stadium* on a Thursday night. The thing about selling is, it's half what you say and half how the customer sees you saying it. The human psyche isn't really as complex as people make it out to be.

"John, it's never too late to get a policy in place. Do you have a specific number in mind?"

If experience has taught me one thing, it's that people have some preconceived number in their head. Most people tend to stick to $500,000 or $250,000, you know, a nice big round number. You know the kind of number, the one that gets flashed around on early morning Television Ads. John scrunched his eyebrows a bit, he had these big bushy black eyebrows. John stared at me for a moment and shuffled around a bit in his chair. Being a salesman, I knew this was signal that he was becoming somewhat uncomfortable. John had his guard up, clearly he had dealt with salespeople before.

"I'm… not really sure."

"John, that's no problem at all."

This was my time to shine. John was showing some hesitation in his remarks, but I knew that gave me considerable room to work with.

"There are normally two kinds of people I work with. The first kind of person knows exactly how much insurance they want, down to the penny. The other type of client comes to me for some guidance…"

I made sure to trail off, to extend an olive branch for John to hop back into the conversation. His hesitation began to dull and John began to let his guard down, just enough to let me know he was paying attention.

"I'm probably the second kind of person, I could use a little bit help figuring it out."

"No *problem*! That's what I'm here for."

Maybe I was coming on a bit too strong, but I felt given the circumstances it was warranted. When I looked down I noticed that John started fidgeting and playing with his wedding ring. Scientists call that a *Sympathetic* response, basically just a nervous tick. At the very least it showed me he was thinking about something.

"John, how much do you think your life is worth? Sorry, what I meant to say was, how much do you think your family would need to continue their way of life in the event that you prematurely passed away?"

I followed this up with a cheesy salesman laugh, you know, the nervous kind of laugh salespeople do when they try to ease the tension.

"I, I really don't know to be honest."

He stopped nodding his head and unharmoniously looked down at the ground. It was clear to me John was out of his element. I had a way of reading people; it was a gift I admired and acquired from Robert.

"Don't worry about it. It's not an easy question to think about."

I took a brief moment to reset the conversation. I shoved some papers aside to make some additional room on my desk. I wanted John to take his mind off the question, at least just for a moment. John laughed out loud as he began to observe my desk.

"Mike, how do you manage to get anything done with a desk looking' like this?"

He smiled for a second, a glimmer of hope. Who would've thought something as silly as my messy desk could reignite a souring conversation?

"John, trust me when I say this, there is a method to my madness."

I stopped moving the papers and glanced back over at John. He was sitting with his legs crossed and hands nestled in his lap.

"Believe it or not, there is no one size fits all approach to figuring out your number."

John didn't say a word, so I took that as an opening to continue.

"In fact, did you know that there are about twenty different methods for determining how much life insurance someone needs? Even the Government of the United States has to estimate the value of a human life."

I always found that people tend to appreciate some brief explanation of the overall process. People tend to be afraid of what they don't understand, so I help them understand it.

"Really?"

"Really, really. To the Government your life is worth over *Seven Million* dollars."

"Seven Million dollars seems like *way* too much money. I was thinking maybe something along the lines of like $500,000."

How strange? One minute he had no clue, the next

he had an exact figure in his head. Either that was a parapraxis or John just randomly threw a number out at me. I started shaking my head up and down to stall for time.

"*Okay.* Let's do a quick calculation and we can figure it out together."

"What's the quickest way to figure it out?"

That was probably John's polite way of telling me to hurry this whole thing up.

"I'm glad you asked."

In reality, I was terrified. I was terrified of losing the sale. I was terrified of looking like a fool. Most importantly, I was terrified of the rejection. People in a hurry rarely ever end up buying, but there was still a chance. Nonetheless, he came here to buy an insurance policy and that's exactly what he was going to get.

"The fastest way is to take your income and multiple it by a factor of *Ten*. The most accurate way to determine your life insurance needs is by breaking down your expenses until your oldest child turns

Eighteen."

I shut up for a second, just hoping I could read his facial ques. His face was stone-cold, like a marble statue.

"Okay, seems simple enough.", he said with a skeptical tone.

I got the strange feeling he was hiding something from me. Most likely, I was reading too much into the situation. Sometimes I get so caught up in the long term, that I forget to think in the here and the now.

"How much would that be roughly speaking? Ballpark?"

John didn't answer right away, he stalled for a bit. Over three years of doing the same thing every day, you tend to learn a thing or two. One of the things that I've learned is that most people don't enjoy talking about their finances, especially to complete strangers.

"*Roughly?* How much are we talking about?", I asked again in a firmer tone of voice.

"I make about *Thirty-Eight Thousand* a year... before taxes."

"Great. Let me do some quick math. Then you would need... if we multiplied 38 by 10... Your number is $380,000."

That was the easy part of the conversation. The next step was vital. The next step was to make this number meaningful to him, otherwise it's just a number. I still didn't know why he needed life insurance. All I knew was that he wanted insurance. I kept reminding myself to focus on the journey, not just the destination. Typically, people react to their 'number' in one of two ways. Most people get sticker-shock from the initial number or they accept it. John decided to accept it, a bit too easily I might add.

"Okay, well... how much would something like that cost?"

Selling is kind of like playing the game of poker. The first rule of playing poker is to play the person and not the hand that was dealt. John had asked what we call in my profession a buying question, which simply means he wanted to buy.

"Here's the thing John. Buying life insurance isn't like going to the supermarket and buying some shampoo or a can of soda. It's not something you can just take off the shelf and purchase. The first thing we have to do is establish how much life insurance you need, which we did. Then we need to figure out how long you want coverage for…"

"Uh. What do you mean by how long I want coverage for?"

It was clear that John, much like 99% of society, didn't know what he didn't know when it came to life insurance. Most people look at life insurance the way they looked at the DMV, a necessary annoyance to be avoided at all costs.

"Here's the thing about life insurance. What you don't know could kill you, financially speaking that is. With auto insurance, the best-case scenario is that you purchase it and never have to use it. With life insurance the worst-case scenario is that you need it, have to use it and it's not there for you."

"What do you mean not there for me?"

"Life insurance can either be temporary or it can be permanent, those are your two options."

"Well, what's the difference?"

"I'm glad you asked John. Temporary insurance is just that, it's temporary. If you don't use it, then you lose it. Permanent insurance is permanent, meaning that it lasts as long as you do. You and it have the same expiration date."

John seemingly understood as he started nodding his head in agreement.

"Well, I think I only need it for a short amount of time. Until my kids go off to college."

A fairly predictable response for someone John's age. I'm always shocked when a grown man with a family doesn't own life insurance. I mean, who does that?

"How long do you think that would take? How long until your kids would be off on their own?"

"Oh... I would say about ten years or so. When they turn Eighteen or Nineteen."

"That's great! John, then I would recommend you purchase a ten-year term insurance policy. Term insurance will get you the coverage you need to protect your family…"

Before I could even finish my sentence, he blurted out, "Yeah… Term Insurance, that's what I need."

"Prefect. So, a Ten-year term policy. Now that we got that figured out, we have to apply. We have to apply for the life insurance and see if the life insurance company is willing to make you an offer."

"Hold on a second. What do you mean by make an offer?"

I was starting to think I had lost him. Most people can't withstand more than ten minutes of insurance jargon before they space out or stroke out.

"Good question John. A quote is just a quote. It doesn't really mean much of anything. It's an indication of a price, but not an official offer to insure you."

John looked at me with a rather skeptical disposition. I could tell he was unconvinced by my explanation.

Nevertheless, his relative level of satisfaction aside, I needed to press forward and close the deal.

"Ah. So, what would something like that cost me?"

He was curious yet oddly confident. The further we jumped down the Rabbit Hole, the most poignant, practiced and piacular his questions became. John had started sweating under his arm pits and had been clutching his phone in his left hand. His phone screen was on, but I couldn't see the detail from that far away.

"John, like I said earlier. Life insurance is something you have to apply for... kind of like a job. You won't get every job you apply for, and you won't know until after the interview. We won't know the cost until you go through medical underwriting... It's kind of like a job interview for life insurance policy."

He interrupted with a somewhat agitated tone, "You mean you can't tell me what it would cost until I sign up? How is that possible?"

"I could give you an estimate, but it wouldn't be binding. It wouldn't even be that accurate. I mean, I can put any number I want on that quote, but unless you qualify it won't matter."

This whole conversation took a sharp turn for the worst. John had purposefully stalled the conversation and started fidgeting in his seat a bit more than before. My only chance was to break the Golden Rule. Go for broke.

"Based on your medical history, and mind you this is purely an estimate and in no way binding. For a 10-year term life policy, it would cost you about $50 per month."

I had fumbled my way into and through a sales pitch. Which from personal experience was the worst way to go about it. What could I say? I done goofed.

Without hesitation he said, "That's a little too expensive..."

Did I miss something? John's posture had changed and his attitude clearly reflected his negotiating position. What was I missing? What was it?

"Before I came in this morning, I got a quote from another life insurance company."

How could I have missed that? Maybe I've become too complacent over the years. Maybe I got tad bit sloppy. I had nothing to say and it was clear as daylight to John that the *Emperor had no clothes on*. Before I could utter a word, John pointed to his phone.

"This quote is for $500,000 in coverage for Thirty years of coverage and only $10 per month."

Animals have three basic reactions to stress; they can freeze, they can flee or they can fight. For me, at that moment, I was like a deer caught in the headlights. All I could think of was to ask for the quote.

"Do you mind if I take a look at the quote?"

The conversation had completely become lopsided and I only could go for the Hail-Mary of Dirty Salesman Tricks. I was going to try and trash talk the other insurance company. That was my plan, to hope for the best. John slowly and cautiously handed me over his cellphone. Part of me thought to just throw it out the window. I looked at the quote in utter disbelief. He had a quote for less money, more coverage and more time.

"Yeah, that is way better than I could do for you... I'm curious though. How did you hear about this company? Flushy, is it?"

In retrospect, what else was I going to say? What else could I possibly do? In all honesty this sounded more like a mobile app, not an insurance company.

"No... But... But, at *that* price, does it really matter? It seems like the best deal I could find."

"I mean, it's a great deal...", I said with a somber tone. If it wasn't clear to John before, I was completely demoralized by what had just transpired.

"Well... is there anything else you have that might be more in line with the Flushy quote?"

He shifted in his seat and turned sideways aligning his body with the quickest path to the exit. I had to make a choice. Do I stall for time? Do I quit? Should I double down? On a good day I consider myself a fairly resourceful person, but today, when it matters, right now, all the clever quips and retorts weren't going to win me this client. So, I did what any noble salesperson would do in my situation. I punted the ball.

"Let me look into some options for you over the next couple of days. How does that sound?"

I found myself cowering behind those once annoying stacks of paper. John shook his head seemingly in agreement. John slowly rose from his chair. He stood up and reached out his hand. I had started to extend my arm out when he said, "My phone?"

"Of course! Sorry about that."

A minor brain fart wasn't going to mar this already stupendous conversation. Somehow I forgot I was holding his phone in my hand. Isn't it funny that something non-existent twenty years ago has now become almost like an appendage to most people?

I handed back the phone and began to apologize. Just as I began to blurt something out, I decided to fold up. That's the thing about sales. Sometimes you win and sometimes you get humbled. Perhaps I'd lost a step or two in my old age. I had a million and one thoughts swirling in my head, but most of all, what in the world was Flushy?

I slowly found my way back to my desk. I was determined to do some research and figure out what just happened. I opened up my web browser and began to search around the web for a supposed 'life insurance' company called Flushy. I was shocked to find article after article about 'the massive success of Flushy'. Before I knew it, two and a half hours had passed me right on by.

I'd be lying to myself if I said I wasn't interested in learning more. So, I clicked on the website. The website was covered in bright almost neon-florescent colors. Color scheme aside, the website was pretty well put together. It had the Flushy logo on the top left of the header and 5 other buttons to select. There was a button that read, 'How did we do it?" There was a button that read, "The Flushy Difference." One of the buttons read, "Our Humbled Beginnings'." There was a 'User Review' section, an 'About Flushy' section and a section that just said 'Contact Us'. Nothing fancy about the site, it was modern and user friendly. This is probably just one of those fly-by-night insure-tech companies. Today they sell life insurance, by next week they'll be out of business or in a different industry. But, you know what? Maybe I should poke around a little more.

As I scrolled down the homepage the site hit me in the face with the 'Flushy difference'. The website read in part, 'Old conventional life insurance is sold and peddled by independent insurance agents for a commission. Because, they are paid on commission, they often focus on selling excessive policies to wealthier people or unnecessary amounts of insurance to people who might not really even need it or even want it.'

"Might not really need it? Excessive?", I mumbled under my breath.

Although that might have rubbed me the wrong way, the site had gotten my attention. It went on to read, 'Here at Flushy, we offer consumers a modernized, mindful, intentional and fully customizable life insurance program to protect the people you care about most.'

"Modernized? Ha! You mean cheap!? What a bunch of garbage..."

Objectivity was never much of a strong suit for me. It would seem these Flushy people meant to upend and simultaneously undermine my entire profession.

I kept reading, 'Our Flushy team members are salaried workers, so they work you and not for a commission. We treat you like part of the Flushy family and that means we won't try to sell you on excessive and needlessly expensive insurance policies. There's no such thing as a good deal for the wrong insurance policy.'

"They stole my line! That's my line!"

I hadn't realized it, but the more I read, the more aggressively I started clicking with my mouse. The thought of being a salaried worker did sound appealing. I scrolled down some more, 'Instead of wasting your money on useless things like claims adjusters, underwriters, management teams and actuaries, we use artificial intelligence and robots. Most insurance companies would still use a quill and ink pad if they could to write you a policy.'

"Yeah, *that's right.* But, how can they possibly get rid of underwriters?"

Maybe they figured out the secret sauce or maybe it was too good to be true. Either way, I was interested in adding Flushy to my line up of carriers to sell. I mean, I'd be foolish not to at least look into it.

My interest was more than peaked, so I clicked on the 'Learn More' tab. When I clicked on the 'Learn More' tab there was a section on the Flushy difference. It read, 'The life insurance industry has a big problem, and it was that life insurance companies couldn't even see the problem. They couldn't see it, because they themselves are part of the problem. We here at Flushy saw an easy way to put a fix to that problem.'

"Okay… what's that supposed to mean?"

I went on to read, 'The old school way of buying a life policy could have taken days, weeks, if not months to complete the process. The old process would involve putting a person through mounds of paperwork, lengthy redundant conversations with insurance agents and almost completely unnecessary medical workups.'

Blood work is unnecessary? Now, I've heard it all.

How in the heck can you write a policy without blood work? This all seemed far too good to be true, it had to be. I mean, *C'mon* you got to be kidding me with all this. I started pouring over the site at an even more vigorous pace. Part of me was trying to poke holes in this obvious charade and part of me was intrigued by the new shiny object.

A little further down it read, 'The old process just wasn't a consumer first or even customer friendly kind of system. We have built the first life company with a consumer-first mindset, not an insurance-company mindset. What we did at Flushy was set an aggressive goal with a simple mission. We set out on a mission to change the way business was done in the life insurance industry. We really wanted to flip the industry completely on its head.'

I took a second to recalibrate myself and digest all of that non-sense. They put the people first? By not doing any kind of due diligence and allowing experts to walk them through the process?

I continued reading, "Flushy single handedly reshaped the way people buy and interact with life insurance companies. We took the process and up-ended it. We kind of look at ourselves like the Mother Theresa of Life Insurance companies. We took the old way of doing things, put it in a box, shook up the box and dumbed it out on a table. We wanted to make a process that puts the people first and not profits."

This sounds like some sick joke. This all sounds like someone made the entire website as an attempt to troll the life insurance industry. Part of me loved that, the other part of me was enraged by the arrogance and sheer disrespect. I took a deep breath followed by a deep relaxing sigh of relief. This must've been a bunch of smoke and mirrors. I sat back in my chair and stroked my chin while I thought it out.

They offer a rock bottom price for more coverage. Now, if they were offering the same coverage for less, I could say that was legit. But, then again, they don't have to pay people like me. But, it did say they have salespeople, just not paid on commission.

There was a section that really caught my eye at the

top and it read 'How do we do it all?' It read in part, "We offer the world's most competitive prices and coverage features. We can do that by cutting out the waste and vaporizing the old hassles of buying life insurance. We put the power in your hands and not in the hands of the insurance agent. We offer the best in class, award winning Flushy service center, which is comprised of a team of non-commissioned licensed life insurance agents ready to help you through the entire process from start to finish. A frictionless experience, that has removed the inherent old-timey conflictions that once plagued our industry."

This whole situation was starting to get me pretty riled up. How is it that not only haven't heard of this company, but they can do all this for much, much, much less than a traditional insurance company? It's not even like it was a little bit less, it was a lot less.

The website went on to read, "Simply put, we are here to put you first. This is life insurance that focuses on your life and not the life insurance company. We do everything differently and all it takes is one quick & easy hassle-free application.

The Flushy experience delivers a 100% completely online insurance application process. We make it simple for you and easy for you to apply for life insurance on your terms, not ours. What could have taken days, weeks, if not months, now can be done with the click of a mouse and under 45 seconds. You have more important things to worry about than paperwork, so let us take care of the heavy lifting. We offer policies that can be purchased like buying a bar of soap at the grocery store. Virtually all of our Flushy applicants can avoid a traditional burdensome medical exam."

"Okay... this is pretty much just a rehash of the stuff on the front page."

I scrolled down with a bit faster pace and stopped when I saw something that caught my eye. It read, 'If you want someone to guide you, and help you along your life insurance purchasing journey. Don't be afraid, because we have a completely licensed staff of completely non-commission life insurance agents that are ready to help you either online or by the phone.'

"Hmm... Interesting..."

I went on to read further and it read in part, "Ultimately, what we would like to do, is to provide you with options, so that you can customize and design the perfect life insurance policy for you. A policy on your terms that fits your specific insurance needs."

I sat back and propped my feet up on the desk. I didn't have much else on my mind, surprisingly this all sounded kind of good. I sat upright again and scrolled down the website. This one section really stuck out to me and it read, The Flush-Lock Advantage.

"What in the heck is that?"

As I read further, "Every single term life insurance policy that we offer comes with the Flush-lock. Meaning that your insurance policy has level premium payments. In simple terms that means the price is the same every single month, guaranteed. As you age, term insurance becomes more expensive, but not with the Flush-lock Advantage. As long as you meet certain conditions, you can qualify for the

Flush-Lock rate guarantee."

"Now that sounds like a bold face lie. How in the world can they do that?"

I scrolled down a little farther and it read, "Not only that, but we offer a Money-Back Guarantee with every single policy for any possible reason. If you are dissatisfied or unhappy for any reason in the first 45 days of your policy, we'll refund your payment in full. No questions asked, no hassle. You are able to cancel at any time, with no cancellation fees or early termination costs. This is all part of the Flushy difference."

"Well, that's just absurd. There's no way they can do that."

This was all turning out to be some terrible nightmare. How could I possibly compete against a company like this? I didn't have a company in my line up with anything nearly this competitive.

One of the headers really caught my eye, it read "Our Humbled Beginnings". This would've been a lot easier to read with a shot of whiskey, maybe a double. This section of the website was engulfed in a completely white backdrop, almost porcelain. Quite the contrast compared to the rest of the website. Clearly a lot of thought went into building this website. The page had a small blurb. It read, "Like any great business it all started out with a simple question. How do we simplify the life insurance buying process, eliminate the headaches and save people money at the same time? Our founding partners David Berrigan and Todd Dupree, both met at the Wharlon School of Business. Mind you, this is all way before Flushy was valued at $10,000,000,000."

"Ah, yes. How very humble indeed. Nothing screams humble like an ivy league school. Two rich kids met and made a company that their parents funded and propped up."

It went on to read, "It was just a humble start-up, much like Apple, Microsoft or even the Catholic Church. At that time, David was struggling to pay his *six-figure* yearly tuition and had to choose between buying previously-owned textbooks or paying his life insurance premium."

"Oh yeah, I'm sure that's how it all went down. Someone paying six-figures in tuition couldn't afford $30 a month for life insurance. *GIVE ME A FREAKING BREAK*. Cry me a river."

Maybe I was digesting this all with a splash of jealousy. This was my expedition into the unknown, it was my journey down the rabbit-hole and I was hooked.

It went on to read, "David didn't realize it at the time but he ended up discovering he was grossly overpaying for life insurance. Turns out David was not the only one being unknowingly over-charged. That's when David and Todd had the 'Ah-Ha' moment. That's the moment when they came up with the idea for Flushy. David took a small loan from his father, a meager sum of *One Hundred Million Dollars*. David made the same mistake millions of Americans made, he purchased life insurance without knowing how much coverage he actually needed. He purchased life insurance without knowing what it was going to cost. Together David and Todd set out to change all of that. What they discovered along their journey was that the old conventional approaches to life insurance had been confusing, costly and even a bit corruptible. David and Todd wanted to really make that all different. So, with a simple vision they both set out to protect families by creating the world's premiere and lowest cost life insurance company."

Where do I go from here? I was at a crossroads of sorts, an inflexion point if you will. At the bottom of the webpage there was a bright red button which was screaming *Press On Me*. This was obviously a big PHD button, it had all the telltale signs of a *Press Here Dummy button*. The button simply read, "Become a Flushy Agent".

"It couldn't hurt for me to hear them out, right?"

Don't get me wrong, I wasn't seeking to join some kind of rebellion against the current way of doing things. I very much like the current way of doing things. On the other hand, I was moderately intrigued by the idea of being part of something bigger than my current indentured servitude. Part of me was scared of not pulling the trigger and being left behind in the dust. Being a relic of a bygone era.

What if I continued down this path? What if I ignored this emerging disruptor? What if I didn't click on it? What if I stayed the course and failed? So, I clicked on the button.

"It would be irresponsible for me to at least not look into it.", I mumbled a terse rationalization.

I wasn't content enough just to become a bystander of this massive looming change. I wasn't put on this earth to merely be a witness to the demise of my own occupation. Maybe I was rationalizing, maybe I was letting uncertainty get the best of me, maybe I was ready to take a gamble.

After clicking on the button another page popped up with a simple message. The message said, "We want you on the Flushy revolution. Help us change the world one policy at a time." I was destined to do something meaningful in life, maybe this was it.

A web application popped up asking me for more information. As I started filling out the application, the door to Bill's office had opened up. Bill started to slowly walk out of his office. He shut his office door and through his sports coat on. As he was adjusting his sports coat he looked over at me. We made this awkward kind of eye contact, I looked like a child who was hiding a bad report card.

"How'd that sale go Mike? Wait, what are you still doing here?", Bill asked impertinently.

He had a briefcase in one hand and his sports coat in the other. He put down the bag and started to put his sports coat on.

"I—I— The client decided to go with a Flushy policy. We weren't even close on the price."

Bill scoffed at my explanation.

"Yeah... that is going to happen. Luckily, we're not in the price business. We're in the peace of mind business, right?"

For a moment there, it looked like Bill was trying to express some genuine tenderness. I quickly turned my computer monitor off, like someone cleaning up a crime scene.

"See you tomorrow Bill?"

Bill did a little thumbs up and headed to the exit.

"Don't forget to lock the door behind you. Get out of here soon kid, it's like 9:30pm. Don't you have a life?", he said while walking away.

That was kind of like the tea kettle calling the pot black. He was right though; it was getting late and I still needed to pick up groceries before I headed home. As Bill was heading to the exit I got up from my chair to stretch and pretended to pack up my things for the evening. One eye trained on my briefcase and the other on the front door. Bill was lazily strolling towards the exit. He stopped at the exit of the salesfloor and put his hand on the light switch. He turned his head to the side and looked at me with one eye. I started sweating bullets, but pretended not to notice and continued packing up my belongings. Bill coughed loudly to get my attention. I was too nervous to even look at the man. I might as well had a big Guilty sign hung around my neck.

Bill asked, "Mike?"

I took a deep breath, and looked up from my desk over to his direction. I still couldn't make eye contact, so I started at the Exit sign instead.

Bill asked again, "Mike?"

"Yeah Bill?"

"On or Off?"

A sense of desperation turned into jubilance in the matter of seconds. All of my anxiousness subsided with a single question. I couldn't help but laugh off his request.

"On, please."

He shot me a thumbs up and said, "Don't forget to lock up for the night."

"Will do boss."

Bill exited stage left. Seconds later I heard the distinct ignition of his Hundred Thousand Dollar sports car. It sounded more like a Jet Engine, rather than a car. That meant I was in the clear to wrap up that Contact Request on the Flushy website. I turned my computer monitor back on and finished up my inquiry.

Chapter 7: The Flushy Pre-Screening

Truthfully, I was floundering at work. My mind was completely pre-occupied with Flushy. I went from a rising star, a person to watch, to the laughing stock of the office. I'd fallen from *Mount Olympus*. The question was, could I get back up? I couldn't close a door, let alone a sale. Every day after work, I would go to the Flushy website and do some poking around. During my lunch breaks I went on my phone and read articles about Flushy. When I was sitting on the toilet in the office pretending to poop, I was trolling on my phone looking at what Flushy had to offer.

I even cancelled my existing life insurance policy with a *Two-Hundred-Year-Old* life insurance carrier and secretly switched it over to Flushy. The savings were substantial. Yeah, I felt a little guilty, but what was I supposed to do? Was I supposed to just sit there and flush my money down the toilet? I finally caved in to my baser instincts.

There was an open job at Flushy that I was mulling

over applying for. For three weeks it was staring me right in the face, popping up in my news feed. I justified and rationalized my decision again and again and again. I went to the Flushy website and hit the apply button. What better day to do it then my day off? The application was your standard boiler plate kind of Human Resources approved landing page. I filled out all of the basic information; name, address, occupation, work history, desired salary, etc. Then I got to the section to upload my resume and a cover letter.

Ironically, I'd never actually gotten around to making a resume. Where does one start? I sat there for 30 to 40 minutes searching for tips on how to build a quality resume. Honestly, I've always found the idea of resumes to be a little antiquated. In my opinion, a resume, like a report card is loosely associated with competency. Nonetheless, it's required. So, I slapped a resume together and hoped for the best. Using the best possible tips the internet had to offer.

"Done and done.", I mumbled to myself.

I submitted the application and sat back in my old

pleather executive chair. The next thing I knew I saw an email pop-up on my phone from Flushy. That was fast, maybe a little too fast.

The email read, "Thank you for your interest in the position at Flushy. The next step in the process, is an *over the phone* interview. If you're interested, please reply to Human_Resources@Flushy.com and let me know the best date and time for me to call you. Monday through Friday, between the hours of 9 am and 4 pm, Pacific Standard Time.

What to expect during your Flushy phone interview?

- The conversation could last up to 120 minutes.
- I will review your employment and educational background, prior to the interview.
- We will ask behavioral-based and non-behavior-based questions in our interview.
- Prior to the interview you need to complete your Flushy assessment. It'll take anywhere from 90 to 120 minutes.

We look forward to speaking with you."

I scheduled my interview with Flushy for the later in

afternoon, it's not like I had anything better to do. Luckily, I called into work and decided to take a sick day. I had five hours to prep for the interview, plenty of time. The email contained a hyperlink to the Flushy Employment Assessment. I clicked on the link and it led me to this website with some basic instructions. At first glance it all seemed rather rudimentary, but then I clicked on the start button.

The test had a giant red countdown timer on the right-hand side that followed you as your scrolled down the assessment. The assessment was comprised of 100 questions, which were a mix of multiple choice, true or false and fill in the blank.

The first question on the test was a bit obtuse. It read, "You're about to board a bus from Los Angeles to San Francisco. You'd like to know if it's raining in San Francisco, so you call four friends who live in San Francisco. There is a 66% chance that each friend is telling you the truth and a 33% chance of telling you a lie. None of your friends are not telling you that it's raining in San Francisco. What is the overall probability that it is not in fact, raining in San Francisco?"

I stared at that question for a good five minutes and I had no idea what the answer was. In front of me, I had five choices and no clue in the world.

A. 1%

B. 22%

C. 33%

D. 66%

E. None of the above

Given I wasn't a rocket scientist; my strategy was to guess. My dad taught me a good rule of thumb when I was eleven years old. If you see a *none of the above* on a test, odds are that's the correct answer. If you don't know the answer, just assume that they are all wrong. So, I did just that.

The drawer in my home office desk had a bottle of bourbon just for this very occasion. I pulled out the drawer and grabbed the bottle of whiskey along with a red plastic cup. I poured a glass of whiskey and started casually sipping. It wasn't fancy, but I needed something to take the edge off.

The next question was a lot of easier.

True or False:

Bob is younger than Donald.

Donald is older than Ronald.

Ronald is older than Bob.

If the first two statements are true, the third statement is:

A. True

B. False

Did I say a lot easier? That was somewhat of an embellishment on my part. This test wasn't nearly as pedestrian as I had hoped. I tried reasoning out the question in my head, like that somehow would help.

"Uh... Okay... if Bob is... Uh.. Ronald is older than... Uh... Okay, *I got it*. I'll just guess. *Man*, forget this!", I blurted out at my computer.

What did I have to lose? I had a 50/50 chance of being correct. Better odds than the lottery. So, I guessed and moved on. I did that for another *ten* or so questions. Until, I arrived at question number fourteen. Let me tell you about question number fourteen. It read, "What kind of Animal are you?" Take that in for a second, I know I did. What kind of animal am I? What kind of non-sense kind of question is that? What would be the appropriate answer for a hipster tech company, what would they want to hear?

Play it safe or bet the farm? I went the safe route. I went with a Wolf. Its pack animal, it's a hunter, it's perfect for sales. I breezed through the next twenty or so questions and half my bottle of whiskey. The whiskey was really starting to take effect. Before I knew it, I was staring down question number 51.

It read, "What *Latin* verb becomes its own past tense by rearranging its letters? (Fill in the blank)."

Latin is a dead language, isn't it? *Hiccup! Belch!*

I was jolted by my own melancholy. Maybe I needed to ease up on the whiskey intake. I decided to leave that answer blank and see what would happen. This test was confiscating what little cognitive power I had left. I was like a car running on fumes, grasping for every ounce of fuel left in the tank. The countdown timer had 30 minutes left on the clock. I started randomly guessing the answers to the next twenty-five questions. It was the only realistic way I could get this thing done within the time window. I got to the final ten questions and took a big sigh of relief. Fifteen minutes left on the clock. Plenty of time to finish strong. I mean, I couldn't do any worse at this point.

Question number 90 wasn't so bad. It read, "True or False: A 4x4x4 square cup can hold more water than a 3x6x3 triangle cup."

I wrapped up the final ten questions and hit the submit button with 30 seconds to spare. I spent the last two hours putting my brain through a hodgepodge of logic games. I stood up quick to stretch my legs, probably a little too quick for how many shots of whiskey I ended up consuming. Nothing like a little day drinking and mental stimulation.

I had about three hours to kill before the initial phone interview. Now that I had the test done I could relax and take a power nap. I had plenty of time. I set my alarm for 2:30pm, which would give me a half hour or so to prep for the interview. Really, I just needed to sober up. I belly flopped onto my bed and instantly fell asleep.

I woke up about as fast as I fell asleep, to the sound of my watch alarm.

Beep! Beep! Beep!

The alarm had a thundering repetitive beep to it. The beep clamored, the beep amplified, the beep intensified. Most likely the culprit was my hangover. The effects of the whiskey started to wear off. I felt fine, more or less, I wasn't crisp, but good enough for an interview. For once, I decided not to hit the snooze button. About five minutes later, after a couple cups of coffee the phone began to ring.

Ring... Ring... Ring...

It was an abnormally loud ring, maybe it was just my nerves. I stared down at my phone and looked to see who was calling. It was a local number, so I assumed it wasn't a scam call. These days my cell phone was bombarded with scam robot-calls.

"Hello?", I answered with a slight hesitation.

"Hi. Is this Mike Allen?"

"Speaking."

"Mike this is Jeanie Distefano with Flushy. How are you today?"

Jeanie had a discernible *East Coaster* kind of accent. She was probably from somewhere around the Long Island area. If I were to guess she was one of the many recent ex-pats coming out of the northeast.

"I'm doing great. Thanks for asking."

I thought it best if I kept my answers short and succinct. I read that somewhere on the internet while I was browsing for interview tips.

"Mike, I'm going cut to the chase. To say we're impressed with your resume would be an understatement."

"Thanks! Believe it or not, that was the first time I

had to put one together."

That probably wasn't the smartest way to answer that question.

"Ah. Well, either way, good job. Aside from your resume we need to talk about your Sales Assessment."

Here it comes... she's about to drop the hammer on me. I was feeling pretty crummy about my overall performance. Maybe downing half a bottle of whiskey before breakfast wasn't a great idea. I mean, I've had worse ideas.

"The results of your sales assessment came back... and they were very strong. In fact, you crushed the Sales Assessment. It's the highest score we've seen all year. Maybe since the test was created."

That revelation was jarred my senses. I couldn't help but utter this pathetic sort of self-congratulatory response.

"I-I... I'm really glad to hear it."

"Needless to say we're interested. We want to offer

you the complete Flushy package. Which includes a; base salary, commission, educational reimbursement, leads, expense account, health insurance and full a retirement package and much, much more."

"That all sounds great. What's the catch?"

This sounds way too good to be true. I was still awestruck by the whole conversation.

"Catch? No, there's no catch. We're looking for the best and the brightest, we're looking for the rising stars, we're looking for the hidden gems. And we are willing to pay for that top talent. That's all. That's it. Simple and easy. Any questions for me?"

"Yeah, when do I start?"

"Sure, let's talk next steps. You'll have to come by the office and interview with the President of Flushy. He interviews all of the *new* salespeople and hand selects are new external candidates. Assuming you make it past that interview, the job is yours."

"Sounds good to me."

"I'll send you a follow up email with all the deets. Tentatively, let's plan on next Monday. If anything changes I'll let you know. If you need anything in the meantime don't be shy about asking. Nice to meet you."

"Nice to meet you as well..."

Before I could finish my sentence she hung up the phone. Things were progressing at a blinding speed. The question I had to ask myself was, could I keep up? On paper, Flushy was a rather compelling odyssey for me pursue. If I wasn't still buzzed, I might be somewhat suspicious. It all sounded too good to be true. I guess I would find out.

"One hundred and six..."

David Berrigan said while swiveling around in his captain's chair. Something he probably practiced over and over again, maybe to convince himself that is how 'powerful' people are supposed to act. Or maybe it was an easy way to intimidate and initiate potential candidates.

"One hundred and six? One hundred and six what?"

"Mike, that number represents how many people die every single minute. Take a moment to reflect on that."

David Berrigan was clasping his fingers together as he looked me directly in the eyes. David paused the conversation there. It was a long deliberate pause. The pause was followed by a loud cough.

"Cooough! Ahem!"

His cough had a raspy echo to it, like the cough of a pack a day smoking habit. He was the kind of imposing figure that reminded me of a villain in an old spy movie. He clearly hadn't shaved in two or three weeks; it was rather distracting. His beard was more stubble than an actual beard. The only thing missing was a cowboy hat and some spurs.

"Better yet, let me ask you something. How much do you enjoy buying life insurance? Or any type of insurance for that matter?"

Normally, I like to take a somewhat measured approach when answering non-conventional interview questions, but with this one, I felt a certain amount of liberty.

"It's right up there with getting a root canal, going to the DMV or shopping for a used car."

There was a noticeable stoppage in the conversation. David took frequent and intentional strategic pauses, probably to create some dramatic effect. So, I decided to really absorb my surrounding and take in the room. David had this imposing yet eclectic office, like an amalgamation of Tony Montana and Willy Wonka.

"Correct! And that is exactly the reason why we created Flushy."

David Berrigan magnanimously explained from his all-white leather captain's chair. The kind of chair that reeked of superiority and an over-abundance of confidence. The kind of chair that cost more than my car. The kind of chair that made a real statement.

"Here's the thing Mike, most Americans view their insurance and the entire insurance industry as a necessary evil rather than how it should be viewed, which is as the pinnacle of social achievement. That's something we here at Flushy plan on changing. We want to be the tip of the spear. We want to amplify the social good that is insurance. Our intended goal if you will, is to revolutionize the insurance industry and turn it on its head.", David Berrigan said with an affirmative and confident tone.

David clutched on to the arms of his chair and propelled himself upwards. He walked towards his window with his hands behind his back, gazing outside as if to take a moment to reflect on his own words of wisdom. After a moment of pause, he turned his head and looked at me with a persuasive grin on his face.

"I just have on question for you Mike. Are you on the in? Or, are you on the out?"

That's how it all started. That's how David Berrigan changed my life, with a simple idea and a smile. He was the salesman of all salesman, he had more of a Rockstar kind of persona rather than that of an insurance guy. Have you ever met someone who was so supremely confident that it made you confident? So much so that you wanted their idea to be your idea? Well, that was David and I was in.

I leaned back in my chair, paused for a moment and reflected for a second. The kind of long winded pause a person has to take when someone has just casually upended their reality. In the span of a two days, I went from browsing the Flushy website to sitting down and interviewing with the President of Flushy. The Flushy Headquarters was one of the many massive high-rises in downtown Los Angeles. It was the kind of building that had a shadow that stretched a mile long. I mean, it's not too often that I'm sitting in what looks to be a $1000 executive leather chair, sitting across from the founder of a billion-dollar insurance start-up.

"I'm interested. I'm very interested. I'll probably have to know a little more about the actual job before making that kind of decision."

David Berrigan chimed back in by rattling on about his mission and the vision for the company he had built from the ground up. I didn't take it he heard the word *no* too often.

"We're challenging everything, we're challenging the status quo by transforming the way insurance companies do business. *And* not only that, we're able to do so at a much lower cost. In some cases, our go to market price is 90% less for the same amount of insurance compared to our other big-name insurance carriers."

"That's all well and good. But, how are we able to do all that?"

Then I caught myself, I was already talking as if I had accepted the offer. I could tell by his facial expression that he picked up on my wordage. David had that kind of effect on people. David Berrigan responded within the blink of an eye and without a moment of hesitation.

"That's the beauty of it all Mike. It's inevitable. People always want me to open the kimono, people always want to peak behind the curtain, but no one ever really wants to know how the hamburger is made."

To be honest, I wasn't sure if I wanted him to pull back the curtain. I definitely didn't want him to open his kimono, or even what that meant. To be honest, I wasn't really sure what I wanted him to say.

"Here's how Flushy is able to do all that. It comes down to our business model, which is based on a peer-to-peer insurance model, which is fueled by a self-service technology platform and powered by Artificial Intelligence."

I took a second and then nodded my head in agreement.

"So if I were to accept your offer... where do I fit into

to the Flushy picture?"

"That's what I like about you Mike Allen, you get straight to the point. No parsing of language, you don't garnish your words. The thing is... the challenge is... for us here at Flushy... when you're too fixated on a problem, when you've zoomed in with a microscope, you sometimes forget to zoom out and view the whole picture. As a result, the larger picture often alludes us."

He seemed to be rambling on a bit, so I thought it was a good time to interject myself back into the conversation. Our rhythm was off, like dancing with someone who had two left feet.

"Zoom out? So, what would I be doing exactly?"

This time I sprinkled on more of a confused tone than my previous attempt. David had a smile ear to ear and turned back towards his desk. He began to slowly walk back to his chair.

"To most people the insurance buying process seems to be somewhat of daunting task. It's like *Latin* to most people, a whole different kind of language, a dead language. A language that very few people can even comprehend. That's where you come into the picture, because you're here to help us zoom out. We rely on outsiders, much like yourself, to come in and widen our view finder."

"So, you're saying that I'm valuable because I do not know anything about Flushy? Or, are you saying my value is in the fact that... Sorry, I'm just not getting it."

Almost too anxiously David replied with a resounding halfcocked answer.

"Precisely that! Precisely Mike. You speak Insurance Agent. We need more of that around here. That way we don't lose sight on what we're trying to fix. Does that make sense?"

"It does... The only thing is... the only real concern I have, is that I'm not a tech kind of person and Flushy is an *Insure-tech*."

David returned to his chair, sat down and leaned over on his desk almost teetering on the edge of his seat. He paused as if he was going to speak with some omnipotent intention. He briefly glanced down long enough to make me aware of his official gold-plated job title sitting off to the side on his desk. It read, 'David Berrigan, the Creator/the Founder'. The way people were talking about this guy in the lobby, it sounded more like he would have preferred it to say, 'The Prophet'.

"Mike... what we did here was bring our own outsider start-up mentality to the insurance industry. We don't need you to be the tech guy, because I got plenty of those guys. Those kinds of guys are a dime a dozen. They practically grow on trees these days. When I created Flushy, I didn't expect it to be such a game-changer. I expected to make a splash, but who knew that we would *Ping the Satellite*? At the same time, to do that, we set out to fundamentally transform the industry from an erroneous process to an experience of a lifetime."

"Uh-huh..."

He completely lost me, like the time my Physics 101 professor attempted to explain string theory to a class of freshmen. I might as well have a giant dunce cap on my head.

"I guess the real question is. What's getting in your way from jumping on the Flushy Revolution? Better question yet. What's stopping you from helping me change the world?"

"How does it all work? I... I still. How is it that Flushy can be so much cheaper than the competition?"

"You're missing the forest for the trees Mike. Why get caught up on all these minute details? Let the actuaries worry about that."

David had a way of varnishing his replies with a healthy dosage of sinister overtones and salesman talk.

"The old way of doing business, with a relationship, a hand-shake and a smile, that's all gone, but most people don't know it yet. Most insurance carriers don't know this fact has now become the new reality of business. People don't want an agent to sell them insurance. Do you think people want to spend hours shopping around for a policy? They want to buy insurance the way we buy a bar of soap, quick and easy."

"A bar of soap isn't as complicated as life insurance. I won't risk my spouse going bankrupt if I purchase the wrong bar of soap."

David Berrigan smiled as if he enjoyed the challenge, like a Lion playing with his food. I didn't get the feeling too many people challenged David.

"Here's the thing Mike, what we did was take the old archaic way of doing things and turned it upside down. This allows us to use data to make informed decisions instead of relying on personal opinions or subjective attitudes. Really, at the heart of it, we're a data company, which means that Flushy uses behavioral economics & machine learning, instead of doing business with middlemen and hoping they place good risks with us. The money we once paid out to insurance agents in the form of commissions, can now be given back directly to the consumer. If there are any leftover premiums at the end of the year, we give it back to the insured and we call that the Flushy Overflow Giveback."

David was attempting to act stoic, clearly he was out

of practice. He wore this deadpan 1000-yard stare and it was aimed directly at me. He was probably just waiting for me to say something. Locking eyes with David was kind of like staring down the barrel of a gun. David started tapping his fingers on his desk.

Tap...Tap...Tap...

"Mike, I did have a question fizzling around in my head though. Do you mind?"

"Sure thing. I'm an open book."

"It seems to me; you are rather successful in your practice now. So, I have to ask, why would you give something like that up?"

"I haven't gone this far in life, to only have gone this far. I want more."

David smiled and took a long-calculated pause.

"I know that look."

I titled my head to the side with a curious expression. What look was he talking about?

"You've got that same look I had all those many years ago. That's the look of ambition. It's written all over your face. That's the kind of look we need more of around here."

I shook my head in agreement. How in the world was I supposed to respond to a statement like that? I felt the best answer was to have no answer at all. I felt the best answer was to bite my lip and hold my tongue.

"Mike, this is normally where people say; when can I start? Or, thank you for this opportunity..."

"I... I Just..."

"If you're not interested... I mean... Look, Mike, there are a thousand other applicants itching at the chance to work here. If it's not for you..."

Tap... Tap... Tap...

David impulsively began tapping his fingers on his desk. David's desk was a single piece of white marble with four legs made out of what looked to be solid pieces of platinum. The passing seconds seemed more like hours and that tapping only inflated my anxiety. I was nervously swinging my legs, kind of like a kid sitting in a Doctor's office waiting to get his booster shots. The pace of David's tapping began to rapidly increase.

Tap. Tap. Tap.

All I could do was awkwardly glare back at him with this stupid confused look on my face. He was expecting me to say something, but I just didn't know what to say. I mean, I'd be stupid to pass something like this up, right? The taps became louder and incrementally more aggressive as the silence persisted.

Tap. Tap. Tap. Tap...

Every time David clanged his fingers on that marble, it completely derailed my train of thought. My inner demons aside, I had to made a decision. It was time to fish or cut bait. I'm a gambler, I take risks, but this all seemed too good to be true. Ultimately, what did I have to lose?

"Okay... tell me about my day to day."

David commenced with his tapping.

Tap, Tap, Tap, Tap...

Then, all of a sudden, he broke his silence.

"Now we're talking!"

David boasted this big smile. It was pretty evident that David took tremendous pride in his personal appearance. His teeth were porcelain white, almost a florescent sparkle. I couldn't imagine how much he spent on professional teeth-whitening services. He paused for a second, I assume to see my candid reaction. I flinched a bit in my chair. It was an uneasy, yet excited squirming.

"Mike, clearly something is worrying you. What is it? Lay it on me."

"No, I'm fine. Really, I'm fine. Can you tell me more about the day to day?"

In reality, I was one step removed from a panic attack. This whole conversation gave me cause for pause. Luckily for me, my sports coat was covering the pools of sweat around my arm pit and masked my heavy breathing.

"Sure thing. As a Sales Agent for Flushy. You will start from the bottom up. We'll need to take your bad habits, break them and then remold you."

His tone was calm, cool and collected. He dropped the salesman shtick and talked to me like an actual human being. In retrospect, I really appreciated that.

"You'll get more details on your first day. But... for now think of this role as my eyes and ears. Think of this role as my Devil's Advocate, so to speak. From my chair, I miss a lot of what's going on at the ground level. I have a 30,000-foot view over the business, which has its set of limitations."

"Ah."

"Mike, what I need to know from you is simple. Are you in? Or, are you out?"

My heart was racing and I began to sweat profusely. I took a deep breath and reminded myself to slow down. See, for the first time in my life, I had a shot to really make a name for myself. I was bestowed with a clarity, a sense of wonderment for what could be. My gut was telling me to do it. If there's one credo I live by, it would be to trust my gut. In one fell swoop, I gave him my answer.

"I'm in."

David beamed a smile at me and stood up to shake my hand. He clutched onto my right hand with both of his and pulled me in close. Close enough to smell his breath as he spoke. With one hand latched around mine, and one on my shoulder, he looked at me with this bottomless gaze.

"Remember this Mike and remember it well. You are either in with us all the way or you are out all the way. Welcome to Flushy. Welcome to the rest of your life. Welcome to the *Revolution*."

The next morning, I found myself lamenting and pacing in the hallway just outside of Bill's office. I must've rehearsed this speech a thousand times on my morning commute. This wasn't my car and this wasn't going to be an easy conversation. I had to do it, all the dread in the world would not dissuade me.

"Bill, I just wanted to thank you for hiring me...", I mumbled while waving my hands around like a mad man.

No matter how many ways I went over this in my head, I knew there wasn't a great way to say it. I knew it was now or never; no matter how much I paced back and forth, no matter how clammy my hands became and no matter how much sweat I wiped from my brow. Like a *Band-Aid*, it was time to rip it off and get it over with. I sheepishly knocked on Bill's door and waited for a reply before entering.

Knock, Knock, Knock.

This wasn't the kind of knock that made a statement.

Maybe, I'd get lucky and miss him. I mean, I could always just leave a note under the door and make a run for it. As it would turn out, I had no such luck. The door slowly opened and Bill invited me in.

"Mike! Come on in."

I entered his office and gravitated toward the nearest empty seat. Well, there's no turning back now.

"Grab a seat."

He gestured over to the most comfortable chair in the office. Normally that spot would be solely reserved for Bill.

"I haven't seen you around the office very much lately. So tell me Mike. What's going on? What is it that everyone else seems to know and that I don't? What alludes me?"

Was I that transparent? He already knew why I was here and why I was pacing outside his office for the last twenty-five minutes. I mean, I left tracks of foot prints, like a snow angel except on commercial grade carpet. In an attempt to conceal the sweat accumulating on my hands, I decided to clasp my hands and started rubbing them together. Bill looked at me and waited for me to say something. To think, it wasn't more than three years ago that I was sitting in this very office for my first interview.

"Bill, we need to talk."

"Isn't that what we're doing right now?"

"What I mean is...I---"

Before I could finish my sentence Bill jumped backed into the conversation.

"Let me guess. You're striking out on your own and starting your own practice? Good for you."

Bill looked at me smug and with very little amazement. It dawned on me that Bill must've had this conversation dozens, if not hundreds of times over the years.

"Not exactly."

"Not exactly? Tell me more."

"I was made an offer yesterday and thought I should tell you right away."

"An offer? From who? Don't tell me one of these other shmucks down the road snatched you up."

"Flushy. I'm going to go to work for FLUSHY."

"What!?!?!"

Bill was struck with utter disbelief. Bill started stroking his beard with a confused gaze, it was really more an overwhelming sense of bewilderment. I didn't really know what else to say, so I waited for him to step back in. Bill's beard had a certain acquired fortitude. The kind that comes with a thick application of beard oil. It had this shiny veneer that caught my eye.

"Mike you never struck me as the kind of guy that was always looking for the easy way out. To be honest, I thought you were a lifer. I thought I saw a lot of me in you. Was I that off base?"

Yeah, I probably deserved that. It was the easy way out. I started nodding my head in agreement, I felt somewhat obliged for the looming verbal beat down that was coming my way. Bill had brought me into the industry and now, I'm about to join up with *the* company dead set at destroying the "old way" of doing things.

He stuck his hands out in front of him and put them about a foot a part from each other. Kind of like he was holding an invisible beach ball.

"This Mike, this is the entire insurance marketplace. It's all in here, within the palm of my hands. All insurance companies, big or small, float between these invisible boundaries. Some are more expensive on the right side and some are less expensive on the left side and some are right in the middle. At some point in time every company is the cheapest, but more times than not, most companies fall on the right side most of the time. Look these *cheap* companies always come and go, but they don't stick it out for the long haul. Trust me, I've been doing this for over thirty years. You know why some companies are always the cheapest? All companies have the same claims costs, it's not like this company figured out how to insure people who don't die. Think about it. How is it possible?"

"Look Bill, if I can't beat them I might as well join

them."

"Mike you've built a practice here. You've got a client list. You've got support. You deserve to stay here. This is and always will be a relationship business, and you've done great so far at cultivating relationships. It takes time to build, and you've already done it in a short period of time. What takes people ten years, you've done in less than three.", he compassionately enumerated my various accomplishments.

"With respect Bill, Flushy is the future and I think the agent model has somewhat outlived its usefulness."

Bill scoffed at my proclamation. He was well within his rights to do so. Here I was some kid, a relative novice by comparison, opining on about something I knew very little about.

"Mike, no one is going to pay you to solve a problem that doesn't exist over at some pie-in-the-sky insure-tech. The agent model is still a viable option, trust me, I've been doing this before you were born."

Bill's impassioned pursuit for the truth was

relentless. Bill leaned forward in his chair and placed his elbows firmly on his desk.

"How can I possibly compete with a company like Flushy? How can any agent expect to beat their prices?"

Bill shook his head in disbelief, like all of his training had gone in one ear and out the other. Part of me appreciated that, his candid nature. I mean, from time-to-time Bill did proportion out more than his share of wisdom.

"Mike, price isn't everything."

"Bill, price isn't everything, it's the only thing. It's the only thing people care about these days. They don't care about having enough insurance. They don't care about having the right insurance. They don't care about understanding their insurance. They care about price."

"Mike, I'd be lying to you if I said price wasn't a factor."

Bill shifted back and forth in his chair. He sat back a bit more, clearly my retorts were making him somewhat uncomfortable. I couldn't blame him. I mean, how could I? I was basically undermining his entire existence as an insurance agent.

"Mike. Do you know when the first life insurance policy was issued?"

"No, I was sick the day they taught history at insurance school. Why don't you enlighten me?"

Bill looked at me with an amused expression. At the very least he appreciated my sarcastic sense of humor. Bill gave me three years of apprenticeship under his tutelage. I figured that lengthening the conversation was sort of my repentance.

"The first life insurance policy was sold in the early 1700's."

"Huh."

"This industry is over *Three-Hundred* years old. *AND* over that 300-year period, that storied history, insurance agents have been there every single step of the way, selling policies and serving clients."

"Mm-hmm."

"The thing is Mike. The industry has changed over that time. People have changed, technology has changed, but what has endured is the agent-client relationship. Insurance agents have been around for hundreds of years and will continue to be around for hundreds of years. I'm sure Flushy has a lot of smart people working there. I'm sure Flushy has a lot of smart technology that I cannot pronounce. I'm sure Flushy has a lot of investors backing its success. What they don't have are the intangibles."

I was beat, bamboozled and befuddled. What could I say? Nothing! So, I didn't. I sat there and took it like a man.

"Human existence, life itself is rather ephemeral. There is a preciousness to it all. And to that end, that is why agents will always be around. People are fragile, life is fragile and people need guidance from an agent. Whether they know it or not."

Bill's impassioned rhetoric wasn't making a dent, my mind was made up. If anything he only solidified my position. As every minute of lecturing passed I found my patience quickly fleeting. This was becoming a rather circular argument and I sensed Bill had realized it as well.

"I get that Bill, I really do. But, Flushy is the future and I don't want to miss out on being a part of that."

"Ah! Another case of FOMO."

"FOMO?"

"Fear of missing out."

"Ah!"

"I imagine you'll need to up your Three-Letter-Acronym game working over at Flushy. Is there anything I can do to change your mind?"

"No. But, I appreciate you asking."

"Well, I didn't think so. You're a man on a mission. That is clear."

Bill stood up from behind his desk and stuck out his hand.

"Mike you've always got a place here and you're welcome back at any time."

I reached out and grabbed his hand. He latched on

like vice grip and put his other hand over the top of mine as we shook.

"Bill I really appreciate what you did for me. But, I'd be a fool to pass up this opportunity."

Bill and I cordially shook hands. It was one of those long awkward handshakes. He looked me in the eyes and smiled.

"Now, before you go, there is just the matter of settling your accounts."

"What do you mean settling my accounts?"

"Your commission draw accounts. You do remember how a draw works, right?"

I was dumbstruck for a quick minute. How I let that one slip through the cracks I will never know. Bill hoodwinked me. I guess, in all fairness to Bill, it wasn't all that shocking.

"Mike, don't tell me you forgot about the draw."

I'd completely forgotten about the draw. So, naturally I did the thing most defensive people do and ignorantly balked. Talk about being caught with your pants around your ankles.

"Don't tell me you forgot."

"Well, Bill. You're joking, right? I mean, after all the money I made you..."

"That was the deal kid. Don't get me wrong, I appreciate the money *WE* made together."

"I mean, it can't be that much, right? How much are we talking about here?"

"Actually, I have the exact figures right here."

Bill handed me a sealed manilla envelope. How in the heck did he have this prepared? As you could imagine we stopped shaking hands. The tone of the conversation became slightly combative, but still friendly. I was starting to come off as that crazy uncle arguing politics over the Thanksgiving dinner table.

"What you didn't think I knew you were looking around? Remember who owns these computers kid. You started looking for jobs on company computers. Computers that I own."

Talk about bush league blunders. Yeah, I messed up. Bill knew he had me dead to rights. I slowly started opening the envelope and decided to stop abruptly. I shook my head and stuffed the envelope into my back pocket.

"So, in the end it's all business to you? What about all of those long hours I put in? All of the birthday parties I missed? All of the family gatherings I had to skip?"

"I appreciate all of your effort. But, that was the deal we both agreed to."

"That's how it is?"

"If we don't honor our agreements, what separates us from the animals? It's not personal, it's just business. It is what it is."

"Fair enough.", I replied back defeated and submissive.

I'd imagine our paths might cross again one day, hopefully in a good way. I pushed in my chair and headed for the nearest exit. For now, it was time to move on and start the next chapter in my career.

What in the heck have I gotten myself in to? I've got a big looming debt hanging over my head and I'm about to step into a complete unknown with Flushy. All I could do is hope for my best, because I certainly just burned that bridge.

Flushy Headquarters, or '*HQ*' as it was often referred to, was located in the heart of downtown Los Angeles. It was right where the 10 freeway meets the 110 freeway. This place was like an 8-hour drive from Silicon Valley, but evidently someone forgot to tell the people who worked there. After suffering through an hour of bumper-to-bumper traffic driving down the 405 freeway I had finally arrived at HQ. This was the first day of the rest of my life. After navigating my way through the massive underground parking structure, I finally made it up to the lobby. The lobby was embossed with a white Marble, possibly imported from Italy, it covered from the floor all the way up to the ceiling.

There was a large hourglass shaped man waiting around for someone in the lobby. He was wearing the most peculiar outfit, a tuxedo t-shirt and flip flops. It was a safe bet that he was waiting for me. He was holding a sign in his hands, like a cab driver picking someone up from the airport. I couldn't read it from a far, as I approached I could see the sign had my last name on it. I found my way through the crowd and walked over to him.

"Mike Allen, nice to meet you."

I stuck out my hand expecting to shake hands, but was met with a fist bump instead.

"I'm Curtis Little. Nice to meet you Mike. How auspicious, you're actually on time. Good."

It turns out my incessant need to be punctual would finally pay some dividends. We fist bumped and stood there awkwardly as Curtis was checking something on his phone.

"Thanks. I'm glad to be on board."

Curtis looked at me briefly and then back to his phone.

"Welcome to the Flushy revolution Mike. Today is the last day of the rest of your life. Today everything changes for you."

It was a little dramatic, but so far so good I thought.

"Mike... what's that in your hand?"

"It's... uh, my briefcase."

I said sheepishly as I guarded my battle-hardened leather briefcase. The years of wear and tear had really begun to make a dent. The leather had cracked from seem to seem, which made these large white almost spider web shaped crevasses.

"Vintage, I like it. But, ultimately its unnecessary. You won't need it here. Everything you'll ever need is already on your workstation."

"Ah... Okay. Great."

We stood there for another minute or so. I wanted to take it all in and get a good lay of the land. Curtis, along with the majority of people bustling through the lobby, was completely fixated on his phone.

"My wife says my people skills are a lot of like my cooking, fast and tasteless. That being said, come this way and follow me. We move fast here and take no prisoners. Let's walk and talk. I presume you can walk and chew bubble gum at the same time."

Without hesitation I followed him down a long white corridor, it looked more like a duckling following behind its mother back to the nest. Curtis had this hysterical waddle to his walk, which I found rather amusing and fitting.

"Today Mike, today is your training day... It's all actually all pretty exciting. You're the first actual Insurance Agent to enter our sales team. Prior to you, our sales team has been comprised exclusively of internal Flushy employees. You made history on your first day, how about that?"

"Really?"

Without explanation our pace quickened, it was all rather enigmatic. The hallway was crowded, I couldn't get over how many people worked here. It reminded me a lot of picking someone up from the fly-away at the Los Angeles International Airport.

"Really really. We prefer to hire from within."

"Curtis, who are all these people?"

"Uh. *What* do you mean?"

He looked at me, almost somewhat insulted by the premise of my question. It probably wasn't the best idea to start pissing people off on my first day.

"Err, I mean, how many employees work here?"

"Ah! *About* ten… ten thousand at this campus. Something like that… I don't really know to be honest. All I know is that we're growing like athletes' foot, that is to say fast and all over."

We stopped abruptly in the middle of the hallway. People were navigating around us, like water flowing around a rock in the river. Curtis had to check his phone, again. He answered it and we started back on our path like nothing happened. We finally arrived at the entrance of the salesfloor. Curtis grabbed his keycard and stood up against a door way for a second. His phone kept buzzing in his hand as he was juggling his keys.

"You're going to need to get one of these eventually."

He dangled his keycard in front of my face and swiped it across the keycard reader.

"For right now, let's just get you to your workstation and set up a learning terminal. Then we can worry about the logistics. We don't want to open the kimono just yet."

Open the kimono? What kind of bizarre metaphor to use in a workplace? I mean, who talks like that? I wasn't the easiest person in the world to offend, but still. Corporate culture was going to be a fun learning experience.

"Gotcha."

Curtis opened the door and escorted me over to an empty desk. He turned on the computer and hit a bunch of keys. I was still a little awestruck by the entire set up. The desk had three LED monitors, a wireless mouse and a backlit Chiclet style keyboard. You know the kind, the kind that makes a loud *CLICK* sound every time you hit a key.

"You're initial training workload will consist of several tranches of interrelated deliverables. In other words, today you'll spend the day watching FlushyTV. FlushyTV is our training repository where we house all of our proprietary corporate training modules. We've developed a completely Artificially Intelligent based training module. Pretty cool, huh?"

Curtis had this weird sideways grin, like a used car salesman about to close a deal. If this was any indication of the sales culture, I could tell that I was in for some turbulence.

"Very cool indeed..."

"Lost for words? I thought you were a sales puke? Don't worry, no one is expecting you to touch the iceberg on your first day."

Curtis went back to typing on the computer. I peeked over his shoulder to get a better idea of what he was doing. I think he caught me in the corner of his eye, because he moved over a bit to obstruct my view.

"Okay... *annnnnnnd...* you're all set up in the system. From here you'll just complete the modules and then we're off to the races."

Curtis slid the keyboard on over to me and sprung up from his hunched over position.

"Thanks. What do I do if I have a question?"

"The computer will answer all of your initial

questions. Mike, it's important that you trust the process. For expectation purposes, we can set a baseline for our initial cadence as you establish more bandwidth post training. Don't overthink things on your first day. No one is expecting you to boil the ocean."

"Okay. What if I need help?"

"Mike, lean into the process, don't fight the process."

"Gotcha. One more question."

Curtis stared at me with this annoyed look on his face. Apparently, a couple of additional questions was a massive time drain for him.

"Yeah, *what-is-it*?"

"Do I get an Employee Handbook or...?"

"Mike, more to come on that. Stay tuned."

More to come? What in the world does that mean? His leadership style was riddled with secrecy and the allure of mystery. To be honest, I didn't hate it all that much. It left a lot of room for me to be my own boss.

"Uh-huh."

"Mike. Let me ask you something."

"Go for it."

"Are you a team player?"

I was a little taken back by the tone of his question. I mean, I've been working here for ten minutes and this guy is asking me if I was a team player?

"Yes..."

"Yes? Yes what?"

Is this guy for real? Does he want me to spell it out like some kind of child? I was new, so I figured my best bet was to just acquiesce to his request.

"Yes, Curtis I am a team player."

"That's exactly what I hoped you say. Look, if you get into trouble. You're surrounded by people who went through the same exact training. Just ask one of them for help. It's not like your conjoined at your hip to this chair. Get up and get around a little bit. When in doubt, as one of your peers."

"Gotcha. Will do. Affirmative."

Before I could utter another word, Curtis looked at his watch and jolted out of the seat. Curtis seemed like a pleasant enough individual, but his personality was camouflaged by his perennial high-strung appearance. Working here at Flushy clearly took a heavy toll on Curtis. I guess his management style was to outsource managing to the people he managed, what a unique change in pace.

"You're on your own until lunch time. I'll be back around noon, more or less. I gotta run. Good luck."

Curtis said as he bolted for the door. I sat down, pushed my briefcase aside and started up the computer module. Curtis didn't have much of a bedside manner, or training acumen, but how hard could it be? What was a computer module going to teach me about selling? I guess I was about to find out. The salesfloor was quiet, like a mortuary before the start of a funeral precession. I mean, you could hear a pin drop from a mile away. Occasionally, I would hear a flurry of keyboard strokes, but other than that it was dead quiet. For a room the size of a moderately sized *Grocery Store*, I figured there would be a flurry of commotion. I guess I figured wrong. There was a pair of headphones on my desk, I plugged them in and went to town on that training module.

The video started with a terse standard corporate disclaimer. The typical 'Legalese' disclaimer that universally precluded all corporate training videos. A cartoon character popped up on the screen and started yammering on about Flushy.

"Welcome to Flushy! Welcome to the company that is singlehandedly spear heading the complete transformation of the life insurance industry!"

I took in a deep breath and an even deeper sigh of relief. I could tell this was going to be a protracted battle between my attention span and this learning module.

"As part of our sales team you are on the front lines of the customer experience. When people think Flushy they will think of you."

I paused the module for a second, took a deep

breath and then hit the play button.

"Even though you are part of the Flushy sales team, it's important for you to remember that Flushy is not an insurance company."

That was a rather startling proclamation. Not an insurance company? That was just the kind of contrivance that I needed to captive my attention. I'm sure that statement works on the typical straight-out-of-college run of the mill Flushy employee, but I wasn't quite ready for Flushy to pull the wool over my eyes just quite yet.

"Flushy is really more of a data company, more of a tech company rather than an insurance company. Flushy leverages best in class tech to help revolutionize the customer purchasing experience. This in turn allows us to save money and give that savings back to the customer. The way it should be."

The way it should be. Right... So, I sell insurance, but we aren't an insurance company? I chuckled a bit and went back to work.

"We do things differently here at Flushy. Your job

isn't merely just to sell insurance. It's to live into the Flushy way of doing things. It's to align yourself with the Flushy core competency value matrix. It's to be a part of the revolution. Everything we do here, by extension everything that you do here at Flushy, is very intentional, cultivated and deliberate. All in order to help us revamp an archaic industry that teeters on the brink of disaster."

I paused the video again and ran my hand through my hair. What in the world did I just sign up for? I didn't realize it, but I started tapping my feet in some kind of nervous anticipation.

Tap... Tap... Tap...

I was determined to make this work and more importantly keep a positive mental attitude. After a momentary lapse I started the video back up and tried to immerse myself in the content. I took another deep breath and reminded myself to focus on the journey.

"Being part of a data company doesn't mean that we are not a people company. We realize the importance of a strong work-life balance. That is why we encourage each employee to take an occasional weekend off from work."

Sorry... what now? Take only *an occasional* weekend off from work? That can't be right. There's no way... I shrugged off the commentary, but I knew better than that. A company this meticulous doesn't make mistakes like that. Every word on this screen was highly calculated, from start to finish the script was probably double or even triple checked.

"As a Flushy team member, we want to help you prioritize all of the things that will make you successful here at Flushy. When our team members are successful, Flushy is successful. For example, we love to measure the productivity of our team members. A productive team member is a happy team member."

I paused the video again and slowly removed my headphones. I subtly and delicately placed them on my desk in front me. After a nice deep breath, I composed myself. I got up and pretended to stretch, but in reality I was scoping out the nearest escape route. I found an exit in the back corner of the salesfloor that seemed to be relatively inviting. I procured my briefcase and pushed in my chair from the desk. I slowly walked towards the exit, inching closer and closer. As I was walking, I felt the sudden need to look back at my desk. Just a quick inconspicuous glance back, like someone who just fled a crime scene. As soon as I did, I slammed into one of my co-workers.

"Woah... watch yourself there bud."

"Sorry about that. I was—"

"You were what? From the looks of it. It almost, it almost looked like a prison escape. What were you making a run for it?"

"No—No—I-- Well, I was, I was doing exactly that."

We both laughed for a second at the absurdity of it all. I mean, I was caught with my hand in the cookie jar. What could I do but laugh?

"The name is Dean. And you are?"

"Nice to meet you Dean, I'm Mike Allen."

"Ah yes... Mike Allen. I've heard of you. You're the

bosses' shiny new toy..."

Dean had an inquisitive tone, like a detective trailing off in mid-thought talking about a theory. Dean struck me as the kind of person who valued being well informed about office gossip.

"You people don't seem to waste any time. I take it that the rumor mill churns quick around here."

"Indeed it does. Well, before you runoff, let me grab you a cup of coffee. That way you can at the very least say you got something out of showing up to work today. How about it Mike Allen?"

Dean was baiting me. In reality, he was chomping at the bits to blabber how the new guy was about to jump ship on the first day. I wouldn't give him the satisfaction. I just needed to reset and a concentrated dose of caffeine was just what the doctor ordered.

"That-- that sounds good. Lead the way."

"*Alriiiight!* Follow me on back this way Mike."

We walked to the back corner of the salesfloor.

There was an entire commercial kitchen attached to the salesfloor. It was like one of those kitchens you'd see on a cooking channel. I was blown away by the welcoming and lavish set up. The grandeur of it all was rather intoxicating. The salesfloor had an open concept and huge twenty-foot ceilings. There were assorted fresh fruits, an endless array of snacks, desserts and even a freaking cappuccino machine. Dean stopped dead in his tracks, looked over at me and pointed at the various coffee makers.

"Here you go."

Dean said as he handed me a complimentary Flushy branded mug. I took a second to examine the mug. I grabbed the coffee from Dean and took an interminable sip out of that porcelain mug. The mug was embossed with this pearl white color to it.

"Mike, why are you here?"

"Uh. To get some coffee?"

Dean grinned at my spontaneous response. He started to laugh as he poured us some coffee. I take it he found my complete lack of self-awareness humorous.

"I meant, why are you here at Flushy."

"Uh. I, I want to be part of the revolution...?", I said as I buried my face back into my coffee mug.

The coffee was a lot like the conversation, that is to say hot and bitter. Dean looked at me as I drank and started snickering under his breath.

"Didn't your mother ever tell you that it's rude to answer a question with a question? No *seriously*, why are you here?", He asked me again with a little more authority veiled behind his question.

His tone became more affirmative as the conversation went on and his pacing noticeably dampened.

"I lost a sale and—"

"You *lost* a sale... *And* what? And you thought the grass was greener on this side of the fence? So what? You thought if you can't beat them might as well join them? Am I right?"

"Well, *yeah*. Basically... that's right!"

"I don't blame you. It's all... so great... working here at Flushy..."

Dean said and then proceeded to take a big gulp of his coffee. Dean had poured a generous amount of creamer into his mug. So much in fact that the color of the coffee in his mug was almost inseparable from the color of the mug itself.

"Mike, being part of the revolution that is... that is so great. Assuming you go back to your workstation and don't decide to rage quit, I'll be two cubicles over from you. Feel free to ping me with any questions that pop up. And, if not, that's cool too."

Dean explained and started walking back to his cubicle. Dean journeyed back to his desk and stirred up some casual chit-chat with some of the other salespeople along his way back. What have I gotten myself into? I decided to grab a seat in one of the many bean bag chairs lying around the salesfloor. I scanned the room to get a better lay of the land. Really, I just wanted a comfortable spot to finish my coffee. The coffee here was incredible, nothing like my old work. Just the ordinary tech company vibe, you know, ping pong tables and goofy furniture scattered about.

After my nerves had settled a bit, I went back to my desk and sat down. I made a commitment to myself to see this through to the end. The way I figured it, every job ends one way or the other. Either you quit, you die, you get fired, your company goes bankrupt or you get downsized.

"Focus on the journey. See it through until the end Mike. See it through until the end", I murmured to myself.

Initially I was a little roused by all of the data-tech speak, but managed to wander back to my desk. Like most human beings, I'm not a big fan of being micromanaged. As a salesperson I wasn't used to the idea of being micromanaged, I was used to the idea of getting people results. This seemed like just the environment I wanted to be. I turned on my computer and started the module back up.

"Nice to have you back Mike Allen."

Well that's just a tad bit creepy. Is this AI? Does the

computer actually recognize me or is this some elaborate training module?

"Here at Flushy. We measure everything and we mean everything. Because, if it can't be measured then it doesn't matter. If it can be measured then we can turn that into useful data. I'm sure you have a lot of questions at this point. Whenever you are uncertain about something, we want you to find creative solutions. Just go ahead and ask yourself this simple question. What does good look like?"

What does good look like? What kind of preposterous question is that? What does that even mean? What an asinine thing to ask? I was starting to get the feeling that this was among one of the many pending useless business clichés that engendered the modern corporate vernacular.

"A great salesperson is a salesperson who takes great notes. A great salesperson is then measured based on notation, timeliness and other critical success factors. A great salesperson sticks to the script. A great salesperson does everything by the book. For quality assurance, we monitor for strict compliance to company best practices."

I had to pause the video again. This was dry, I mean brutally dry content, even for a learning module. At the very least it was on a video. I couldn't imagine having to read this nonsense in some kind of book or training manual. I put my hands together and cracked my knuckles.

CR-RACK-KK!

The noise echoed across the entire salesfloor. There was an eerie quietness to it all, like a library on the weekend. I clicked the video back on.

"We base the predominate amount of your success around industry leading Key Performance Indicators. For instance, we measure you on how fast you respond to a customer quote request. This is one of our best indicators of sales success. We also monitor how well you document each of your sales conversations. A well-documented conversation is a successful conversation. Even though every one of your interactions is recorded, for posterity we find it important for you to document each of your sales calls."

Wait. Wait. Wait. So, each call is recorded and automatically documented, but I have to manually enter in call notes on top of that? For a tech company that seems like a rather redundant and useless exercise.

Knock... Knock... Knock...

I almost jumped out of my chair after being awaken to that thunderous knock. It was Dean standing next to my cubicle.

"How's it going Mike?"

"It's going..."

"Yeah? Because, five minutes ago you were thinking about jumping ship."

Dean clutched onto his coffee mug and took an audible gulp of coffee. I took it that he tended to do that as a way of demonstrating his self-appointed superiority. It was probably something he gleaned from one of those old cheesy late 80's sales movies. He was almost a character Ture of a prototypical sales bro.

"Dean, are they serious about all this?"

"Serious? About...? About all what Mike?"

Dean was leaning up against my cubicle drinking his coffee, cool as a cucumber. Just another day for him on the salesfloor, you know, not making sales. What was this guy hourly?

"Well, we're salespeople, right?"

"Yeah... What'd you mean by that?", he replied slowly and with discretion.

I gauged by his response that he was slightly confused by my inquisition. That was turning out to be a common theme with this company. I felt like the caveman who discovered the wheel trying to explain to another caveman why the wheel was so great.

"It's seems, from the training, that we're measured on a lot of things that have absolutely nothing at all to do with sales."

"For instance...?"

"Well, it looks like we get measured on how fast we

notate a sales conversation. What's up with that?"

Dean drank some of his coffee and pondered my question. I was getting the feeling that I was testing waters with Dean's tolerance for griping. The way I looked at it, griping was a way of life. I mean, a good gripe was the fuel that promulgated most of my working life.

"Tell me more…"

Tell me more was the proverbial punt the football of the business industry. I was starting to pick up on the jargon, but I still had to read between the lines.

"What does that have to do with sales? Shouldn't we get measured on actual sales?"

"Ah… you're one of those people I take it. Look. Here's the thing. This is the way we do things here at Flushy. If you can't handle it, then go work somewhere else… People would kill to have a chance to work at Flushy. People would die for the opportunity to work here."

That wasn't the most inspirational of answers, and needless to say I was dumbstruck by his retort. Go work somewhere else? What I can't ask questions? I was starting to piece together that the Flushy culture did not reward independent thought, in fact, they probably discouraged it.

"Well, I'm just curious. That's all."

"Mike, if you can't handle it. Maybe you should start refreshing your resume."

I scoffed at his response. It was more like a snarl really. What kind of answer was that? Who talks like that?

"What I can't be curious about something? Weren't you the least bit curious?"

"The only thing you should be curious about is the pending IPO and how much your stock options are going to be worth when we go public."

"So, you're not curious why we track all these non-sales metrics? As a salesperson, that doesn't interest you at all?"

"Not at all. Not in the least. I do my job and I do my job well."

Dean put his coffee mug down on my desk and folded his arms across his chest. I was trying his patience, to the point where I was riding the line of good taste and being a complete annoyance. The way I looked at it, I wasn't the one who strolled over to his desk to stir up random conversation.

"Let me ask you something Mike. Do you like money?"

"What?"

"Do you like money? It's not a complicated question."

"I mean, it's not the most important thing in my life."

Dean smiled and picked his coffee mug back up from my desk. It left a large circular stain on my desk. Coffee rings were the battle scars of the insurance industry. If you didn't have a coffee stain on your desk, you weren't much of an insurance salesman in my book.

"Well Mike, to me, money isn't everything in life. It's the only thing in life."

"Uh-huh."

"Mike, that makes me think. Where's your manager at?"

"Curtis?"

"Yeah, that guy is like the Heisman Trophy winner for the office."

"What?"

"Anytime someone has a question he stiff-arms them and runs for then nearest exit."

"HA!"

"Don't believe me? Next time you have a question and don't come complaining to me, try asking him something. I guarantee you, the next words out of his mouth will be; more to come or stay tuned or tell me more..."

I stopped laughing, because that all seemed to track from what I knew about Curtis. Albeit my experience was rather limited, it seemed to be consistent with what I knew of him so far.

"Okay-okay. Fair enough."

"Just remember this Mike. If you want to be successful here at Flushy. You need to be the CEO of your workstation. Be the CEO of your desk space. I mean, you are a team player, right?"

Knock... Knock... Knock...

Dean daintily knocked a couple of times on the side of my cubicle with his middle finger and began to walk away. All I could do is shake my head and get back to work. I put my headphones back on and went back to the indoctrination process. To my begrudging dismay the video went back on.

"What we've found is that all these behaviors drive positive sales results. We measure everything here at Flushy, because we are a data company. If it can't be measured it can't be objective."

In my head, I knew this was all just part of the process. I mean heck it was only my second *real* job. I'm sure all big companies are like this. I spent the next ten minutes or so just spacing out at my desk. Before I knew it, it was time for lunch. An instant message popped up on my computer monitor. It was from Curtis.

"TTT?"

I tried to reason out what that meant in my head. TTT... T... T... T...? What the heck does that mean? Curtis impatiently replied back in bold font.

"TIME TO TALK?"

Clearly I had to up my three-letter-acronym game. When it came to acronyms people didn't seem to mess around at this company.

"Sure thing!"

It wasn't like I had anything better to do, I mean aside from eating my lunch alone in the cafeteria.

"Great. Turn around. I'm at the espresso machine in the breakroom."

I turned around and looked over towards the breakroom area. There he was, standing around fiddling with the espresso machine. I took my headphones off, stood up and started walking over to the breakroom. As I approached the breakroom, Curtis turned around and we did that awkward half raised hand kind of hello that people do.

"Mike, how's it hanging?"

"I think I'm starting to get used to everything. I'm excited to get going."

"Glad to hear it! I know how it is the first day. It takes a toll on the best of us."

I couldn't tell if he was being sincere or not, I wasn't able to get a good read on him. That was just the kind of guy Curtis was. He was an enigma wrapped in a spinach flavored burrito covering. What I hadn't quite figured out was whether or not he was one of those corporate stooges. You know the kind, the kind that just walked around placating people for the sake of placating.

"What uh... what did you want to talk about?"

"Let's do a working lunch. How's sushi sound?"

"Well, that all depends."

"Depends on...?"

"You paying?"

I was half joking, but not really. Sushi was a little rich for my blood and I just started a new gig. Curtis didn't to seem my mind my tampered down attempts at humor.

"It's on the house. Whatever you want. It's one of the best parts of working for Flushy. David and Todd really spare no expense when it comes to employee happiness."

"Sounds good to me."

"Walk and talk Mike... Walk and talk. I mean, you can walk and chew bubble gum at the same time, right?"

"Sure can!"

We started walking, to where I had no idea. We exited the salesfloor and headed down a seemingly endless hallway. We embarked down a staircase, up a staircase, through one corridor and out another.

"Mike, don't take this the wrong way... but, you strike me as a belt and suspenders kind of guy."

"Thanks?"

As we started walking I noticed Curtis had started playing around on his phone. The hallways of Flushy were bustling with people, almost bursting at the seams. It was a mad house and everyone seemed to be in a hurry to get somewhere. Curtis walked and I followed for another five minutes or so. We took a left, a right and two more lefts to an open elevator. We stepped in and headed up to the cafeteria.

As the elevator doors began to shut I looked over at Curtis and he was still pre-occupied with his cellphone. The doors shut and I started scanning around the elevator hoping to drum up some small talk. Not a single person wasn't staring down at their mobile device. I was intrigued by the synchronicity of it all. What could they be all looking at? What was so captivating? Before I knew it, we arrived at the cafeteria level.

There was a loud *DING!* Which was accompanied by a female voice over the loud speaker.

"You have arrived at the Cafeteria, please enjoy your lunch", the voice announced in a soft-spoken tone.

Curtis put down his phone and right as the doors opened everyone piled out of the elevator.

"*C'mon* Mike."

As we exited the elevator, I stopped for a second to take it all in. The cafeteria was a smorgasbord of different cultural delights. It was like the *United Nations* of food cafeterias. Curtis put his hand on my shoulder, in a seemingly friendly manner.

"Welcome... Welcome to Flushy. Welcome to the good life."

"Glad to be here."

"Let's go and eat. *Avanti*!"

Curtis started walking and I started following, again. We vigorously started navigating our way over to the Sushi restaurant. We grabbed a seat at the Sushi bar and both took a sigh of relief. Apparently, we both needed to catch up on our cardio.

Curtis yelled out to the Sushi chefs, "*Hiroshi!*"

The sushi chef's all greeted Curtis in kind and a bellowing chorus of greetings rang out around the restaurant. I surmised this was a regular outing for Curtis. I was half expecting to be eating a baloney sandwich out of a brown paper bag this morning, and somehow I'm about to get treated to Sushi. He was right, this was the good life.

"Been here before, huh?"

"Oh yeah, this is the best sushi you will ever eat. I'd bet my life on it. Heck, I'd bet your life on it to for that matter. For whatever that's worth these days, I don't know. You work somewhere for so long, pour your life into something and for what? What was it all for?"

Curtis started this incoherent indicatable rambling. Honestly, I didn't pay much attention to it. I was enamored by my surroundings. All I could eat sushi? For free? This was paradise as far as I was concerned. I couldn't help but let curiosity get the better of me though.

"Can I ask you something?"

"Mike, you can ask me anything. However, I do reserve the right to now answer, depending on the question of course."

"Of course... Thanks... It's just... it's just that. Curtis...

how are we able to afford all of this?"

I didn't see much need for beating around the brow. The shortest distance between two objects is always a straight line. So, why not just get to the point? Curtis was completely unphased by my question.

"Mike, it's free, remember? It's part of the benefits package. Didn't you read that thing?"

"No, I didn't. What I meant was, how can Flushy afford all of *this*?"

"*Ha!* You're kidding me, right?"

I put my hands up and bashfully conceded my point.

"You've worked here for a whole fifteen-seconds and that is the kind of question you have for me? However David and Todd are doing it. They are doing it and making globs of money."

"I-I just... I was just curious. That's all."

"Look, Mike, you don't want to know. However were doing it, were making money hand over fist. Trust me, you're better off not poking the beehive. Don't bite the hand that feeds you."

"You're not a little bit curious about how we do it?"

"Not-at-all. The only thing I'm curious about is what kind of sushi roll I want to eat with my *Sake*."

Curtis didn't instill a considerable amount of confidence in me with his answer. He grabbed a set of chopsticks and began anxiously investigating the menu. I thought it best to drop the subject for now. Was it all rather lavish? Was it all looking too good to be true? Probably, but why should I care? I kept reminding myself to focus on the journey and stop over-analyzing every little thing.

Curtis motioned over to the waitress, held up two fingers and yelled, "Saki! Give me two please."

The waitress pleasantly approached us to sure up his demand.

"Saki? Warm or Cold Saki?", the waitress asked in a polite tone.

She probably found that being polite to someone as brutish as Curtis would disarm him from using any colorful commentary. In sales, language is everything. How you say something often matters much more than what you actually say to the person.

"Give it to me Warm!"

The waitress acknowledged his order with a polite bow and headed back to retrieve our order.

"Mike, what do you figure my job is here? What is it that you think I do?"

"Aside from eating sushi and drinking Saki all day?"

"Well obviously that is a big part of my job, but what do you figure my purpose is? Why do you think Flushy pays me the big bucks?"

"Curtis, I honestly have no clue."

"Clearly. You've got clueless written all over your forehead."

"Well then, why don't you educate me?"

"Don't mind if I do... My job is to help you be successful here at Flushy. I'll introduce you to the right people, help you navigate through the office politics, and along the way I'll probably have to bail you out of tough situations."

The waitress dropped off our Saki and Curtis handed her the filled-out order sheet. Curtis happily grabbed the *Saki* from her, like an actor latching onto an award.

"Cheers Mike! Drink up. This is the beginning of the rest of your life."

"Tough situations?", I asked and then down the *Saki*.

The Saki went down about as smooth as some old coffee syrup. Curtis started playing with the brim of his shot glass. He was methodically spinning the glass on the countertop. Making these figure-eight counter clockwise motions, like a figure skater or something.

"Forget I said that. What I meant to say, was that sometimes people make mistakes and if you do, I'll be the one that has to bail you out of trouble. You don't want the brass breathing down your neck here. Trust me kid, fly under the radar."

We awkwardly stared at each other for another minute or so. His pupils started to dilate; the Saki was starting to have some effect.

"What kind of trouble? I'm not following."

What in the world was this guy talking about? I mean, this was insurance not the Department of Defense.

"What did I just say. Forget I said that. Let's just put it this way. You don't want to find out. You don't got to worry about it."

"*Okay...* Hey you mentioned David and Todd earlier. David seems to be the face of the company. I haven't heard a peep out of Todd so far. What's up with that?"

"There you go with the questions again. What's up with that? Why? You writing a book or something? Are you a biographer or what?"

"Eh. I'm just curious."

"Nobody is paying you to be curious."

I shook my head silently, holding onto hope for some basic answers.

"Todd... Todd is on an extended vacation in the Europe. Forget about that. Let's eat man."

"Sounds good to me."

After a few minutes of pigging out on Sushi, he jump-started up the discussion in typical Curtis fashion.

"Mike, I fancy myself a pretty good judge of character. I can read people like a book. Cover to cover baby!"

"Ah. So, what's your read on me?"

"Well, since you asked..."

Curtis smiled and downed his *Saki*. He slammed the Saki on the table and put his hands up. He was forming a picture frame with his hands and looked deep into my soul.

"You are clearly a very passionate person and surprisingly intelligent. You aced the interview and the big man upstairs said you were somewhat of a rising star to be on the look for. With that intelligence, you often find yourself stepping in *it*. It's part of your bombastic nature. That's all pretty obvious by how you carry on a conversation."

"Go on…"

This guy read me like a book. I was impressed, but that might have just been the *Saki* talking. I found it comical how every salesperson thinks they are the modern-day Sherlock Holmes. If I had a dime for every time a salesperson thought they could read someone like a book, I'd be a rich man by now.

"Was I spot on or what?"

"I mean, yeah. Spot on."

Curtis nodded his head to the side. He was thoroughly impressed with himself. In all fairness to Curtis, he had enraptured my attention with his showmanship.

"I'm curious how many other tricks you have up your sleeve? Now that you've told me what you know, tell me what you don't know."

"What I don't know. What I don't know yet, is that being a former 'sales bro', no offense…"

"None taken."

"I don't know if you can cut it in a tech firm. This is a

data company, not an insurance company."

"Can't cut *it*?"

"Being a former insurance agent, being self-employed, I don't yet know if you can play well with others. That's what I'm here to figure out. Anyone can fake it till they make it and get a foot in the door. Lasting at this place is the challenge."

He motioned over to the waitress and blurted out his order. And started making all sorts of lazily put together hand gestures.

"More *Saki*! Let's keep this party going!"

The waitress scurried on over and re-filled our shot glasses with a bottle warm *Saki*. I can't remember the last time I drank this much during a business luncheon.

"The thing is Mike. Being part of Flushy, isn't like going out and slinging life policies at some networking event over in *the San Fernando Valley*."

Curtis took a second to down his *Saki*. To Curtis, Saki was like mana from heaven.

"You are now part of the resistance. You are now part of the revolution. You are now part of something much bigger than you, bigger than me and bigger than anyone in this room. We are all just cogs in the wheel. Replaceable. Interchangeable. Expendable..."

Curtis doted off for a second, he was lost again in his shot glass. Swiveling the glass in a hypnotic circular motion on the countertop. He was mesmerized by something stirring around in his head.

"Are you gonna drink that?", he asked.

Curtis asked as he pointed to my Saki glass. I was pawing it and he clearly noticed or had an obvious drinking problem. I couldn't tell which. Curtis was the king of non-sequesters. I thought my attention span was bad, maybe I found my doppelganger.

"I'm pacing myself..."

"Do you mind if I have it?"

"Uh... sure. No problem."

I said as I handed over the shot glass. Curtis quickly downed the shot glass and slammed it on the table.

"Bottoms up!"

We drank and ate, drank and ate, and repeated that cycle for about an hour or so. We finally hit rock bottom and called it quits. Theoretically, we both had to get back to work at some point. Curtis unfolded his napkin and wiped his mouth from ear to ear. He placed the napkin neatly on the sushi bar and looked over at me.

"What kind of questions do you have at this point in the game?"

"What's it like working at Flushy?"

"Ah. Oh, yeah. Now that's a question. Well, working at Flushy... Its... its..."

BELLLLCH!

Curtis rang out a thundering burp. The other patrons started staring at us and chuckled.

"Pardon me."

Nothing cuts the tension from an awkward moment than a random change in topic. Curtis's face rapidly redden like a ripe Roma tomato.

"What's it like working at Flushy? It's all just, well, all just *so* amazing. Being part of the revolution. Being somebody..."

"Uh-huh. Well, I guess the other questions I have are more process related in nature."

"Such as?"

"Well, what are my hours?"

"We expect that you have a healthy work-life balance. That being said, typically, we don't expect new associates to work more than 16 hours a day."

Curtis started staring down his empty shot glass, without so much as an accidental glance over at me. Clearly, he was conflicted with some serious inner turmoil.

"We want you to have a life outside of Flushy. We want you to have life... Have *a* life I mean."

"What about working weekends? I heard something about that earlier."

"Well, that depends all on you."

"How so?"

"It depends on you. Some people can make their quota by just working weekdays and some find it easier to work a few weekends a month."

"Uh-huh…"

Inside I was terrified, what did I just sign up for? Six glasses of Saki and my poker face had completely disintegrated.

"Don't worry about it. The only thing you should be worried about is how much money you want to make. Do you know why people come to work for Flushy?"

What was the politically correct answer? I think politically correct was a few bottles of *Saki* ago. The best I could muster is a standard company line.

"To be part of the revolution?"

Curtis titled his head in astonishment. He was pleased that I was toting the company line this early in the game.

"You're a quick learner. I think you'll do just fine."

The truth was he saw right through me. I was full of

it, and a bit tipsy. Ultimately, who cared though?

"People work at Flushy for two reasons and two reasons only."

Curtis had started to waiver a bit. He stuck his hand in my face and made a big peace sign.

"Two reasons…", he noticeably started to slur his words together. He paused for a second to regain his composure.

"First and foremost, people work here to be part of the revolution. People also work here to become exceedingly wealthy."

"Wealthy? Really? I like the sound of that."

"I'm talking *Accountants for your Accountants* kind of money. The kind of money that changes people… the kind of mon…"

I tilted my head back for a second in disbelief, but then realized we just ate like a $500 lunch which was completely free of charge.

"We pay better than any other insurance carrier. It's part of our employee retention strategy and our recruitment strategy. See we steal the best talent from the industry and have them come work for us. We have a salary match guarantee. If another company makes you an offer, we up it by 10% for IT and 25% for executives..."

"How?"

"How what?"

"How in the world are we able to do that?"

"Mike, if I told you, I'd have to kill you..."

We had a long awkward pause and both kind of shook our heads. Talk about an uncomfortable changeover.

"Well, it's about time to get back to work."

"Sounds good."

Curtis stumbled out of his chair and barely managed to get to his feet. He brushed off his lap and started patting down his legs in an attempt to compose himself.

"Remember, we are not paying you to think Mike, we paying you to make sales. So, go get to it. Go make some sales. Sell more Flushy!"

Sell more Flushy? The lazy battle cry of a Do-Nothing-Manager. Curtis stuck out his fist and we bumped fists. It was time to get back to work so we both went our respective ways.

Chapter 11: Things change quick, like the flip of a switch.

The next week of my life was going to be a real barnburner. I didn't pick up the phone, I didn't insta-chat, I didn't respond to customer emails, I didn't quote, I didn't do anything remotely sales related. I sat in my cubicle and watched training modules on a computer screen for *twelve* hours a day. I took the training modules to be no more than the conduit for indoctrinating new employees to the Flushy way.

I noticed after the first couple of days of training that I started using these meaningless business terms. I was telling people about the various *use-cases* for Flushy, the *P/E Ratio*, touching the iceberg, *EBITDA* and how the Insurance Industry has a corrupt and conflicted cabal of conspirators running the show behind the scenes. I was finding new ways to move the dial. I was finding new ways to lift and shift. I was preoccupying my time with how I could move the needle. I was all-in.

The word around the water cooler was that Flushy

was setting up to go public on the NYSE. After a quick internet search I found out that stood for the New York Stock Exchange. Up to this point, the enterprise was funded on combination of Angel Investors and short-term debt obligations. It was all rather complicated stuff. All I knew was that it would take some time to get there. I got my foot in the door. I was on the ground floor. So, I needed to keep my head down and grind my way to the top. It was eight fifteen in the morning, my second Monday working at HQ. When all of a sudden an instant message popped up on my computer monitor.

It read, "What's happening bud?"

What a great way to start my day. It was Dean! He raised his hand above his cubicle and started waving in my direction. I could tell it was Dean given how hairy his arm was and the platinum-plated wristwatch. The watch was one of those European style brands, I can't recall the name. It made this clanging sound every time he waved, almost like someone opening an old school cash register. I never fully understood the male obsession with wearing a fancy wristwatch. I made sure to reply in kind. No reason to start of the morning on the wrong foot.

"Not much. What's going on with you?"

"Another day another dollar, my friend. If the sun is shining people are dying. Time to sell some life insurance baby!"

To say you acquire a dark sense of humor working in the life insurance industry would be somewhat of an understatement. It goes with the territory. It is very much an acquired taste. I tried to change the subject the best I could.

"This is my last day using the training module."

"Good for you. Time to take the proverbial training wheels off and put your big boy pants on. Time to sell some Flushy."

"I guess..."

"You guess?"

"I mean, I'll do my best."

"Ah. Well, just try to not embarrass yourself. Sell more Flushy."

"That's the plan.", I said to my own chagrin.

"I've been meaning to ask you something Mike. What do you do for fun?"

"Besides being part of the revolution?"

"Obviously. Yeah. Besides that."

"Lately I've been really into playing board games with my roommates."

"Board games? Like what?"

"I'm big into chess right now."

"I don't want you to take this the wrong way, but I had you pegged as more of a checkers kind of guy."

I didn't reply back. I mean, how could I? Dean was trying to get an early morning rise out of me, he easily succeeded. He was keen to my delicate sense of self.

"I don't play Chess myself. But, I do know that chess is in fact a lot like selling. Chess is a great way to understand people in general."

"What'd you mean?"

"Well, if you play Chess with someone long enough. You tend to notice something about the person you're playing with. Do they open more offensively? Are they more defensive? How do they handle their queen? When you play with someone long enough you quickly find out that they tend to open in the same way. That's the key. Figuring out how people play the game and then exploiting that."

"Exploiting them... In the game...?"

"Well, yes. But, in life as well."

"Oh."

"Enjoy your modules. Get at me later."

"Thanks. I'll hit you up later."

The chat ended abruptly and I went back to booting up my training modules. With my arms fully outstretched I took a deep breath and yawned at the top of my lungs.

Yaaawwwwnnnnn!

The peanut gallery around me started throwing balled up papers my way and began a round of golf claps. You could hear the entire salesfloor clapping along with a resounding appreciation for my yawning.

"Way to go Mike.", someone yelled under their breath.

"You the man!", another hollered.

I put my head phones on and went back to work. The module started with a large banner scrolling across the screen.

"Welcome to Your Final Course!"

Which prompted the A.I. to pop up on the screen and start speaking to me. Initially, it was creepy, but I got used to it.

"Way to go Mike Allen! You're almost done. You're almost aligned. Today you will learn the **Top Secret**: Flushy Proprietary Sales Method."

Alright, I finally get to get my feet wet. Time to dip my toe into the pool and get wet.

"A team of consultants and scientists have studied every level of human interaction to create the most efficient sales process in the world."

They did, did they? I wasn't the best salesman in the world, but selling isn't a one size fit all kind of thing. It's not like you can study people long enough and just create some cookie-cutter sales system.

"I know what you're thinking Mike Allen. C'mon, you've got it all figured out? For now, don't worry about it. For now, lean into the process."

That was a rather eerie response. It's like the AI module was able to pick up on my facial ques or something.

"Selling isn't as complicated, nuanced or as sophisticated as most salespeople would like to make you think. Anyone can do it! That is of course, all it takes is having the right training, the right company and the right systems in place."

Demeaning my entire profession with one fell swoop. Wonder what else I was in store for today? Sure, anyone can do it. No problem! How hard can it be?

"Contrary to popular opinion we believe that selling is an exact science. It's not some mystical or whimsical art. There is really nothing to it, but to do it."

An exact science, is that right? To say the least, I was thoroughly unimpressed. Barely a week into the program and I was jaded. Who would've guessed it? Surprise, surprise. I kept convincing myself to just sit back and enjoy the journey.

"We've identified a major challenge facing consumers when buying life insurance and the problem was/is the industry itself. That's why no one was talking about the problem. That is, except the actual consumers themselves. We set out on a way to remedy that problem."

This was starting to sound a lot like the research I did online. A splash of hyperbole, a dash of over-dramatic language and a pinch of cult like mentality.

"In the old days, life insurance took days, weeks, if not months to complete an application. We set out to transform all of that. And thanks to our proprietary technology, data sophistication and Artificial Intelligence, we have done just that. Think of it like our own secret sauce."

Have you ever talked to someone and they blurt out a bunch of seemingly impressive sounding business language, but it all just comes across like meaningless gibberish? Welcome to my time so far lodged in the bowels of Corporate America.

"I know what you're thinking. How does it all work? It's actually all quite simple really. The first thing we did was think about the process from the consumer perspective and not the lens of profit. We redesigned the entire process from that first inquiry to the application to issuing a policy."

The end was near, I could feel it. I was chomping at the bit to prove myself on the salesfloor and be rid of these pesky modules. I didn't have a good barometer for how long this module would persist, but I could feel the end was looming. I could feel it in my gut, or maybe that was just the lack of food.

"There are hundreds of life insurance carriers and over one million licensed insurance professionals in America. So, let's get down to business. Why do people buy from Flushy? Why will they buy from you? The primary reason that people buy from

Flushy, is because of the price. We are able to offer them a customized, special and exclusive rate."

I was praying that Dean would swoop in to end my suffering, or at the very least ease it with a coffee break

"Congratulations! You've completed module 1 of 205. Click *Next* to continue..."

My only option was too take a big deep breath and remind myself that this was all temporary. This was all just part of the process. I could tell this was going to be one of those painfully protracted kind days, like going in for a root canal kind of days. You know the kind, the kind that you end up looking up at the clock every *Thirty Seconds* and hoping for the time to change. Against my better judgment, I decided to take a coffee break and walk around the office. I mean, the way I rationalized it, I had all day to get these modules completed.

I got up from my desk chair and wandered over to the breakroom area. There wasn't a soul insight, which I thought was kind of weird considering how big the office was. This morning we had our own personal Barista making pour overs and severing cold-brew. I wasn't much a fan of cold-brew. It's not that I care for the taste, when I drink coffee I want it to burn my mouth, scorched earth baby. I grabbed a cup of coffee and headed back over to my desk.

In my first week I gained over fifteen pounds. Sitting on my butt all day and eating free sushi wasn't helping my waistline. By the time I arrived back at my workstation there was an upswell of commotion over in one of the cubicles. A bunch of sales guys had huddled around a cubicle to shoot the breeze. So, I slowly inched toward the group to find out what all the fuss was about. As I got closer someone awkwardly invited me over, into the fray.

"Hey... new guy. Get over here!"

"What's going on fellas?"

"Didn't you get the memo?"

Dean asked as he walked into the crowded cubicle. Dean was hovering around the periphery of the cubicle and decided to come into the fold. Dean struck me as the kind of person who always sat at the back of the classroom. That way he could always see everyone coming in and out.

"Uh. I did not. Why? What's up?"

"It's Curtis."

"Yeah, what about him?"

"What about him? Well Mike, he's a claim."

"A claim?"

"Man you are dense."

The group laughed and started filling in the blanks for me. In the only ruckus and rowdy way a sales team could.

"He's six-feet under", one of the salesmen shouted.

"He's checked out of the hotel", a saleswoman proclaimed.

"He's swimming with the fishes", another salesperson chimed in.

"He's D-E-A-D. Dead", another said.

"What? I just had Sushi with him last week?!?"

One of the salesmen said under his breath, "More like a last supper."

Dean made sure to establish himself as the Alpha dog of the group by shaming the salesman into submission. He instantly admonished the other salesman and said, "*Too* soon man... *Too* soon."

The rest of the group stood there silent. The atmosphere in the room began to sober up. I decided after a brief moment of silence to keep the conversation going.

"That's hard to believe. How old was he?"

"That's a good question. Curtis was, probably like 40... or 45? Around here that makes you more or less a senior citizen."

The group disbanded one by one and everyone somberly went back to work. I mean, this news really killed the mood on the salesfloor.

"Did he have life insurance?"

"Mike! Dude. That is savage. I mean, you're cold."

"I just meant..."

"I know what you meant. Didn't you read your benefits package?"

"I perused it."

"Yeah, I'm sure you did. Well, here are the cliff notes. All Flushy employees have life insurance. The company highly encourages it. Rumor has it that for upper-level employees, the company takes out life policies on them whether they like it or not."

"Nice!"

"No kidding."

"So, they buy life insurance on the employees?"

"Yup. It's one of the many, many, many, many, many benefits for working for Flushy."

"Isn't that like some kind of conflict of interest?"

"Mike, a man just died. Have some sympathy for heaven's sake."

Dean verbally berated me about my apparent lack of decorum. In truth, I think he was just having a bad day.

"Fair enough. It's just a little unusual that's all."

Dean walked back to his desk without saying another word. I slowly meandered back to my cubicle and plopped down in my chair. I started my computer back up and turned on the learning modules. I wasn't approaching the learning with the same zeal or vigor that I once had. I mean someone just died, granted I didn't know him that well. Even still, a colleague was dead.

"Welcome back! This section of the training module will cover the Flushy approved talk-paths."

What the heck is a talk-path? After doing a rudimentary google search on business jargon, I found that it meant a script. Why can't people just say what they mean?

"Selling insurance is as easy as knowing when to say the right things in the right order. *That* is called a talk-path. At Flushy we use a very specific sequence of talk-paths that create the ideal customer-centric experience when someone is buying life insurance."

I wish selling was that easy. I spun around in my

chair and started drumming my hands on my desk. My concentration was totally shot. The reality was, this all seemed like a big waste of my time. I know how to sell insurance. I don't need some artificially created robot to tell me how to sell.

"Don't be afraid, we have broken selling down into easy digestible modules for you to learn. The first module we are going to discuss is Rapport Building."

What in the world can a machine teach me about building rapport with a human being? This will be rich. I outstretched my arms like a cat waking up from a cat nap. Just as my cynicism subsided, a notification popped up on my screen, it was probably the email about Curtis.

It read in part, "Dear Flushy Family, It is with mixed emotions that we announce that Curtis has passed away. Curtis was an invaluable asset to Flushy and he will be missed. We ask that any employee who needs assistance with this contact HR. Effective immediately Bob Lundi has been promoted to fill the vacant Sales Manager role left vacant by Curtis. Bob has been employed with Flushy for almost two years and currently serves in our Information Technology Architecture unit as Assistant Scrum Master."

Well, that escalated quickly. Dean messaged me seconds after the email came out. He said, "The new boss should be coming by soon. Make sure to look busy."

"That's pretty crazy, huh?"

"Right? The guy's body isn't even cold yet and they already replaced him. Make sure you make a good impression. Bob is an enterprise-wide talent."

"Is it normal that they replace salespeople with tech people?"

"Oh yeah, half the people on this salesfloor came from the tech department."

The door to the salesfloor opened up and everyone stood up from their cubicles. Most of the salesfloor was leering over their cube walls to see who it was. In the middle of replying back to Dean I decided to stand up and see what all the fuss was about. Presumably, it was the new boss. It was Bob. Bob was 6'1 and about 150 pounds soaking wet. He wore a typical tech guy get up. He had a long-sleeved buttoned-down shirt with a pocket protector.

Might as well start off on the right foot and introduce myself. I wanted to make a good impression. As I approached to introduce myself, Dean side stepped right in front of me.

"Dean, nice to meet you", he said.

That *SOB*. As Dean and Bob started some cordial small talk I stood off to the side to wait my turn. As soon as they were done talking, I stepped in to introduce myself.

"Mike Allen, nice to meet you."

I extended my hand and he said, "Go back to work and I'll eventually get around to touch base with everyone."

That was a bit unexpected, even for the bed side manner of a run of the mill tech guy. I mean this was a salesfloor, not a prison yard. What in tarnation is going on here? So, I went back to my desk and sat down. I finished that email to Dean.

"It's bizarre to me that organizations in general have so little respect for sales as a profession. They think any employee can interchangeably go out of one department and into the sales department with the expectation that they should succeed with no prior experience or training. I mean it's not like I could just go into finance, I don't know finance."

I sent the email and breathed a comforting sign of relief. I guess I was still a little flustered from the announcement. Sometimes I just wrote things to help me blow off steam. Retrospectively, I wasn't in the right state of mind to be working, or sending emails for that matter. So, I spaced out for a while at my desk. I put my head phones on and stared at my screen for twenty minutes or so. I was tuning out the world, when all of a sudden I got jolted by a finger poke on the back of my shoulder. It was Bob. What a lovely surprise.

"Bob Lundi, Sales Manager for the floor, nice to meet you."

"Mike Allen, nice to meet you."

"What are you working on here?", he asked while

gesturing over to my blank computer screen. He had his arms crossed, which immediately tipped me off that I should lie. Having arms folded while talking to people usually is a good tell that the person is either cold or in a bad mood. I'm assuming it was the latter, because about an hour ago this guy was working on building cloud architecture and now has to manage of a bunch of sales pukes.

"I'm in the process of rebooting my computer, it froze on me. I've been going through so many modules that the software must've crashed."

"Seems to be working fine now. Modules… why are you doing that?", he asked precipitously.

I couldn't tell if he was being serious or not. So, I played the new guy card.

"I'm the new guy."

"Ah. Training modules. Got it. Well, hurry up and get that done. We need you selling not lollygagging around. We have aggressive sales goals this year."

This guy has been a sales manager for an entire five minutes and is telling me about sales goals? Now

I've seen it all. Either way, I wasn't in much of position to complain, I just started.

"Sure thing Boss."

"Uh. One more thing. Why are you sitting alone?"

"Don't ask me, I just work here."

Bob stared at me for a few seconds before responding. He methodically raised up a single eyebrow. I take it my attempt at humor fell flat, Bob was seemingly unentertained by my comment.

"This is a cube, there are four corners and I see one person. We need to optimize this workspace. I'll move over two or three people. It'll help your training process go smoother."

I wasn't sure if he was fishing for some kind response, so I decided to just nod my head like a bobble-head doll.

"Are you going to sit there and stare? Or do you plan on getting back to work anytime soon?"

"Sounds good Boss."

Bob shook his head and walked away. He didn't say

goodbye. He just shook his head and walked away. *IT* guys...

I spent the next five hours completing learning modules. I knocked them down like dominos, one by one. At the same time, one by one people inconspicuously started slithering off the salesfloor. By the time I finished the modules it was almost 8:00 maybe 8:30 or so. When I got up to look around it a veritable graveyard. The new boss snuck out the backdoor around 4:30 pm or so, typical management, you know the kind, the last in the office and the first to leave the salesfloor.

I was completely on my own. In every sense of the word. And for the first time in my life I appreciated the irony. I had been dealt a tough hand. Here's a riddle for you. What am I? I've had ZERO prior sales experience, I've never sold an insurance policy, I've never talked to a customer, I've never been licensed, I've never went to business school, I've never managed salespeople, I've had no clue what I am doing? What am I? If you guess a front-line manager at Flushy, you'd be correct! Well, I could get busy complaining or get busy wrapping things up for the day. I gathered my belongings and headed for the exit like everyone else.

Chapter 12: Out with the old in with the new.

I once read an article from an Ivy league university titled, 'why is my boss is so wildly incompetent?' The long drive in gave me some real time for self-reflection. I had a clueless manager, that lacked any kind of rapport or basic understanding of my job. What could I do? I could sit around and pout or I could go to work. So, I found solace in my mundane routine. There was a warm comfort in the ordinary way of doing things, the Flushy way of doing things. I warmed up my computer and grabbed some coffee. When all of a sudden there was a upswell of commotion on the salesfloor. It sounded like a rabid pack of hyenas chasing down a gazelle. People started stammering up from their desks and hordes of employees rushed into the hallways.

"Where's everyone going?", I murmured aloud.

Dean jolted up from his desk and started power walking towards the nearest exit.

"Dean, what's up?", I yelled.

He didn't flinch an inch. I made sure to yell to get his attention.

"Yo-Dean! What's up man?"

He looked back at me for a second and said, "Don't you read your emails? You gotta keep up with those Mike."

He turned back around and headed towards the exit. As he got close to the exit, he turned back around and shouted, "There about to make a big announcement in the conference room. It's an all-hands-on-deck bulletin company conference call. There should be close to 10,000 people on the call."

Dean followed the outflow of people leaving the salesfloor and didn't look back. I hurriedly packed up my stuff and ran out after him. I followed the crowd in to the nearest open conference room, one of hundreds in the building. This place was packed, like a pizza with way too many toppings. The boardroom table was a single 50-foot piece of redwood, the table sat around sixty to seventy people, yet not one open seat in the whole room. So, like the other 100 people jammed into the room, I stood on the preliterary of the room and waited patiently. What was I waiting for? I had no clue.

A nudged the guy next to me and whispered, "Hey. What's going on?"

He pointed up to the ceiling said, "*Quiet,* the 'man' is listening... the man is always listening."

I titled my head, just enough to look up without drawing attention.

"Ah..."

The boardroom was covered in whiteboards and computer monitors with adjoining web cameras. As far as I knew, this was just one of many conference rooms at HQ. All of a sudden on the conference table speaker a voice chimed in.

"*And now* the President of Flushy."

The president simultaneously popped up on all of the computer monitors. I wasn't used to being cornered. To say it was intimidating was an understatement. With no further introduction he screamed out, "We need results. We need a game changer. We need to think outside the box people. We need to turn the dial. We need to move the needle. We are just one week from announcing our next venture funding round. That's right! We are opening up our Series B funding round. Our most recent round of funding produced a valuation of $5,000,000,000. We are hoping to get a valuation somewhere in the ballpark of *One Hundred Billion Dollars*."

Half the people in the room needed bibs, because drool was spooling out each ends of their mouths. I looked around at the room and had nothing but questions. David let his statement simmer without uttering another word, it worked. Because, every single person in that room was nearly foaming at the mouth, chomping at the bit to get a piece of that eventual IPO money.

"But, wait there's more...", I whispered aloud.

The guy next to me immediately took a side step away from me. I wasn't quite sure why. Was it my breath? And then...

"Speak up on it. Who said it? Time to step up or shut up."

The President began berating the room. I nearly soiled myself. I sheepishly raised my hand up in the air.

The president pointed at me and said, "You... Give us an idea."

My body instantly went limp. To stall for time, I pointed at myself and looked around. As I looked around people began to step back from me.

"Oh yeah. *You*. First of all, who are you?"

"I'm Mike Allen. I'm the new guy."

"Perfect. The new guy. The guy who speaks up on conference calls. Just what we need."

David started uncomfortably laughing, like a generic kind of corporate laughter bosses do from time to time. Other people around me shared an obligatory laugh at my expense. The noise quickly quelled and I was once again face to face with the president of the company. Time for me to step up to the plate and take a swing.

"Well... We save people time and we save people

money... How about...? Why Flush your time down the toilet buying life insurance the old school way? Try Flushy."

There was an awkward pause. A moment of kindling silence. The President began to tap on his desk.

Tap... Tap... Tap...

I took it he wasn't pleased with my answer and started looking down in shame. People around me further distanced themselves.

"I, I like it. I like it a lot! Time is money and money is everything. That's what I'm talking about Mike Allen. Keep coming up with ideas like that and I'll be out of a job soon."

The President laughed again, the room obliged and followed in sequence. David began to again scan the room looking for something. As long as I was off the hot seat that's all that mattered. The President started to squint as he sized up the room. He pointed over to someone at the end of the boardroom table. It appears David found his next victim.

"Jerry... this guy Mike over here, he's been with the

company, what a couple of weeks by the look of it. He came up with a brilliant idea on the top of his head. What do you have for me? Inspire me Jerry. Tell me something good."

Animals have three reactions to danger. They can fight, they can run or they can freeze. In this case Jerry was frozen stiff, might as well had a cardboard cutout in that seat. I didn't know the guy or nothing, but he seemed to be one of our many overpaid managers.

"Uh... What about life insurance... life insurance that..."?

Jerry was stumbling through his words, desperately trying to come up with a creative idea. Clearly, he hadn't used his brain in quite some time. He must've been a manager.

"What about, what about life insurance for your pets?", Jerry proclaimed magnanimously.

Jerry really thought he knocked that one out of the park. Jerry likened his idea to the caveman smart enough to rub two sticks together and create fire. He leaned back in his chair and ran his hands through his suspender straps. The room was dead silent. People were looking around to gauge the reactions. The President leaned back in his chair and a large disappointing sigh was all that anyone could hear. It wasn't looking great for Jerry. The President started aggressively tapping his fingers on his leather chair.

Tap... Tap... Tap...

"Jerry... That was... That *was* probably the worst idea in the history of ideas."

The President clasped his hands together and titled his head back looking up at the ceiling. He was deep in thought and we all started looking around. I felt like a witness pending an execution.

"Jerry, you realize that uttering something that moronic has consequences, right?"

Jerry began to sweat profusely, like he just ran a marathon. This felt more like a scene out of a mafia movie, rather than a brainstorming session. The room had gone completely silent with anticipation.

"Jerry you're fired! You have ten minutes to clean

out your desk and leave the building."

Jerry, along with the rest of the room looked completely stunned. Initially, he sort of laughed it off and shrugged. When he looked around the room people were afraid to make eye contact or say anything. Jerry ran through the typical phases of denial.

He scoffed and said, "Uh. What? Are, you serious?"

"You've now got 9 minutes and 45 seconds."

"You're joking, right? But... I've given this company the last four years of my life."

"You're not got 9 minutes and 20 seconds."

Jerry frantically looked around the room and realized he had no allies and no options. Clearly, this reality had set in as his tone became somber and face expressionless. Jerry found the courage to collect himself and slowly rise form his chair, like a loaf of sourdough bread beginning to rise in the oven.

"Jerry, let's get moving already. Go before I have to call security. Let's not make this more embarrassing than this has to be. Believe me this is hard on all of us."

Jerry's eyes noticeably started to water up. He got up. Stood up tall and headed towards the exit. He mustered what strength he could and politely excused himself from the meeting room.

"Now, listen to me and listen carefully. This is a revolution people! Sometimes you gotta crack a few eggs to make an omelet. No one said it would be easy. We're out to change the world. Now people, let's lock arms and make this happen. If you can't handle that or if you're not down with that, I suggest you all start refreshing your resume and find somewhere else to work."

The meeting abruptly came to a halt and the President disconnected from the conference call. Not a word was said as people started vacating the conference room. I scanned the room as people began to spill out into the hallway. Dean was at the other end of the conference room. He was twirling a pen and staring at a blank monitor. I could tell he was thinking about something. After a conference call like that, who wouldn't have a few questions? He got up and started walking over towards me.

"Walk with me Mike. Walk and talk. C'mon, I think we're heading in the same direction anyway."

"Sure thing. I hope so."

Dean patted me on the back and we set out on our journey back to the salesfloor. Dean could tell I wasn't my usual self; tempers had flared and my anxiety was spiraling out of control. I guess it was written all over my face.

"What's on your mind?", he asked quietly.

"What's on my mind? Are you for real? What the heck was that all about? Firing people on a company-wide conference call? Who does that?"

"Ah... yeah. Granted, that was all a bit unorthodox. It's kind of just the way we do things around here. Believe it or not, Flushy was ranked the number 1 most desirable place to work for the last 3 years in a row."

We stopped dead in our tracks. I took it that Dean

was waiting for the hallway to empty out. As the commotion died down, Dean began to comfort me.

"Number 1 place to work, in the world. Not in Los Angeles Mike, in the entire world."

"Yeah, that was mentioned during the interview process."

We picked up the pace again. This time with a little more vigor. I'm not sure if that had anything to do with the subject of the conversation or the meeting.

"The thing is Mike... Let me ask you something, have you worked at a Start-up company before?"

"No... I can't say that I have. This is only like my second real job out of college."

"Figures. Here's the thing Mike. If you want to work at a Start-up you have to align yourself with the company culture. It's an agile work environment. You have to learn to lift and shift. Things happen quickly and you might have to pivot on a dime. You have to be able to adapt and overcome. And if you can't do that go work somewhere else."

"I think I'm starting to understand that now."

I guess that's what I signed up for. I could accept that reality or move on. This wasn't like my old job, I mean, it was insurance, but it wasn't really insurance. Ultimately, this was my dream job. If I screwed this up, I screwed up the opportunity of a lifetime. People would give an arm and a leg to be in my position.

"You good Mike? Or..."

"Uh-huh. Well, I did have one more question. What's the whole 'Series B' thing about?"

"Man, you really are *that* new. Wow. I really envy you Mike Allen. It's the way Start-Up companies raise capital without going to a bank or making an initial public offering. Basically, you just go through different 'series or rounds of funding."

"Oh. Yeah that all makes sense."

"The last time Flushy did the company valuation the street put the estimate around two and a half billion dollars, but we exceeded those expectations by like one thousand basis points or something crazy like that."

"Street? Like, as in Wall-Street?"

"Now you're getting it. I don't care what anybody else says about you Mike, you're alright by me."

We rounded the final turn that led to the salesfloor entrance and rooted in place for a while as we shot the breeze.

"See the thing is Mike. None of that matters. Do you remember back in the day when you had your first job? Not the job before this one, but your first actual job."

"I do. I worked a paper route believe it or not."

"Well, let me ask you something. Did you ask about what the editor wanted to put in the paper?"

"No. I was a kid. All I cared about was doing my route."

"What was the job? Why did they pay you?"

"It was to deliver papers..."

"If you want to succeed here. If you want to end up

like Jerry. If you want to climb the corporate ladder. If you want to cruise like me. Whatever you want to do here. Put your head down and do the work. The company isn't paying you to ask questions. The company isn't paying you to think. They pay you to execute. They pay you to sell policies. They pay you to go deliver papers."

"Was that some twisted version of a motivational speech?"

"Listen or don't listen. It's up to you. I've seen a lot of people come through those doors and just about as many go right out. Word for the wise. Don't listen to me or do. Frankly Mike, I don't care. But, don't come crying to me when it all falls apart and the wheels start to come off the bus."

"Uh-huh."

"Do you know the worst part about being right all the time?"

"No clue. I'd imagine it's rather repetitive. The realization that you're smarter than everybody else?"

"Smart, real smart. The worst part about being right

all the time is having to say I told you so. It's so exhausting."

We both shook our heads and went about our day. I sat back down at my computer and started working my email que. Before I could start responding I heard call for me, it was a feint echo of my name.

"Mike... Mike Allen."

"Mike, I need to speak with you in my office", Bob shouted with both hands clasped around his mouth like a blowhorn.

"Yes... Yes, sir. Give me a second to close down my terminal."

"Not one second from now, I said now. My office. Let's go!"

I turned off my terminal and started walking towards Bob's office. Looks like I couldn't catch a break. I opened the door to Bob's office and peered my head through. I looked around and saw Bob with his back turned. Seemingly he was finishing up some work on his computer.

"Can I come in?"

"Grab a seat and close the door behind you."

"What a crazy meeting, right?"

Bob looked at me for a second and shook his head in disbelief. Then out of nowhere he said, "You can't pull stunts like that."

"I.. I... stunts? Sorry, I don't follow."

Honestly, I was confused by his tone. As far as I was concerned I thought that meeting went pretty well for me. I mean, I wasn't the one who was publicly humiliated in front of the entire company and subsequently fired on the spot.

"Mike, you're still new here so I shouldn't put too much blame on you. This is something that comes with professional maturity. You have to learn when to shut your mouth and when to speak up. You have to learn when to lead, when to get out of the way and when to follow."

I stared at Bob with a blank expression. I mean, who did this guy think he was? Professional Maturity, is this guy for real? I mean, this is a workplace not a bordello. I decided to let cooler heads prevail and hear him out. In retrospect, it would have been easier to punch him in the face and quit. What followed was a flurry of curse words and overly dramatic language. Bob was highly expressive with his hands, waving them around like a nineteenth century dictator. I tried my best to block it all out. I tuned back in to Bob about a minute later still wording through his seemingly endless vengeful diatribe.

"Mike, when you speak, you represent not only yourself, but what you say directly reflects my leadership. You made a mockery of that conference call!"

There we go. He finally got to the point. Apparently, I embarrassed him. I nodded my head in agreement without saying so much as a word. Clearly, I had outshined him and he took it personally. I guess somehow it was my fault that I was more qualified to do my bosses job than my boss was. It would seem I was entangled in a rather large quagmire. I sat quietly for the next thirty seconds to let the proverbial rage balloon deflate. I knew that if I smiled and shook my head long enough it would appease Bob into routing his attack.

"Mike, are you getting me? Do me a favor and take that smug grin off your face. What's the matter with you? Are you getting me?"

I had two choices to play out in my head. On the one hand, I could engage in a back-and-forth argument. Or I could just sit there and take it like a man. I knew making the wrong choice would set the entire tone for our professional working relationship and set a precedent for future situations. I had to reconcile this. I mean, give it some real thought. Grapple with the implications of my decision.

Bob's face had become noticeably redder as the conversation regressed. It was almost like talking to a big red tomato. His belligerence increased with every passing second. It looked like my silence played a large role in his instability. What's wrong with me? I didn't use to be such a glutton for pain and belittlement.

I decided to speak up and ask, "So, you're saying I

shouldn't speak up when the President of the company calls me out to speak up? How can I ignore the President of the company?"

Bob was stunned someone actually had the gall to stand up to him. It was clear by his facial expression this wasn't what he expected me to say. He shouted his reply at the top of his lungs.

"I'm saying you should never get called on in the first place."

Bob was clearly flustered and when people are angry they tend to make bad decisions. So, I decided to say the most placating thing I could think of to a supervisor.

"Sure thing Boss."

I slid back my chair and stood up. I stuck out my hand to shake his hand. He didn't reply in kind. Not in the least.

"Did I say you could leave?"

Bob had his arms folded, his hands thoroughly entrenched into his arm pits and this rather dreadful look on his face.

"No, no you didn't. Can I go back to work? I'd like to make this company some money? Or should I not sell any policies today?"

Bob waved me off and I went back to my desk. I needed to collect myself and reset. So, I decided to take some sound advice. I decided to take a break and finally get around to reading that email I missed earlier this morning.

The email read, "Well, who would've thought? What can we say? It's been an interesting week within an interesting month within an interesting year. I wanted to take this moment to connect and contribute some of my reflection of my own in hopes and dreams. Firstly, I'd like to commend each of you, my employees, for your individual leadership as we navigate through these craggy waves and jagged bluffs. Despite the recent news, you have each maintained a clear commitment to the task at hand. While this may seem small to you, even trivial, I can't tell you how huge it is in the game of life and especially in business. The ability to focus and execute amidst turmoil is a sign of a true leader.

For me, I have experienced a wide range of thoughts and emotions over the last couple days. As a leader, it's important that we express and consider all of these thoughts and emotions. At the same time, you don't have to invite them in for tea and crumpets. It's ok to feel confused, worried, excited, happy, angry, sad.

One thing I like to remember is that the power of the mind is to be able to *acknowledge* these emotions without allowing them to incapacitate you, disrupt your flow state or dampen your attitude.

Speaking of attitude, this shouldn't come as a surprise to most of you, but reading *The Art of War* is another helpful practice that helps me stay focused and centered every day especially amid these challenging times.

One thing to keep in mind is that the only way to eat an elephant is to start one bite at a time. For instance, let's say you want to run your first marathon. The point is not to run a marathon, it's to become a runner.

Life happens, nothing is by accident. In order to lead this revolution it takes a commitment to be the best every single day. Let's all just stay focused. I'm asking you all to trust the process. We are well on the way to our One-Hundred Billion Dollar vision, but without sacrifice that'll remain just a vision. With that, once again, THANK YOU for leading. Thank you for being self-aware.

We have hands-on-deck company conference call in Thirty minutes. Please come prepared to discuss how we achieve our $100B vision. Failure is not an option, it's a choice. We can either choose to be great or choose to be obsolete.

Respectfully,

David Berrigan"

What could I say? I guess Dean was right, I should make it a habit to read my emails.

Chapter 13: What comes around goes around.

Believe it or not, that conference call really lit a fire under my butt. I was overcome with this feeling over euphoria, I was marinading in it. I was crushing my sales goals. I was on track to hit a new company sales record. People were starting to notice, especially to my chagrin one person in particular, his name was Bob. I was hitting my stride and it felt really good. I finally found my groove and did it all in spite of my boss. Sure, he didn't make it easy on me, but Bob wasn't going to be the end of me at Flushy. He didn't let off the gas pedal, but it didn't matter. It took me a bit to get off the ground, but ultimately the wait was worth it. I was taking on additional responsibilities, heck I won three consecutive sales competitions.

Another day at Flushy, meant another day to change the world. At first, this day seemed like any other. I got my coffee, started up my computer terminal and waited for my computer to load. The previous night I worked until about 11:00 pm. It wasn't glamorous, but the money was phenomenal. Sure, I didn't have much of a social life, but how many twenty-five-year-old kids do you know that can buy a sports car?

I logged into my computer around 7:45 am, I remembered the exact time because Bob had actually shown up early for once in his life. I thought it must be Christmas, because it was a miracle to see a manager show up before the starting bell. Good on him. Maybe he was turning a new leaf.

Bob casually strolled on over to my desk. He dropped off a large white piece of paper at each desk along his way. For once, he didn't give me the stink eye. This was all so reminiscent of back in grade school when a teacher would drop an exam on your desk. He dropped off my sales numbers and a performance evaluation. I flipped it over and like usual had crushed my sales targets. The striking part of the review was that under the overall performance for my evaluation it was marked, 'Performance Rating Not Acceptable'.

"Not acceptable? I'm crushing my sales targets...", I protested aloud.

When I read further into the assessment it pointed to concerns around my documentation of sales calls, response rate, adherence to the approved talking points, sub-optimal quoting and lack of utilization around the company script. So... let me get this straight. I'm being heavily measured against things that are not sales, even though I am selling policies.

I realize this was just business, but I felt slighted. This all felt deeply personal and nowhere near professional or objective. I know in business, people say don't take it personally, but this was personal to me. On the bottom of the review it read, "Mike you lack focus, intention and professional maturity. Please pivot to focus on what you can control and conquer. Don't focus on the uncontrollable aspects of the job. Needs to focus more on the task at hand and not the bigger picture."

Bob was hovering around the other salespeople trying to drum up small talk. In reality, he was circling the wagons. They were far too polite to tell him to go pound sand. We briefly made eye contact and I motioned him over to my cubicle. He pretended not to see me and walked away.

"What a coward."; I said.

What was I supposed to expect? This guy was highly suspect. I just got bad marks and I'm the highest performing salesperson on the salesfloor. I started making various forms non-sense noises as I was thinking. I began rocking back and forth in my chair. I put my hands together to form a triangle and thought about all of the things on this review. I stood up with the review in my hand and started scanning the room again to see if Bob was still around somewhere. He had retreated back into his office, so I got up and found my way over to his office. My performance review in hand I barged my way into his office to begin my tirade. Bob was waiting for me.

"What's going on Mike?"

"What's going on?", I asked in a sarcastic tone.

I held up my review and pointed to it.

"This... this is what's going on Bob."

"Your review? What about it?"

"Let's drop the charade Bob. What is this?"

"I've been meaning to set some time up to discuss it with you. As you can imagine given that it's our monthly review, I've been quite busy around the office."

Bob glanced down at his computer monitor and clearly pretended to start searching through his calendar.

"How about we set something up for next week? How does that sound? I can fit you in on Monday at 10:30 or Tuesday at 11:00. Which do you prefer?"

"We're gonna deal with this right now."

"Mike, I'd love to. But, I'm a little busy at the moment."

Before he could finish his sentence, I cut him off.

"You're right. You're busy, busy with me right now."

"Mike... you barged into my office. There's got to be something important on your mind. What specifically do you seem to have a problem with? How can I help *you*?"

"This… this review is the most subjective piece of garbage I have ever laid eyes on."

"Tell me more."

"Tell me more? Are you kidding me? Well, firstly, you said that only 90% of the time I use the approved company script. Why does it matter what percentage of the time that I deviate from your pre-approved line of questioning? I have the highest closing ratio in the office."

"Ah. So you want me to open the kimono. Statistics have shown that the best salespeople are those who stick to the company approved script 100% of the time. They perform more efficiently than those who don't."

"I'm the number one salesperson here. I won the last three sales competitions. I'm the highest producing salesman in company history…"

"We know *AND* we appreciate that Mike, just how effective you can be. Just imagine how effective you could be if you just stuck to the approved company script. Imagine Mike, not at 90%, but at 100%."

All I could do was blink and take deep breaths. Long protracted breaths, almost like a yogi. Maybe I would take David's advice and do some yoga.

"So, what you're saying is that sales don't matter? Is that what you're trying to tell me Bob?"

"Not at all Mike. What matters is that you learn to do as you're told. You need to lean into the process and not fight it. What matters is that you need to be coachable and learn. If you don't like that then you can go work somewhere else. If you don't like that, then I suggest you start refreshing your resume."

Bob was clearly starting to bait me into an argument, so I decided to end the conversation and go back to my desk.

"Bob, as always, it's been enlightening speaking with you", I said sarcastically.

I did an about face and headed back to my desk. Bob was completely unphased and just went back to pretending to work. This guy had to be one of the least self-aware people in the history of human beings. Even for a manager, this guy was dense. He had a way when it came to dealing with people, to say it nicely he was a blunt instrument. He viewed programming computer software no differently than influencing human behavior. As far as I could tell he looked at us like a bunch of ones and zeros. When I got back to my desk, I put the review right where it belonged, in the trash bin. I booted my computer terminal back up and started sipping on my coffee. It was barely room temperature, but I forced it down anyways. The way I figured it Bob was setting me up to fail. It is what it is.

My computer took a little longer to boot up than normal. Ordinarily I would have thought nothing of it. Maybe Bob fired me and didn't tell me. When my computer loaded, a rabid sequence of notifications popped up on my screen. There were 50 unread emails in my inbox, all of which marked urgent. That was a little out of step, but nothing too extraordinary.

The first email read, "Message: Request to Recall - Confidential." I figured it was a phishing email or some kind of spam. At first I hesitated to open it. The email body was blank. I scrolled through email after email, all with similar headlines. I mean, what in the world was this about? After digging through the emails, I finally found the source. The email header read, "Confidential – Senior Leadership Eyes Only". So, naturally, I clicked on it immediately.

The body of the email read,

"Mark,

We've been subjected to another 'routine' audit by the Department of Insurance. They're poking around, I think they're just on a fishing expedition. Allegedly, they have seen an increase in the number of consumer complaints due to non-payment of claims.

They're asking for the following:

1. Our Claims Settlement Ratio
2. Our process for claims handling
3. The Investment Income
4. Our Speed to Pay Ratio
5. An explanation of our key account's loss ratio
6. Current GAAP financial statements
7. An On-site audit of company records

8. An explanation of the deficit in the employee life accounts

We need to clean this up before we file with the Securities and Exchange Commission for our Initial Public Offering. If we don't respond within 10 business days it will result in a $100,000 per day penalty. We need to figure this out quick. We've been punting this ball for far too long. I can move some things around until the IPO, but that won't make it go away.

One more thing. This is the stickler. They are asking for an in-person audit led by Todd. How in the world do you plan on accomplishing that with Todd on his 'Vacation'?"

I wasn't 100% certain about a lot of that stuff, but it doesn't sound great. An instant message popped up on my screen, it was the President of Flushy, David Berrigan. The president of the company was instant messaging me. Wait a minute, the President of the company was instant messaging me? Why in the world?

"Mike, it's been awhile. How's everything going?"

I replied back, "Everything is going great David. How are things with you?"

"Great... Great... It looks like an email meant for Mark Alias was accidentally sent over to you this morning. He's the head of Compliance and Finance. What I'm going to need you to do is go ahead find it and delete it."

"David. Uh. There's a problem. I opened it and read it."

For the next five minutes. The chat read, "David Berrigan is typing..."

"You did... I see. Why'd you do that?"

This was the President of the company, not one of my knuckle head buddies. This guy was a big freaking deal. This wasn't shooting the breeze with Dean at the watering hole. I had a massive decision to make. Do I lie or tell the truth? Sometimes doing the right thing isn't really doing the right thing, especially if it ends up getting me fired. So, I lied.

"It was an accident. My bad."

The chat abruptly ended and my computer terminal shut down. Okay that was weird. I decided to get up and stretch my legs. I think that conversation earned me another cup of coffee. I strolled on back to the breakroom kitchen and refilled my mug. As I moseyed on back to my desk, about ten or fifteen minutes later, I looked up and there were two nameless suits towering over me.

"Uh... How can I help you fine gentlemen?"

"Are you Mike Allen?", one of the suits asked.

"Yes... I'm Mike Allen. How can I help you?"

One of the suits pulled out his phone and started whispering to someone on the other line. I didn't realize Flushy had a plethora of 1940's style goons on the company payroll.

"So... Can I help you?"

"We need you to vacate this space and come with us immediately.", they said in unison.

"Hahaha! Really funny. Are you guys from IT? My terminal shutdown and..."

"Immediately. Come with us. As in right now."

One of the goons gestured with his arm over to the nearest exit. I started following them down a series of corridors. I figured this was either some mafia style hit job or they were possibly escorting me out of the building. We walked for another ten minutes. The whole excursion was rather exhausting. We walked through doors, upstairs, down stairs, up elevators, down elevators. They didn't say a word the entire time. We finally arrived at a large silverish looking elevator. This was a guarded elevator, it clearly was private, it was clearly important.

"Fellas, where we going?"

The two suits both gestured over to the elevator and politely escorted me in. The elevator looked like it was made of platinum or at least platinum plated. I looked over at one of the suits and he had a clear bulge by his upper torso. I wasn't a rocket scientist, but I'm pretty sure that was a gun. I started getting increasingly nervous, sweat was dripping down the back of my neck. The elevator was going up to the 20th floor. The elevator had arrived and the doors opened. I started to walk forward and one of the suits grabbed my shoulder.

"Not yet. Mr. Allen."

Two people holding briefcases got onto the elevator and we continued to go up to the 30th floor. When we arrived at the 30th floor the doors opened and another two people got on. We went up again, this time to the 40th floor and the suits escorted us all off the elevator.

"This way please.", the suits said in unison to the entire group.

People began to pile out of the elevator and the suits escorted the group down a narrow corridor. The 40th floor was baron, aside from the brand-new furniture which was still wrapped in plastic. At the end of the hallway there was a large double door entrance to what I assumed was an office or a conference room. Turns out it was a 180-degree view conference room.

The suits opened the doors and led everyone in. In the corner of the room, there was a stenographer sitting, presumably waiting to take notes. There was a large conference table, that looked to be a solid piece of Hickory. The chairs were carved of what I could only describe as a pure ivory type material. This conference room was nicer than my apartment, heck this conference room was nicer than my dream home. The two suits sat me down at the middle of the table. Me on one side of the table and everyone else on the other side. All of a sudden, David Berrigan kicked open the doors of the conference room and everyone stood up. That was rather magnanimous of him, how fitting.

"Please, sit. Everyone down... Sit down..."

David Berrigan took the empty chair exactly opposite of me. I was face to face with *the power*. I was used to dealing with peons, people like me all day long and on occasion Bob. But, nothing like this. I wondered if he even remembered me during that interview we had.

"What is this? The meeting of the *5-families*? Am I about to be made an offer I can't refuse", I said jokingly to break the ice.

The room was dead silent. Everyone was looking at David Berrigan for cues. David Berrigan smiled and started to chuckle. Which was followed by a bevy of uncomfortable corporate style laughter. You know the kind, that obligatory kind of laugh people do when someone higherup laughs at a bad joke.

"Mike, the first thing I need you to do, right now, is sign this NDA."

He slid what looked like a phone book over to me.

"I know it looks intimidating. The best way to approach it, is by just flipping to the last page and sign where it says signature."

Everyone awkwardly laughed out loud.

"Is that an order or a suggestion?"

"I mean, you don't have to sign the NDA. You can always go that route and see where that takes you."

I quickly flipped to the last page and signed the NDA. I didn't want to be pushing up daisies, so to speak. David Berrigan quickly took the signed NDA and slid it over to someone at the end of the table. By the way she was dressed, I assumed that to be one of our many corporate attorneys on retainer for Flushy. The attorney at the end of the table flipped over to the last page to verify the signature.

"Great. Now that is out of the way. On to the business at hand. Mike, I just finished reading your last performance evaluation on the way up here."

The attorney at the end of the table slid over a bunch of copies to the center of the conference room table.

"You know what I think about your performance review?"

I wasn't quite sure where this conversation was going. So, I decided to just shake my head.

"I think it was a bunch of rubbish. Ain't that right boys?"

David polled the room and encouraged people to speak up in agreement. He glanced around to make sure people were in line. There was a chorus of murmured agreement around the table.

"In fact, I think you are just the guy we have been looking for to spear head our experimental agency distribution channel strategy. What we're talking about here is the transformation of our sales department. Your results are impressive what else can we say."

I looked around the room waiting for the punch line. To my pleasant surprise, nobody was laughing.

"David, I don't know what to say."

"Then, just say yes."

"Yes. *Wait, Wait, Wait.* So, you want me to take Bob's job?"

"*No, no, no.* We want you to be our Senior Vice President of Agency Sales Distribution."

"Agency distribution? I thought, I thought we didn't have agents?"

"You're just the man we need to spearhead this new division. And do you know why? Why Mike Allen is the right man for the job?"

"I-I...", I couldn't even complete a sentence.

"It's because, well, you get results. The best results in fact. The other reason is that you speak the language of Insurance Agent. You know the lingo; you walk the walk and talk the talk. You know how to connect with *those* kinds of people."

I was visibly awe struck. I was half expecting my first corporate execution over here and I stumbled my way into a promotion. This has all got to be some deranged candid camera show, right?

"So, what would I be doing exactly?"

"That's all in the details. Don't worry about it for now."

David Berrigan started snapping his fingers and his secretary came over with a packet. He handed me the packet and said, "This is the comp package. Go ahead and open it."

The offer would give me:

- Company car
- Private corner office
- A private secretary
- A secretary for my secretary

- A parking spot with my name on it
- Access to the company gym and spa
- 100% paid health insurance
- Group Life insurance
- An executive key man life insurance policy
- Unlimited PTO (Paid Time Off)
- Paid Company holidays
- Equity sharing
- 100% Tuition Reimbursement
- A monthly bonus
- 100% 401(k) matching
- A Company Pension, fully vested day 1
- Three Hundred and Fifty Thousand Dollars a year starting Salary
- Guaranteed 10% per year salary increases

"That uh, that is one generous offer."

"Glad to have you as part of the SLT… that stands for Senior Leadership Team, get used to it Mike. Welcome to the good life. As the newest addition of the SLT we will need to get you up to speed on the business. On how the company makes the hamburger, so to speak."

Someone at the end of the table slid over a giant packet, along with another Non-Disclosure Agreement for me to sign.

"Read that packet and get up-to-speed by... what is it now about 2 pm? Let's say zero-nine-hundred tomorrow morning."

I assumed it was one of those asks that was more of an ultimatum rather than an actual request. David had a way of mincing his words.

"Tomorrow were calling you up to the big leagues. Time to get off the bench and get in the game. You'll meet with each member of the SLT and they'll give you a crash course in each department. Right now, we don't need you to be proficient, we just need you to know enough to be dangerous."

David Berrigan grabbed the edge of the conference room table and stood up. He extended his arm across the table to me. I reached out and he grabbed my hand. We shook hands, he put on his aviators and he whisked out of the room. Everyone else stood up and followed David out of the room. I couldn't help but stare down at the packet on the table. Before I looked back up the room had completely emptied out.

I quickly grabbed the packet off the conference table and headed back down to the salesfloor. You ever drive home from work, and not remember the actual trip? Like, not remembering the actual drive home. Yet somehow you arrived back at your home safe and sound. That was me walking back to the salesfloor. Everything and everyone just sort of passed me on by. I had blinders on, before I knew it, I was back at my cubicle. I started gathering up my stuff and began to shove it into a cardboard box. Dean had slithered on over to my desk. He immediately began to barrage me with a flurry of questions.

"Mike, what in the heck happened? Where'd they take you? What's with the box? Did they let you go? Talk to me man, what's up?"

I looked over at Dean without saying a word. I kind of grinned at him while shoving the various knickknacks on my desk into this box.

"Oh, man. I'm so sorry man. That really sucks. They

let you go, huh?"

He put his hand on my shoulder and patted me on the shoulder for a second. It was a lite patting, just enough to get my attention.

"Dean, it's not exactly what you think."

"Did they at least give you some severance pay?

I cracked a smile and said, "Believe it or not. They actually gave me a promotion."

Dean shook his head in disbelief and he said, "You're kidding me, right? They promoted Mike Allen. To what? Head of Sanitation?"

I cleared my throat and said, "My new role will be as the Senior Vice President of Agency Sales Distribution."

Dean started laughing out loud, so much so that the entire salesfloor could hear him.

"You had me going there for a second Mike. C'mon man. What really happened? We don't have agents. You, a Senior Vice President? Bah!"

I looked at Dean dead in his eyes and reiterated,

"Senior Vice President of Agency Sales Distribution."

Dean's tone quickly course corrected to a more serious disposition. I took it he started to believe me. He stood up a little taller, brought his shoulders back a bit more and said, "Wow... I don't know what to say."

"How do you think I feel?"

"How'd you find out?"

"David presented me an offer like thirty minutes ago. What was I going to do turn it down?"

"David, David Berrigan... You mean the President of the company? What're you guys on a first name basis?"

"Dean, I'd love to chit chat with you. But, I gotta go take a private elevator to my new office."

I snuck in a smile as I was shoving things into my cardboard box.

"Oh, it's like that. Mr. Big Time over here. He gets a big fancy promotion and then forgets who mentored him along the way. It's like that, huh?"

"Don't worry Dean. I won't forget all the little people that helped me along the way. I mean, I do need a secretary if you're interested."

I stopped packing my things for a second and we both laughed at how absurd an idea that would be.

"Although, it sounds tempting, you know, being your peon and all. I'll have to pass for now. I kind of like my little slice of Flushy Heaven here on the salesfloor."

"If you ever change your mind..."

"Uh. Does Bob know yet?"

I smiled and completely stopped in my tracks.

"Oh yeah... Bob... We have some unfinished business to discuss."

I put my box down and walked over to his office. It was a short walk, I made sure to have an audible thudding knock on his door. The kind of knock that made an impression.

Knock... Knock... Knock...

I pulled the door open and saw myself in. Bob turned

around in his chair.

"Oh, Mike. What do you want?"

"Did you hear the news?"

"What news? Unlike popular belief, I'm a very busy person. Get to the point or get out of here."

"Sure, sure. No problem Bob."

I got in nice and close, violating any kind of personal space boundaries we had. I wanted to make sure he heard me loud and clear.

"Watch your back Bob.", I whispered affirmatively.

"What did you just say to me? Are you out of your mind?"

I smiled and said, "You heard me. And if you ever talk to me like that again. One time. Ever again. I'll have you fired Bob."

Bob stood up out of his chair. He practically thew the chair to the side in a pathetic attempt of intimidation. All I did was shoot him back a big smile.

"Who do you think you are talking to me like that? You're fired! Go clear out your desk! Now, before I call security."

I got right up in his face and fronted up on him. We squared off and it seemed to have the desired effect of having him peep down.

"Who do I think I am? I'm your new boss."

Bob squinted his eyes and clearly was dumbfounded by my declaration.

"Yeah. That's right. You didn't hear the news. I'm part of the SLT now. I'm untouchable."

Bob scoffed and laughed under his breath. I don't blame him for not believing me.

"Now, sit down Bob. Or I will sit you down. Pick up your chair from the floor or I'll put you down there with it."

Bob had this look of complete bewilderment on his face. It was priceless. He didn't quite know what to do. I started snapping my fingers and said, "Bob did I stutter? Pick your chair up and sit down."

He picked up his chair off the floor and acrimoniously sat back down. He grabbed his phone and started dialing up HR. Mind you, Bob hadn't uttered a word. I sat back in the chair and smiled as he called his Human Resources.

"I'm calling H.R. right now. You can sit there with that stupid grin on your face all you want."

Ring... Ring... Ring...

"Hi, this is Bob Lundi..."

He was blood thirsty tirade was interrupted by the person on the other line.

"Well, I've got Mike Allen here in my office and I need to process his termination effective immediately..."

"Uh-huh... Yeah, but... Uh-huh... I understand..."

He sat there silent for some time. His life drained from his body. I stuck out my wrist and pointed down at my watch to let Bob know to hurry up. I was getting impatient, so I just started talking again.

"See the thing is Bob. You have a choice to make. Do

you want to go out on your back or get on your knees and beg me for your job?"

Bob hung up the phone. He gulped and stared at me with this lifeless expression. His skepticism had subsided, but had not quite fully receded.

"Don't worry Bob, I won't make your life half as miserable as you made mine. That'd be inhumane. That'd be arbitrarily cruel. That's be someone who lacked professional maturity."

I started laughing with sinister overtones. The power was overwhelming. This is what power feels like. I'm beginning to like it. I think I could get used to this. I noticed Bob had a sandwich on his desk. Turns out he was about to start his lunch when I barraged in on him.

"Is that your lunch?"

"Yeah... It's a pastrami sandwich from Palino's down the street."

"Oh... Palinos! Do they deliver?"

"No. I had one of the interns wait in line to pick it up

for me. Around this time it takes about an hour or so."

The chitchat made Bob calm down a bit, like a cow being led to the slaughter house.

"An hour? Wow. That must be one great sandwich."

"It is."

"Is that like your favorite place or something?"

"It is. Mike, what's your point? Why are we talking about my sandwich?"

"My point is Bob. My point is, shut up and give me your sandwich."

"What? No! I'm not giving you my sandwich. That's my lunch."

I tapped my fingers on my leg.

Tap... Tap... Tap...

"*See* the problem you have right now is Bob, is that you still think that you matter. You think that you have power. You think that people care about what you have to say. Well, Bob, you don't. I'm not going to ask you again. Give me your sandwich."

Tap... Tap... Tap...

Bob degradingly slid the sandwich over to me without making eye contact.

"Put the sandwich in my hand Bob."

He begrudgingly picked up the plate and put it in my out stretched hand. I took a big slow bite of that sandwich, all while looking Bob dead in his eyes. I slowly chewed that pastrami sandwich. He was right, this place was worth that wait.

"Wow, that's a good sandwich!"

I said obnoxiously with a big chunk of sandwich still in my mouth. I stood up from my chair with the sandwich still in my hand. Turned around towards the open door. I took the rest of the sandwich in my hand and hurled it across the office. The sandwich broke apart and scattered across the floor.

"Now, Bob, considering your fancy lunch, I'm assuming it was very expensive?"

"It was a $30 sandwich..."

"Now, Bob, considering your $30 sandwich is splattered across the salesfloor, as your boss, I recommend you go pick it up."

I licked my fingers clean and didn't break eye contact with Bob. Bob didn't flinch one bit. Bob was unmoved by my request. So, I asked more affirmatively.

"Go pick up your sandwich."

"What? No. I'm not doing that.", he protested like a child refusing to clean up his room.

"Oh, you're going to pick up the sandwich. And I mean, you are going to and not some poor intern."

"No. Don't be absurd. I'm not a janitor."

I could tell Bob was going to persist on with his little protest in order to retain what was left of his manhood. If there is one thing I've learned from my managers is that you can't let your employees have free thought. You had to break their will, make them absolutely submissive and eliminate any free thought. Oh, I put him in his place.

"Bob. You're going to pick up that sandwich. Or else."

"Or else what? Picking up a sandwich isn't in my job description."

"Well you can pick up the sandwich. Or choose not to and see where that takes you."

Bob slowly stood up and hunched his shoulders. He escorted me out of his office and went to go pick up the sandwich. It was my first taste of power, maybe a bit vengeful and maybe a bit brash. What could I say? He deserved it. I deserved it.

"Great. Don't forget to scrub the carpet when you're finished. It looks like that deli mustard got pretty deep into the crevasses of the carpet. I'm sure you'll do a great job Bob. You always aim to please."

I got my stuff and headed up to my new office. When I stepped off the elevator, I was greeted by my new secretary.

"Mike?"

"Yes! Nice to meet you..."

"Hi, I'm Gilroy. I'll be your secretary. Follow me please."

We walked through rows of empty cubicles. We walked for like ten minutes, until we arrived at two big beautiful white doors.

"Is that Marble?"

"Nothing but the best boss."

I opened the doors and slowly peaked my head in the office. It was baron, nothing but a desk, a chair and an empty bookcase. At least it was a large space with lots of potential. From wall to wall the office probably measured forty feet part. I put my stuff down next to my desk and pulled out the packet. Gilroy was standing in the door way waiting for something. I wasn't quite sure what she wanted, or what I was supposed to do with a secretary.

"Gilroy, what do I do next? I mean, how does having a secretary work? I've never had one before."

"First. I'm an executive assistant. So, let's correct that. I'm not a secretary. This isn't the 1950's..."

"I-I'm so sorry. I didn't mean it like that."

Gilroy started laughing out loud. Clearly, we were going to work well together.

"No. I'm just messing with you. Why don't you start with that packet and if any questions come up, ping me and I can help you find an answer. My desk is right outside your office. I'm on call from 7 am to 7 pm."

"Yeah. The packet. That sounds good."

Gilroy shut the door to give me some privacy and went over to her desk. I opened the packet and it only had a few documents in it. I guess this insurance stuff isn't so complicated after all. The first document was the company business plan, or at least a synopsis of the business plan.

The first paragraph was titled, "Mission, Vision and Values." It was your typical run of the mill corporate style writing. The kind where you put a lot of words down on paper that mean absolutely nothing of substance. Kind of like when a Non-fiction writer starts writing Fiction for the first time.

It read, "Mission: To provide the best in class, easiest to purchase and lowest cost life insurance experience in the world. Vision: To revolutionize and dominate the insurance industry."

The writing was fairly simplistic, no three syllable words or anything like that. I mean overall it felt like it was written at a fourth or fifth grade reading level. Whether this was done on purpose or not I had no idea.

"Values: at Flushy we value being a first mover, acting fast and being agile."

Nothing mind-blowing here, mostly mundane corporate-speak. I'm not really sure what I was expecting. That was it. I mean, that was it. That was the entire first page. I flipped over to the next page and it continued. This all kind of felt rather pedestrian. Almost like a rough draft or some kind of redacted version of a business plan. The next page listed key financial data and had a large red 'CONFIDENTIAL' diagonally stamped across the page.

It read, "Context: Flushy is a bottom-line company.

We care about the bottom-line above all else. Insurance companies have two predominant sources of revenue generating vehicles. The first way is through writing policies and collecting policy premium from customers. The second way is by taking that collected premium and investing it in the stock market."

Listed below that statement was a series of key financial ratios. Although I had a business degree, I hadn't familiarized myself with any of those ratios in some time.

It read, "Policy Retention Ratio: 99.9%, Expense Ratio: 7%, Loss Ratio: 15%, Combined Ratio: 23%, Solvency Ratio: 100%, Commission Expense Ratio: 5%, Claims Settlement Ratio: 81%, Claims Resolution: 51 days, Investment Yield: 47%."

The section below that was the valuation section. It read, "Flushy has a current valuation of $5,000,000,000 and expects a velocity on that figure to be 20X by the Pre-IPO funding round. We have established an anticipatory runway of late Q3 or early Q4."

That was it. That was all the second page had to offer. I flipped through to the next page and it had an explanation of the business model.

It read, "In our industry there are numerous ways to Win. The key is to find a clear way to Win, a clear way to differentiate. At Flushy we have created an incredible use-case for customers. Our industry is a crowded space, it's hyper competitive, fragmented and is undergoing massive disruption. Every insure-tech has great people and great tech, so we make a consorted effort to admire and acquire both great people and great tech from our competition. The Insure-tech space is now a $100B industry, and Flushy is in the vanguard to blow that number up. Our vision is to be the first Trillion Dollar Insurance carrier. The old model of collecting premiums and doing nothing for clients is about as archaic as a Fax Machine. We intend to upheave all of that, by bringing the industry the likes of which it has never dreamt of. A lot of what we knew to be true or our perceived biases need to be challenged. Consumers are more educated, price-aware and demanding than ever."

After reading all that, I figured it was time to take a break. I mean twenty minutes ago I was berating my old boss and tossing his lunch across the salesfloor. Now, I'm three pages deep into a business plan that I can barely comprehend. I stood up for a second and stretched my legs out. When I looked up to stretch my neck out, I noticed a security camera staring me right in the face. Directly above my desk there was a security camera with a red-light blinking. That's a little weird. I stepped outside my office to get a good lay of the land. When I started looking around, I noticed that there were security cameras just about as far as the eye could see.

I turned to Gilroy and asked, "What's up with all the cameras? What's the deal?"

She laughed, "Did you not notice them all over the salesfloor? They're set up all over the building like that."

"Can't say that I did. Creepy."

Gilroy laughed and went back to typing up something on her computer. I stepped back into my office and lethargically continued through the business plan.

The next section read, "Strategy: Our strategy is to offer the lowest price insurance, through better pricing synergies, better tech, better data, creative financing and strategic partnerships."

What in the world is a pricing synergy? The remainder of the packet was more of the same. I finished it up in less than an hour. I decided to call it an early evening and headed out around 8:30 pm. When I emerged from my office, Gilroy had already taken off for the day and the office was completely emptied out. I broke for the exit and made sure to turn off all the lights on my way out. Who knows what I have in store for tomorrow?

Chapter 14: An Education Fit For an Executive

Per my usual routine, I arrived at work early the next morning. Dealing with traffic in Los Angeles is possibly one of the most daunting crucibles a person ever has to endure in life. I wanted to avoid the perennial traffic jam on the 405 freeway, the 405 can be pretty unforgiving during rush-hour. I hit the lobby around 7:00 am and was greeted by a new face.

"Hi Mike! Mark Alias. Nice to meet you."

Mark was one of the least imposing people I had ever met. He stood about 4-foot and 12-inches and couldn't weigh more than 125 pounds and that is with his three-piece suit on.

"Mark... Oh yeah. I got your email the other day, by mistake."

"*Yeah*... Well, I'll be working with you this morning and getting you up to speed on the finance side of the house."

"Sounds fun. Kind of like seeing how the hamburger

is made, right?"

"It's a little less bloody than that Mike. But, yeah basically. Let's walk and talk. You can walk and chew bubble gum, right?"

"Sounds good to me."

"Mike, if you were to guess, how many insurance policies do you think go unclaimed each year? What do you think? If you were to estimate it?"

"I have no clue. How many?"

"Guess. I've seen your pedigree. You've got enough industry experience to make an educated guess."

"Mark, honestly, I have no idea."

"More or less than 10%? Over or under? What's your bet?"

"It's got to be under 10%. I don't know maybe 1% of claims. Who doesn't collect on their life insurance? Why would you pay all those years and not collect?"

"Believe it or not, the answer 5%. Across the entire life insurance industry, on average it's about 5% of death benefits go unclaimed. That's how many people never collect a death benefit."

"No… 5%? Really? 1 out of 20?"

I was shocked. I mean, that seemed absurd to me that so many people would pay for a policy and never collect the thing they paid for.

"Let's walk and talk. Here's the thing about Finance. It's not an exact science how we price insurance policies. When done correctly, think about it more like an artform."

"Got it. Art not science."

"Yes, well. We have to ride the line between the two. Ultimately, what we want to do is blur the lines a bit."

"Blur the lines? How so?"

"Good question Mike. Let's say 5% of policies go uncollected on average. What we want to do is simply push that line a little bit further out than the average. Push the goal post."

"What'd you mean? I don't follow."

"The thing is Mike. People don't care about their

insurance policies. People care about the type of phone they buy, the car they drive and the house they live in. Insurance is a nuisance as far as most people are concerned."

I nodded for Mark to continue his rant. Mark was right. Insurance is right up there with getting a root canal to most people.

"To get to that magical 5% average some companies are above the 5% and some are below the 5%. Ultimately, the customer will never know the difference. We want to be the kind of company that is above the 5%."

"So... what are you saying exactly? You're saying..."

"I'm saying we want to be above the 5% average, that's all. When we're above 5%, we're able to provide significantly greater returns on economic capital, which means greater returns to our shareholders. We are bottom-line company."

"Okay... So, how do we do that?"

"How?! However we can Mike. However we can."

"Uh-huh."

"That is of course without going to jail or getting the attention of the regulators."

"Of course."

"That's really where the artform comes into play. We want to blur the lines, bend them without breaking them."

"Mm-hmm."

"Let me ask you another one. What percentage of Term Insurance Policies payout?"

I was afraid of where this conversation would lead, so I stalled for a moment to think.

"Ugh. I have no idea. You stumped me, how many?"

The truth was that I wanted to have no idea. It was starting to seem that ignorance was bliss.

"Less than 1% of all Term Life Insurance policies ever pay out. That's across the whole industry. By in large, most people, 99% that is, outlive their term insurance. In fact, almost all people who buy term insurance never die during the term."

"Let me guess, we want to be above 1%, right?"

"Oh. Look at this guy. You're a quick study Mike. I don't care what anybody else says about you, in my book you're alright."

That wasn't the first time someone told me that around here. I guess I had gotten somewhat of a colorful reputation on the salesfloor. Throwing a man's sandwich across an office probably didn't help instill a lot of goodwill in the Flushy community.

"The thing is Mike. The longer we can stretch out paying a claim, the longer we can keep investing that money and in return earning investment income on that money. We want to delay claim payments as long as we can, within the bounds of the law of course. In other words, blur the line."

"Uh-huh."

"Look, you're the shiny new object around here. We need to align on something and we need to align on it fast."

"And that is... what, exactly?"

"Ask for forgiveness and not permission."

"What?"

"Have you heard of the first mover advantage?"

"Err. I read about it the packet. That's about the extent of it."

"It's simply being the first to go-to-market with something. The advantage of doing something first, before everyone else. Well, that is Flushy doing it first. If you see a way to capitalize on something and increase the intrinsic value of the firm, do it."

"What are the bounds of the laws? I mean there has to be strict laws around that, right?"

"Oh, I didn't realize you went to Law School. Where did you get your law degree from?"

"Uh... I-I didn't."

"Oh? Then let the lawyers be lawyers and how bout you do your job?"

"Sorry, what I meant was, aren't there regulations or laws that we have to be mindful of?"

"*Ehhhh.* Sort of. It's kind of a grey area. It's not really that black and white. Let's leave all that legal stuff to the lawyers. What'd you say?"

"Yeah. That makes sense."

"Look your job is to recruit as many insurance agents as humanly possible. And do that as quickly as possible."

"You say jump and I say how high? Right?"

"Good answer. I like your style Mike."

"In a nutshell, here is our roadmap to success. We're going to start purchasing insurance companies. We're going to start by purchasing insurance agencies. Think of it like a reverse merger."

We stopped abruptly in the hallway. Mark was deep in thought, he looked at me and said, "You familiar with Olympic Rowing? The sport of Rowing. Do you know the strategy behind being the fastest boat?"

"I'm more of a Baseball kind of guy to be honest. But, I'd imagine they win by rowing faster than the other boats."

"*Ha!* That's priceless. The team that wins, does so by rowing together as a team and following the direction of the captain. It's important that we all row together, as a team. Can you do that Mike? Can you row together?"

"Yeah. I can do that."

"Mike, I need to make sure we're aligned on this."

"Perfectly. As aligned as aligned gets."

Without notice we started walking again. Mark had this grimace look across his face. This guy was stone cold, I mean all business all the time. He might have been doing calculations in his head for all I knew.

"Another way we earn income is through the Flushy re-investment fund."

"Which is what exactly?"

"Flushy as an employee benefit purchases insurance on each employee. In the untimely event of a premature death of an employee, Flushy receives part of the death benefit and part of the benefit goes to the beneficiary of the employee's choice."

"Is that *legal?*"

I was a bit startled by that proclamation. How could an insurance company buy life insurance on its own employees? Isn't that a massive conflict of interest?

"Legal. Mike, why wouldn't it be legal?"

"Uh... it just seems unusual."

"Mike, believe it or not I had the same exact questions you had when I started. Don't worry about it. It's important that we're all on the same page. Know what I mean?"

"Got it. Yeah, I'm still getting used to all of this."

"It is what it is. Trust me when I say that it's better to get these kinds of questions out of your mind sooner rather than later. We get a lot of young up and comer type executives. I swear, it's like some of these guys just love to ice skate up hill. You know what I mean?"

"Yeah... For sure."

In reality, I had no idea what he was talking about. I was mostly nodding my head like a trained seal begging for fish at the aquarium. From everything I've seen around here, barking like a trained seal might be a core competency.

"Mike, do you mind if I ask you something. You're kind of in over your head, aren't you?"

"Was I that transparent? Mark, where my shortcomings end, my ambition tends to pick up the slack."

"That's rather auspicious when it comes to being successful. At least, successful here at Flushy."

"What is auspicious?"

"You being that resourceful is auspicious. People come and go quick around these parts. Don't be another statistic Mike."

"I'll try not to."

We shared a laugh for a moment.

"I have been meaning to ask you Mike. What'd you think of that email you stumbled onto earlier in the week?"

Mark was starting to ask some probing questions. I

made sure to be tactful about my answers, I didn't get an easy feeling about him. Sure he was very lax, but why was he so lax?

"Which one do you mean?"

"Which *one*? Which one do you think I'm talking about? The one you were not supposed to see. The one that was meant for me."

"I didn't think much of it. I'm just a sales guy."

Mark started shaking his head and said, "Yeah... we do a lot of that around here. We speed people up the org and randomly replace positions within nincompoops. The number one qualification around here seems to be whether or not your somebody's niece or nephew."

Mark trailed off and his tone became rather somber. Mark took a deep breath and followed by a slow sigh. There was something bothering him, but I had no idea what it was. Normally people are very candid with me. I guess they figure that if left my guard down so should they.

"Mike... I think we're good for now. Why don't we do

a working lunch somewhere off campus?"

"*Perfect!* How's like 1 pm? Mark, why don't you come by my office and we'll go get something to eat. It's my treat today."

"That'll be great. I'll see you then."

I felt like he was holding something back, or maybe he didn't trust me. I was probably just reading too much into the whole situation. We both parted ways and I went back to my office. As I was walking back to my office I received a text message.

It read, "Mike, I'm Naomi Watson. I'm the Chief Claims Officer for Flushy. I'll meet you on the 10th floor in about 15 minutes. Meet me outside in the lobby."

So, I quickly ran up to my office and dropped off my briefcase. I shot on back down to the 10th floor, which was the infamous claims department. I stood around waiting for about thirty minutes for Naomi. I figured she forgot about me, so I shot her a reply-back text. The doors to the claims department quickly opened up and out walked Naomi Watson.

She smiled and greeted me. She stuck out her hand and latched on to mine. We exchanged the normal pleasantries and she led me back to her office. We passed rows and rows of empty cubicles on the way to her office. Nothing out of the ordinary, it was still kind of early in the morning.

"This way Mike."

She motioned me over to her office. Her office was a complete disaster zone, it was like a bomb went off or a tornado ripped through her office. I mean, to put it simply, it was a dumpster fire. To be honest, part of me loved it. It reminded me of home, it reminded me of my old brokerage. Simpler times.

"How's everything going so far?"

"It's, uh. It's going great so far."

"Great. Welcome to the revolution! The first thing we need to talk about is teamwork. Teamwork is very important around here. In fact, teamwork is the glue that binds us all together. You do want to be part of the team, right Mike?"

"For sure. Of course I do. Mark and I went over that

in some detail."

"Oh yes, Mark. I'm sure he did a splendid job at explaining the importance of teamwork."

Naomi approached the oversized liquor cabinet situated in between her desk and the door. She pulled out two crystal glasses and what appeared to be a bottle of bourbon. She held both glasses in her left hand and giggled them my way.

"Oh, no thank you. It's too early for me."

She sighed.

"Mm-hmm. Well, your loss."

She began to pour herself a shot of bourbon. Well, I suppose it's 5 o'clock somewhere. Naomi slowly poured the bourbon into her glass. As she began to pour I noticed her shirt sleeve start to reveal an elaborate tattoo on her arm.

"It's a peacock."

"Uh, what?"

Apparently, she noticed my prowess for observation.

"The tattoo on my arm. In case you were wondering. I saw you gawking."

Gawking might have been an overstatement. It was more of an observation. We both laughed a bit as she finished pouring her refreshment. Naomi waddled back to her desk. She was one of the only people around here not to be in a hurry to be someplace. A loud thud rang out as she put her glass down on the desk. Naomi left quite the impression on me, she looked more like a runway model rather than an insurance executive.

"Mike, how much do you know about claims?"

"Not much. I'm just the sales guy."

"Oh, right. Well, in the claims department our job is to resolve claims. Sounds simple enough, right?"

"Resolve?"

"You don't miss a thing, do you? One out of Twenty life insurance death benefit claims go unresolved each year. It accounts for about 5% on average. Over time, over the history of the industry, that 5% has added up to billions upon billions of dollars to insurance companies."

"Billions?"

"Yes, we're talking about billions of dollars Mike."

"I mean, that's all legal, right?"

"Mike. Don't be silly. It's not like we purposefully withhold the money. Well, not permanently at least. Our job is to resolve claims and sometimes that means paying them and sometimes that means denying them and sometimes that means paying them on a later date."

"Later date? That sounds complicated. Err. Why don't you tell me more about our claim's philosophy?"

"Our claim's philosophy, oh, that's precious. I'd say that our claim's philosophy is to automatically deny claims as they come in. We do this in order to make sure the claim is legitimate and not fraudulent. I like to think of it like the justice system. The burden of proof that we need to pay a claim is on the plaintiff, not the defendant."

"Are you serious?"

"Serious as a heart attack. You don't think we should be paying fraudulent claims out, do you?"

"Err. No of course not. I just…"

I was left somewhat speechless. The further I worked my way up the food chain, the more people tended to throw ethics right out the window. I mean, it's like the day they taught ethics in business school everyone skipped class.

"The longer we can stretch out the Days to Resolve a claim, the greater investment returns we can earn for the company. The more investment returns for the company means a higher valuation and the higher the valuation the higher your bonus will be at the end of the year. Make sense?"

"Yeah, so, to clarify. We're only denying, in order to make sure the claim is a real claim. I mean, it's not like we're arbitrarily outright denying claims for no reason, right?"

Naomi took a sip of her bourbon, which left a florescent purple lipstick stain on the brim of the glass. She swirled the glass around in her hand and rubbed her tongue on the tip of the glass. I wasn't quite sure what to think of it.

"No Mike, it's certainly not an arbitrary process. There is a method to the madness."

I looked to my left and looked to my right. The was one of the best non-answers of all time. I felt the need to ask, "What's not arbitrary?"

"Why we deny claims. It's not arbitrary. It's to help push up the valuation of the firm. There is a reason. We don't just run around doing things here. C'mon give us a little bit of credit."

"Let me get this straight. Are you saying that we deny claims to inflate the value of the company?"

"Sure. All companies do it. All companies deny claims. C'mon Mike, don't be naïve. Do you still believe in Santa Clause and Unicorns?"

"Uh-huh. How does that work?"

"Ultimately, what it comes down to is how the policy is written. We use a broader definition of the language around the Contestability Clause."

"The suicide clause is kind of black and white, isn't it?"

"Eh... Its more flexible than you would think."

"How so? Its standard language isn't it?"

"Let me clear up some of the confusion for you. Your traditional insurance contract has a two-year contestability clause."

"Yeah, I'm familiar with the concept. You can deny a claim within the first two years, no matter the reason, even suicide."

"Precisely, but after two years we cannot contest or deny claims. So, what we did was expand the view finder a little bit. We blurred the line."

"Blurred the line?"

"Well, for instance, we added some ways of dying that are excluded from the policy, even during the contestability period. Like, dying while skydiving, scuba diving, being in a war, flying on an airplane, being inside a building, etc. Things like that."

"Is that legal?"

"Mike, if it were illegal do you think we would be doing it? Give us some credit. I mean, we've been able to do quite well before you showed up. We only built up this multi-billion-dollar enterprise."

"Fair enough."

"We want to prevent any kind of motivation to use the insurance policy, so we removed things like death due to homicide, death due to illegal activities, death due to drug use, death due to alcohol use, etc."

"Ah. That makes sense to me."

In reality, I had my reservations about all this. I mean, who wouldn't?

"It's all part of the process. Every insurance company does it. Trust the process Mike. Are we aligned on this?"

I put my head down and nodded. Naomi looked at me somewhat concerned. She could tell that I wasn't fully sold on the process.

"We need you to really lean into the process Mike.

Can you do that? Can you be a team player?"

"No problem. I got it."

Did I just sell my soul to the toilet bowl? What did I get myself into?

"Look, I was in your shoes once. I was new, young, a little too eager, maybe a little brash at times and outspoken. I asked far too many questions above my pay grade. Don't try to eat the whole elephant in one bite, eat it one bite at a time."

I shook my head in agreement. She was right, I was getting a little to excitable.

"In a nutshell, that is the claims department. What else do you have lined up today?"

"Well, I have a lunch scheduled with Mark and then I have to cover corporate strategy with David Berrigan later in the day sometime."

"Classic Mark. Always taking lunch breaks. So, that's it. That's claims. I did my part. As far as I'm concerned you are up to speed. Now get out."

We both stood up to presumably shake hands. When

I went in, she went in further and hugged me. It was one of those unexpected awkward business hugs. Why people felt the liberty to hug in a work environment was beyond me. I think she picked up on my uncomfortableness, because she let go abruptly. She smiled and I turned for the door. As I was walking away she yelled, "One last piece of advice Mike... Don't be a claim."

I shook my head and gave her a thumbs up as I walked away. That's a little dark. Don't be a claim? What kind of advice was that? I finally had some time to breath and more importantly think. I went back to my office, I decided to take the stairs for a change. It took me about 30-minutes or so to climb those stairs, but it was just the mental disconnect I was craving. All the agitation, all the corporate non-sense, all the angst was immediately wiped away from my mind. Every now and then a nice walk was just the mental reset I needed.

I walked over to my office, more of a lazy stroll than a walk. Gilroy was out to lunch, so the entire floor was empty. I opened my office door and there was a 7-tier fruit basket on my desk. This thing must've cost hundreds of dollars. There was a gold encrusted card on the top of the basket. It read, "Welcome to the revolution! Glad to have you on board."

Even more impressively, it was signed by each member of the senior leadership team. I plopped myself down in my executive leather chair and stared up at the ceiling. It felt good to stretch out my neck and forget about the day. I slowly looked over at the door and Mark was standing there staring at his phone.

"Lunch time kid. Let's go."

"Sounds good. Where we going?"

"Does it matter? Let's roll."

"Not really. Let's get out of here."

Mark and I silently walked for like twenty minutes or so off campus to find a spot to eat. It was rather awkward, at certain points during our journey he mouthed some words without being able to complete full sentences. We finally made it to a hole-in-the-wall restaurant.

We stopped and Mark said, "Here it is! The Spot. I hope you like street tacos Mike."

"Mark it's Southern California. Of course, I do."

We grabbed a seat at a bench near the restaurant. For the next twenty minutes of my life, I was in heaven. We sat there and ate street tacos on the side of the road. It was pure bliss.

Mark took a mouthful of *Carne Asada Taco* and said, "How do you like it so far?"

"These tacos are incredible. Love 'em."

"No! Being part of the SLT. You're elevator really doesn't go to the top floor, does it?. How do you like working here so far?"

Mark had a mouthful of street taco as he began berating me. Mark wiped his lips and started laughing. Mark found imposing his intellect on people to be a leisure activity.

"It's *so* Flushy to pick someone to be that dense as part of the SLT. You'll fit right in kid."

"It happens a lot *I take it*?"

I wasn't offended, I mean, not really. Clearly something had been bothering Mark and I wanted to figure it out. I was more curious than anything.

"Mike, I've got a Master's Degree in Accounting and Finance, an MBA from a *Top* Business School and over 25 years' experience. Let me guess. With you, someone walked around the salesfloor and just looked for the one person not sleeping or picking their nose, am I right?"

"I mean, well, yeah that is exactly what happened. How-did-you-know?"

I beamed a big old smile while jamming the entire half of a taco into my mouth. We both laughed it out for a few seconds. Mark appreciated my terrible sense of humor.

"Sorry to be so pedantic with you Mike. It's... It's just..."

Mark trailed off and went back to eating his taco. Given his attitude I didn't make much of it. Mark was oblivious to the Salsa Verde spilling on his pants. I figured it best to just let him monologue and enjoy his meal.

"Mike, what do you think of all the things I've been telling you? What do you think of everything?"

"The insults?"

"No. What you've been learning about the company. The confidential information. The culture. The way we do things. Only if there was enough time..."

Mark was starting to trail off, so I took that as a que to lead the dance and step back into the conversation.

"It's all a bit new to me. It's all a bit foreign to me conceptually. I'm a fast study though... Wait, what do you mean by more time?"

"Does anything seem out of place to you? You've been in the industry long enough now. What's your take on everything that we're doing here?"

I'm not sure if he ignored my question, or didn't hear me. So, I decided to not press him on it.

"I'm just a sales guy. I don't know if I know enough yet to have an opinion."

"Just a sales guy? I don't think so. I think you can actually do some good here. Some good, yeah. I thought that's what I signed up for. See Mike, the grass isn't always greener on the other side. Sometimes things aren't what they seem."

"Did we come to eat tacos or philosophize?"

We both took a moment to finish up our tacos. Nothing like an ice-cold cola and some street tacos. This reminded me of the good old days growing up in SoCal without a care in the world. I wanted to get to the bottom of this, we've spent enough time shooting the breeze.

"Mark, I did have a question."

"Shoot."

"When do I get to meet Todd?"

Mark scratched the back of his neck and started staring up at the sun. It was starting to bake; the pavement was cooking in the Downtown LA sunlight. He sat there kind of rubbing his hands back and forth thinking of something to say.

"What were we talking about? Oh, Todd. That's right. Umm. Todd is on an extended leave of absence. He's with his family in the Caribbean on vacation."

Todd began to erratically scope out his surroundings.

"Vacation? Sounds nice. Yeah, that makes sense."

Mark started fidgeting with things in his pocket and pulled out a toothpick. He vigorously began cleaning his teeth. He was fixated on distracting himself.

"Mark, am I missing something here? To be honest, this all kind of seems too good to be true."

I figured it was time to stop dancing around my lamenting concerns. I was never much for brow beating or dancing around topics. I figured that if I wanted to make mistakes, I could sprint into them or slowly and painfully experience them. Mark looked at me and just as he was about to speak a panel van pulled up in front of us. We both simultaneously looked up, it was a large black van with tinted windows. It was clearly expensive and looked foreign. We both looked at each other for a second, Mark was slightly less confused than myself. He stood up and the passenger side door opened up.

"It looks like our ride is here?"

Mark rose from his seat like someone getting up from a long plane ride. A large private security guy exited the van and opened the sliding door for Mark.

As I got up the security guy gave me a stiff arm and said, "I'm only cleared to let Mark on."

Mark looked confused and then looked back at me, like a dog going to the veterinarian. I'll never forget that look.

"Uh... Mike... I..."

Just as he was about to say something the security guy shut the van door. The van sped off and left me with a dizzying stream of curiosity. So, I started walking back to the office. I started finding my way back to the office and decided to stop and take in the view. Life was short, why not enjoy it a little bit. I wasn't even really sure what my job was yet, or at least what I had to do. I guess all I had to be concerned with was surviving the corporate gluten. What in the world could be so important to whisk someone off like that?

This day was getting stranger and stranger by the minute. About fifteen minutes or so into my trek back to Flushy HQ, I got a series of text messages. I didn't bother to read them. I was really just trying to clear my head and enjoy the views. A lot of people give downtown Los Angeles a bad rap, but it's actually quite nice in the spring time. As I strolled down the main drag, I think it was Flower street, I could see the office in the distance. People were rushing into the building, swarming like a bunch of worker bees returning to the hive. What's that about? I guess I was about to find out.

As I entered the building, the lobby was dead quiet and empty. I mean, the kind of empty you'd see in an aisle after a blue light special. I found my way to my private elevator and headed back up to my office. As I headed up, the elevator stopped on the 4th floor and a suit stepped into the elevator.

"Great, I get my own private security detail. What happened now? Did I get promoted again?"

"Mike, I've been advised to tell you that your

presence is required up on the 40th floor. Your attendance is required for an emergency SLT meeting."

"Do I have a choice?"

The suit turned to me and slowly shook his head at me. Obviously, this was important. I wasn't sure how people expected me to get any work done with all these pointless meetings. I took it that was just how corporate America was, a lot of busy work.

"Lead the way... Can I ask what this is about?"

The suit turned to me and slowly shook his head at me in disapproval. We arrived at the 20th floor and a couple more people hopped on the elevator with us. Some familiar faces from before. We were crammed together like a can of sardines, otherwise I would've started striking up some good awkward elevator conversation.

We finally arrived at the 40th floor. The group was scurried off to the conference room. The conference room was rather lite today. Which made me question just how important this impromptu meeting was. The suit started handing out phone book sized NDAs and pointed out each signature line. Just as he started handing them out to the attendees, David Berrigan entered the room. He entered the room like a conquering King back from a protracted war, magnanimous as always.

"Thanks for meeting on such short notice. Please sit down."

The room went silent for a moment as David approached his chair. Whether he was going to sit or not was another question altogether.

"Well, there is no easy way to say this. We are meeting today, because of some somber news. It's with mixed emotions, I'm sorry to say that on his way back to the office, Mark was involved in a fatal car accident."

"What?!?", I accidentally blurted out.

I was just eating tacos with him 30 minutes ago. What in the world happened?

"Mike, don't you read your text messages?"

There was no good answer to that question, so I just decided to keep my mouth shut. The suit came around and started collecting our signed NDAs. He was shoveling them into a briefcase.

"Like I said, before Mike interrupted me, Mark was involved in a fatal car accident on his way back to the office. He will be missed."

Naomi chimed in and said, "I think in times of great uncertainty. We should all try to mellow out and be positive. We should relax, mediate and do some yoga. This is a time for reflection and introspection."

Yoga? What kind of non-sense is that? A man just died. His body wasn't even cold yet, and people are talking about yoga.

"Now, now, no point in us crying over spilt milk. We have a business to run. We have a revolution to lead. Like any revolution there are necessary sacrifices that must be made."

I surveyed the room, I was glancing around to try and read facial cues, everyone was just nodding in agreement. This was the entirety of the senior leadership team and people were barely phased by the news. I mean, his body isn't even cold yet and were acting like everything is just business as usual.

"During this transition period, until we find a replacement for Mark. We need to take drastic steps in order to thrive together. We need to lock arms and lean in."

The group of executives nodded in agreement. David snapped his fingers over at his secretary and she brought him glass of water. David clasped onto the glass and held it close to his lips without drinking.

"Let's get down to nuts and bolts. We have a unique window of opportunity. In fact, I'm stepping up to lead through the fog. In fact, we all need to step up in our own ways. That being said, I'll be enveloping Mark's role and responsibilities into my day to day."

David began drinking the water and some of the executives started gauging the room and looking around at each other. Not a single member of the senior leadership team raised on objection.

David finished drinking and said, "Just to make sure

everything goes smoothly for our next rounding of funding. Are we aligned on this?"

Everyone in the room nodded and murmured support for his initiative. David wasn't pleased and repeated his request, "Are we aligned on this people?"

"Yes," a member of the SLT said.

"Yes," a member of the SLT said.

One by one each person in the room verbally acquiesced. David smirked and continued his dialogue.

"Okay, now we have that all settled. Let's talk strategy. Let's talk big picture."

David snapped his fingers again, like someone snootily ordering a waiter an upscale restaurant. His secretary jolted into action and brought over another glass of lime infused water.

"We've got a gamechanger of a strategy coming down the pipeline. We need to execute a best-in-class action plan. This strategy has a lot of moving parts, which is why we need alignment on all the deliverables."

David began to drink his water, which I saw as an opportune time to invite myself back into the conversation. I sheepishly raised my hand to get David's attention. He looked at me with this bizarre expression.

"Mike, you don't have to raise your hand. This isn't kindergarten. What's on your mind?"

"How do we do all that?"

"Ah. You're a big picture guy, eh? Well, I'm glad you asked new guy. You can do one of four things to get ahead in this industry. You can be smarter, you can be first, you can cheat or you can out hustle. Since, I don't feel like cheating, let's figure something out."

The senior leadership team started to look around the room, one by one, each nodding at one another in agreement. It was pretty clear to me that not one of them had the feintest clue as to what David was talking about. His speeches were more like authoritarian dictator style diatribes. Somehow they always ended up being a malaise of business jargon and or meaningless platitudes.

Growing up, as a kid, you always think that adults have their stuff together. In reality, when you grow up, you realize just how wrong you were about that. When looking from the outside in, at a corporation, I always thought the same thing about CEO's. I always thought they had their stuff together, now I realize just how wrong I was about that. I mean, it turns out they're just as clueless as the rest of us.

We sat there for a couple minutes and David Berrigan turned on one of the projectors. We went through a corporate legally approved Presentation. The presentation took about an hour or so, in reality it felt more like days. The Presentation led us through the roadmap to the IPO. We had super aggressive growth goals for the year. I wasn't quite sure how we planned on achieving them. David Berrigan talked about the evolution of the industry, where we fit into the puzzle and then, he finally arrived at the newest part of the strategy.

"And that is why, today I am unveiling the newest Flushy strategic initiative. For too long we have been trying to move too many footballs one yard at a time. Today, we are focused on moving one football one hundred yards, not 100 footballs one yard each. Our plan, is to aggressively start recruiting independent insurance agencies. This is a key part of our omni-channel strategy. Time to go deep and go home."

"Independent Insurance Agents? Now you're talking my language. So, how do we plan on doing that?"

David Berrigan looked right at me and said, "I'm glad you asked. That my friend is precisely where you fit into the picture."

David took a second to lazily take a sip of his vitamin and lime infused water. My eagerness prompted me to propel the conversation forward.

"What exactly is our recruitment strategy?"

I sat on pins and needles waiting to hear some magical explanation.

"You, Mike Allen, you are the recruitment strategy."

"I'm the recruitment strategy?"

"Correct. We can touch base offline about the details."

Of course I am... I shook my head in agreement. My leg was starting to fall asleep, so I shifted in my chair. It must've seemed like uncomfortable fidgeting to everyone in the room. David snapped his fingers again and his secretary leaped into action refilling his glass.

"You see Mike. We didn't pluck you off the street merely for charitable purposes. We saw raw-untapped potential. You know how to speak to these people. Insurance Agents have a certain way about them. They have a certain language and way of dealing with people. Frankly, some just have brain damage from working with bad insurance companies."

Brain damage? What a preposterous thing to say about an entire profession. Obviously, this was hyperbole and not meant to be taken literally, but still. Who does that?

"David, that sounds good on paper. Getting them onboarded is one thing. How do you plan on retaining them? I'd imagine we have a well thought out retention strategy, right?"

"We do. You, you are the retention strategy Mike."

"Mm-hmm. I see."

"Mike we can align on the deliverables offline. We need to make sure that we are all singing from the same hymn sheet."

In reality, I hadn't the furthest clue what that was supposed to mean. How am I the retention strategy? This is a multi-billion-dollar insurance company. How am I the retention strategy? What does that even mean?

"Well people, it's like I always say, tough times never last, but tough people do. Let's go change the world. I'll email out your perspective initiatives and deliverables throughout the day."

I wasn't very sure what the strategy was, or what our plan was. I was pretty sure he stole that quote from some airport hotel motivational speech. David called an end to the meeting. We quickly adjourned the meeting and the room cleared out. I sat back in my chair for a few minutes to think. The automatic room lights had turned off, so I was sitting there alone in the dark. The conference room was dead quiet, I mean I could hear a pin drop it was that quiet. It was the perfect environment to space out and take it all in.

The next morning I decided to step out of my comfort zone, I decided to take a different route to work. I thought it would help spark some creative juices. Sometimes the best way to jump start my brain was injecting some randomness into my routine. The altered route only added 15 minutes or so to my drive. To my surprise, I found a new hole-in-the-wall coffee shop.

I giddily pulled into the parking lot and grabbed a spot in the back of the coffee shop. I made sure to find a spot over in the rear corner of the parking lot. I always tended to park away from other cars. The way I figured it, it reduced the chance of an accident and I got to get some extra steps in. I found the perfect parking spot. It had an empty spot on each side and was screaming my name. I backed my car into the spot, you know, in case I had to make a quick escape.

As I shut off my engine, another car raced into the

empty parking spot to my left. It was an early 2000's Royal Blue Crown Victoria. I wouldn't have paid much attention to it, but the windows were completely blacked out, like the tint on a limousine. As I got out of my car I started thinking about all the new possibilities for my caffeine fix. Latte or Cappuccino? Maybe I'll get a Macchiato. A new coffee spot presented all sorts of interesting opportunities for me.

As I got closer and closer to the door, someone yelled from behind me, "Hold up. Grab the door for me."

I turned around and it was the guy who parked next to me. He was wearing these large aviator style sunglasses and a classic three button two-piece black suit. This guy had a 5-o'clock shadow, slicked back hair, and was probably around 240-250 pounds. Why would someone so well put together be driving a car like that? I guess some people just cared more about their personal appearance than their ride. I grabbed the door for him and he followed me into the coffee shop. Sometimes the small overtures in life have the biggest payoffs.

"Thanks man. I really appreciate it."

"No problem. After you.", I said politely.

When I got inside, I was struck by how long the line was. It was about 15 or 20 people deep waiting to order coffee. In that instant I had to make a judgment call. If I wait this out, there is a high probability I will be late for work. If I left, I wouldn't get my coffee. I figured it was best to see it through and take the risk. What did I really have to lose? I mean, besides my job.

As I was standing in line I started looking around and took in the atmosphere of the coffee shop. At first glance, it was like any standard coffee shop. Plenty of hipsters and the fresh aroma of finely ground coffee beans.

As I began to peruse the menu, I was interrupted by Mr. Royal Blue Crown Victoria, "I hope it's worth the wait."

I turned around and it was the driver of the Crown Vic. I beamed the obligatory smile his way and awkward head nod.

"Me too. I don't remember the last time I waited in a line like this, at least not for a cup of coffee. What're you thinking about getting?"

"Coffee, black coffee."

"Uh-huh. Hmm..."

"Hmm, what's hmm?", he asked with a certain fervor.

"Black coffee, it's a very safe pick. It says a lot about you as a person."

"Does it, really?"

"Sure does."

"How do you figure?"

Granted, I'd strayed away from the normal stranger small-talk, but I had time to kill.

"Well, you wear a very traditional suit. You carry yourself with your shoulders back, which means you probably take care of yourself. You drive a low-key car. Your tastes are simple, to the point. Nothing flashy, nothing that will make a lot of heads turn. It tells me a lot about you."

"Uh-huh. It does, does it? For instance?"

"For instance, if I were to guess... I'd say you're former military? I can see my reflection in your shoes. You wear your wristwatch facing inward not outward. What I don't know is what you do for a living."

"Wow. You can tell all that from my coffee order. Impressive."

I stuck out my hand and introduced myself. Yeah, I was impressed with myself. Who wouldn't be? Deductive reasoning had become one of my strong suits and made for a good conversation starter.

"Mike Allen, nice to meet you. It was nothing but an educated guess."

"I'm John Daily. Nice to meet you Mike."

We both finally got up to the barista and we placed our orders. As we walked over to the waiting area, I asked, "So, what do you do for a living John?"

"Oh... Me... I'm in the insurance business."

Typically, when people phrased it that way and

dressed the way he did, I figured they worked for some large life insurance multi-level marketing scheme. John struck me as more of a compliance kind of guy, rather than a salesman.

"You do? Me to. Small world."

My order was ready, so I picked up my Cappuccino from the countertop and dropped a tip in the jar.

"Great meeting you John! Have a great day."

As I began to make my way back to my car, I was juggling car keys in my right hand and my cappuccino in my left hand.

He yelled out, "You to. Oh, by the way Mike. How do you like working for Flushy?"

I waved instinctively and stopped for a second in the middle of the coffee shop. Shrills ran down my spine. I just met this guy. How does he know where I work? I slowly and cautiously turned back around towards John. I looked him right in his eyes, he lowered his glasses.

As I approached him, I asked, "How did you know I

worked at Flushy?"

"I'm in the insurance business Mike."

I looked with more discontent. Did that mean I was supposed to recognize this guy? Was this one of the suits following me from Flushy?

"Why don't we grab a seat and chat for a bit? It'll only take a minute of your time."

I was hesitant, but reluctantly agreed. He motioned me over to an empty table and we sat down. He took a giant gulp of his coffee and we sat there silently for a couple minutes.

"Did you know the traditional way of thinking is that the first person who speaks during a negotiation loses?"

"Is that what we're doing? We're negotiating?"

"No, not at all Mike. We're just talking."

"Look John, I don't have all day. So... what's your angle?"

John smiled and looked back at me.

"Mike, have you met Todd?"

"Todd? That's what's this is about? Todd Dupree.

"The question still stands. Have you met him yet?"

"No. I haven't. He's on vacation."

"Mm. I hear that the Caribbean is pretty nice this time of year."

"Europe. He's in Europe with his family. What's your point?"

"Is he? Oh, my mistake."

John smiled again, but this time it was more of a smirk.

"You've been working for Flushy for a few months now. More or less?"

"*And,* what of it?"

"It's quite incredible to see someone rise through ranks, really in such a meteoric fashion. I mean a couple of weeks ago you were a sales puke and now you're part of the Senior Leadership Team. Especially for someone who hasn't even met one of the cofounders of the very business he works for."

This is wasn't quite the conversation I was expecting. Serves me right for changing my routine. This is what I get for trying new things. I really couldn't read this guy and for some reason that bothered the heck out of me.

"Mike, how do you think something like happens? The whole thing seems rather fascinating to me looking from the outside in."

"It's just hard work. That's *all*."

John smiled from ear to ear and shook his head.

"Yeah, hard work. That's it. And you believe that?"

"Look, I don't have time to sit here and listen to some kind of lame attempt at a motivational speech or lame sales pitch. Can we get to the point already?"

"Your concern albeit intoxicating, if aimed at me is completely misplaced. What you should be concerned about is working at Flushy."

"What? What kind of nonsense is that? How so?

What are you trying to recruit me or something? Man, if this is some half-baked job interview, I can stop you right here and now."

People in the coffee shop were starting to stare at me, so I toned down the rhetoric. These days one bad camera phone video can ruin your career in the matter of seconds.

"I sell Insurance Mike. That's it."

I stood up and kicked out my chair. I wasn't going to waste my time anymore listening to this guy.

As I began to walk away John asked, "How many people have to die before you open your eyes. How many before you're next?"

I looked back at John, paused for a moment, picked my chair back up and sat back down.

"Oh, I have your attention now? You sales executives are all the same. What I mean is, Flushy has a great way of thinning the herd."

"What'd you mean by that?"

"Don't tell me you haven't noticed anything weird

going on. Don't sit there and tell me it hasn't concerned you seeing all these young healthy people dying in mysterious circumstances."

"Does the insurance you sell come with a free tin-foil hat?"

"Jokes, yeah you got jokes. I'm happy you can joke around."

John slammed a file folder on the table and began to take another big gulp of his coffee.

"See this?", he asked and pointed to the folder.

"Yeah. It's a manila file folder. So what? What is it?"

"What is it? Use your imagination Mike. Use your deductive reasoning skills."

John slid the file folder over to me. I slowly opened the file folder, at first it didn't seem like much. It was a list of Flushy employees who died just after two years, and they all died under mysterious circumstances. Upon further inspection I realized it was full of what appeared to be crime scene photos, coroner reports and various witness statements.

"What-what is this? Why are you showing me this?"

I knew exactly what it was, maybe part of me just couldn't handle what it was. Part of me didn't want to know what it was. I felt an upswell in my stomach.

"You know what it is. Don't you? It's your future Mike. Another name in my file. Another chalk outline of a body on the pavement. Another accidental car crash waiting to happen. Another insurance claim waiting to happen."

"Who are you?"

"Special Agent John Daily. I'm an insurance fraud investigator with the Federal Bureau of Investigation. We have reason to believe that Flushy is involved in some kind of intra-insurance company money laundering fraud scheme. We believe they are systematically killing off their employees for financial gain, among many other financial crimes."

I burst out laughing and even had some of my cappuccino come out of my nose. I started looking around, this had to be some kind of candid camera show.

"The FBI? You had me going there for a second. Insurance Fraud Investigator, I got to remember that one, that's rich! Flushy masterminding some giant cabal of death. Well, it was good talking with you bud. That was entertaining. You really made my day."

John's reaction wasn't exactly what I was expecting. His demeanor hadn't change at all. Nothing, not even a wink and a smile. He was looking at me with this a serious disposition. After the laughter subsided John said, "Are you finished?"

"Look, John, this ain't funny man. I haven't worked at Flushy very long, but don't you think it would be pretty obvious that the company is playing an active role in murdering its own employees? C'mon man!"

"I know how it all must sound. It's all *100%* true. You can choose to help us or not. Either way this house of cards is going to come tumbling down. Kid, you really just got to ask yourself one question."

I took a sip of my cappuccino. I figured I'd play

along a little while longer. What could it hurt?

I asked with a pompous tone, "And what is that? What is that one question I should be asking myself?"

"When that house of cards comes falling down, where do you want to be? On the inside or the outside?"

It was hard for me to believe this guy was an FBI agent, granted he had absolutely no fashion sense and a flair for dramatic language. He took a long sip of his coffee and slammed it down on the table.

"Well, I'm done with my coffee. I'll let you back at it."

John got up from the table and handed me a business card.

"Remember, I sell insurance. Insurance, Mike. When you want to talk, hopefully it won't be too late to get that insurance. Don't let them drag you into deep waters, there will be a point where not even I can save you from drowning."

All I could do is scoff. I was struggling to find the words. At this point, I couldn't even make eye contact with John. Who knew if John was really his name?

"Oh. One more thing. Mike, are you familiar with the concept of a Tontine?"

To say that I was dumbfounded would have been an understatement. I had a pretty robust understanding of the modern insurance vernacular, but was completely unaware of a Tontine. John scoffed at my unmistakable display of ignorance. All I could do was shrug my shoulders and look away.

"That's a real shame."

John shook his head, did a one-eighty and walked away.

"Well, that will teach me to try new things. Never again."

I tucked his business card it into my back pocket. I took a deep breath and a sigh of relief. I sat back in my chair and took some time to think. Did I miss something? Is this guy for real? What was my next move? I finished up my cappuccino, but it's not like I could even enjoy it. Is there really anything worse in this world than a wasted Cappuccino? What time is it? I looked down at my Smart Watch and it read, "8:00 AM". I decided to head back to the office. Better late than never. It's not like being 15 minutes late was going to kill me.

As I approached the building, I decided to park in the normal employee parking lot, with the common folk. After hunting for a parking spot for about ten minutes, I managed to find the perfect one. I parked my car and headed for the lobby. The lobby was in a state of complete disarray. There were people and construction materials scattered all about. I shook it off and creeped towards the private elevator. I took out my key card and right before I could swipe it, the elevator opened up for me. As the elevator doors opened further, I noticed they had installed some new security features. The most notable was the facial recognition system and the wireless microphones hanging from the top of the elevator. I put my face close to the scanner, and it made a loud BING sound. A voice came over the loud speak,

"Welcome Mike Allen." The doors to the elevator closed and it rapidly ascended to my floor. As the doors re-opened, I thought this was kind of peculiar timing to be installing new security features. It was safe to say my day was ruined before it began. Either way, I better play this whole FBI thing pretty close to the vest.

To my surprise, there were a couple of new faces on the office floor. It looks like someone finally decided to fill up those cubicles. I started walking around the office, more of a brisk stroll than a walk. I navigated my way past all of the cubicles and made it to my private office. Gilroy was typing away on the computer, at what I had no idea.

"Hey!"

She looked up and said, "Hey to you as well. What's up boss man?"

"What's with all the new people?"

"Didn't you read the memo? They gave you ten direct reports."

"Who is *they*?"

"I don't know, I only work here. That's above my pay grade."

"Okay... But, what do I do with them?"

"I mean, they're your employees."

At this point, I had a pretty flimsy understanding of my overall job. How in the world was I supposed to manage and lead ten people? Especially, if I couldn't lead myself?

"Gilroy do me a favor and gather the troops for me. Round 'Em Up."

Gilroy stopped typing, calmly stood up, let out a big whistle and then in her best attempt at a baritone said, "Gather round y'all. Team meeting!"

People slowly got up from their cubicles and started gathering around me. In front of me stood my team, *Ten* fresh-out-of-college mouth breathers. The group stood in front of me waiting for me to say something. If there's one thing I knew about being a manager, it was that you want to give rousing and inspirational speeches. Being a manager was all about form, not content. The best managers tended to know the least about a subject, but knew the most about how to talk to people.

"Listen up you people. You work for me now. We have one key priority in this department. We are here to grow a completely new distribution channel for the company."

People starting nodding in agreement. I could tell they were captivated right off the bat. One of the members closest to me took a slight step back. I didn't realize it, but my lunch must've left quite an offensive odor seeping out of my mouth. My atrocious breath aside, I still needed to give a rousing speech. For courteous sake, I took a slight step back from the group.

"Take a second and wrap your heads around that. It won't be easy. I won't have all the answers, but we will do our best. We have to lead through the fog. In times of great uncertainty, winners are either made or destroyed."

Gilroy leaned in and whispered to me, "Good stuff."

"Our strategy is simple. Three words.", I said holding

up three fingers.

I could tell I had them handing on my every word.

"Three simple words… S.M.F. Sell More Flushy! I want you to remember those words, nay I need you to remember those words. Whenever you have to make a decision, ask yourself, does this help me Sell More Flushy or does it get in my way of Selling More Flushy?"

I took a sip of my cappuccino and waited for a second to let that maturate. The group was nodding in unison, so I decided to continue.

"We're going to start aggressively acquiring insurance brokerages. We're going to convince them to sellout. In exchange for their clients, we'll offer them gainful employment with lucrative equity positions here at Flushy."

I could really get used to this whole Senior Vice President thing. I could tell that I had a real knack for it. Say a bunch of fancy words, throw out some half-cocked ideas and yell at people to keep them inline.

"Think of it like a reverse merger. It's all about synergy. Our department is tasked with a two-pronged stratagem. We are going to divide and conquer. The plan is to buy insurance brokerages and switch clients over to Flushy. We'll make sizeable offers, offers that Agent's would be foolish to pass up. We'll then steal market share from our competitors, and then, after stealing enough market share from other carriers we can offer to buy the carriers for pennies on the dollar. In fact, some of these carriers will hemorrhage so much premium that they will be begging to sellout. That's the plan."

I gauged the room to make sure everyone was following me. In reality, I just made all of that up on the top of my head. This company didn't have much of a coherent strategy. It was deemed confidential so nobody ever actually bothered talking about the strategy.

"Any questions? No? Okay, let's get to work and find some insurance agencies to buy! Sell More Flushy!"

Someone in the background raised their hand.

I pointed at him and yelled, "Yeah. You. What is it?"

"Mr. Allen. How do we plan on doing that?"

"The first deliverable is to make a list of insurance agencies. The second deliverable is to right-size that list. The final deliverable is to send out an email blast out to that list with the plan."

Someone else raised their hand.

"Guys, don't raise your hand. This isn't preschool. Just speak up."

"What do we say in the email?"

"What do you mean?"

"What's the content strategy for the email blast?"

"You are the content strategy. Why do you think I have you all around? Go figure it out."

I thought was a good place to end the conversation. So, I clapped my hands together and headed back to my office. In my head, it all sounded like a good plan. The group disbanded from the crescent moon shaped circle and everyone went about their days.

Chapter 16 – If we can't beat 'em then we might as well buy 'em.

"Mike, we need to talk about the acquisition strategy."

"Can you wait about an hour? I'm only on my first cup of coffee."

David stopped typing in the chat. Clearly he wasn't amused by my early morning sense of humor. Maybe it was the lack of humor that displeased him.

I replied back, "Now is fine. Where should we start?"

"Let's square the circle. What's the plan? Talk to me."

"That's really the $64,000 question, isn't it? The plan is to *Sell More Flushy*! The plan is to go deep and to go wide. We want to lift and shift. At the same time we don't want to boil the ocean."

Yeah, that all sounded smart. I mean, smart enough to pass the smell test.

"I like it. Tell me more..."

"See David. It's all about synergies really. Synergies and scalability that leverage our omni-channel approach."

"Yes! I like it. I like it a lot."

"Thanks!"

"So, what barriers are getting in your way?"

"Uh... None that I know of."

"Well, go out and do that. Let me know how it goes. We have high expectations for you."

"Will do Boss."

"Over and out."

Thinking it over, the strategy wasn't all that bad. We wanted to attack the castle from all sides. We wanted to acquire clients from three revenue streams. We wanted to acquire clients through marketing, through acquiring brokerages and acquiring small insurance carriers. The ironic part is, if a carrier turned down our initial offer, after we've stolen enough clients we could then come back with a much worse offer that they would have to accept. I mean, it was all really quite genius.

Monday was already off to a fast start. After wrapping up that quick strategy convo with David I decided to clear out my inbox. To my surprise, I had over one hundred unanswered emails waiting for me. All that by the time I got to the office, not bad. Apparently, the email campaign we sent out was pretty successful.

We had RFPs from all size firms, 100-man firms to 1-man firms. Really, a request for proposal, is just an excuse for business people to mock up presentations. One of my peons had put my work email address as the automated reply, big mistake. What a genius...

"Who in the world thought it was a good idea to put my contact info on this email?", I shouted across the office floor.

A hand slowly raised above the rows of cubicles. I pointed them out and shouted at the top of my lungs.

"*You!* Get over here."

If there's one thing I've learned from being in *Corporate America*, it was to never give your contact information directly to the customer. Otherwise the customer is going to be bothering you every five minutes for this, that and the other thing. The employee walked over to my office, I realized I hadn't even bothered to learn anyone's name yet. The one thing I had learned is that all good members of the Senior Leadership Team have to be able to make examples out of their employees.

"What's your name?"

"Jeff Stulowski..."

"Jeff, did you put my contact info on this email?"

"I did..."

"Can I ask why you did that?"

"Well, I figured that way in case they have questions about the program..."

"You don't figure Jeff. No one is paying you to figure. We're paying you to execute. I do the figuring around here. If you don't like that I suggest you go refresh your resume."

Jeff's face went pale and he froze up. I couldn't blame him; I wasn't being my normal self. Maybe I was projecting my own nervousness onto Jeff. I shifted my tone down and asked, "Do you get what I'm laying down? I don't have the appropriate bandwidth to be dealing with customers."

"I do."

"I don't have time to sit here and comb through emails, not to mention all of the follow up emails. I'm the closer. By the time it gets to me I need it teed up and ready to close."

I was getting used to this whole manager thing. The power was addictive, the ability to make people bend to my will. It was exhilarating, it was like a drug. Upon inspection of the emails, I found that most of them were obvious attempts at trolling. One of the return email addresses read, muhbuth@email.com. Apparently, the email campaign wasn't as successful as I initially assumed.

However, one of the emails did catch my eye, it was

from 'Daily Insurance Group'. No... That can't be right. My phone started ringing; it was the front desk. I was hesitant about picking it up.

The receptionist said, "Sir, a John Daily with Daily Insurance Group is here to see you."

"Don't let him up. I'll, I'll come down to greet him in the lobby.", I said and quickly hung up.

"Gilroy, do me a favor and hold all my calls. I've got a meeting down in the lobby with a potential broker."

I made my way down to the lobby and standing next to the receptionist was John Daily. John was smiling ear to ear and chatting up the receptionist. The most prudent course of action was to speak first. That way I didn't give him a chance to make a scene. If I could only get rid of him and make this all disappear.

"Can I help you sir?"

"That depends. You sent me an email about a potential business opportunity."

I took a deep breath and whispered, "What do you want John?"

"I want to *Sell More Flushy*! As you so eloquently put it in the email."

I grabbed John's arm and whisked him to a remote part of the lobby for more privacy. I subtly scanned the room, to see if there were any microphones present. It looked like the coast was clear and we could speak in a modicum of privacy.

I whispered to John, "Is this your idea of discrete? Do you know how much trouble I can get into if they found out I was talking to you?"

"Mike, you're wearing a $10,000 wristwatch. You didn't strike me as a person who liked to keep a low profile."

The conversation went silent for a second. As an act of insecurity, I plunged my hand in my pocket to hide my watch. Two groups of people entered the lobby and started slowly walking over towards us. Not in an intentional way, but slowly navigated over to us. I noticed it, but didn't think it was anything to worry about. Just in case, I moved further over to some dead space in the corner of the lobby. John made sure to pursue me as inconspicuous as possible.

"Why are you here?"

"I'm here to follow up on our last conversation. Did you give it a second thought?"

"This isn't the place... we can't talk here."

"Well, where can we go to talk? How's the 40th floor sound? I hear some interesting stuff goes on up there."

"Not here. Not now."

"If not here, then where? If not now, then when?"

"I'll call you."

John laughed and shot me a smile. He didn't flinch an inch. Large droplets of sweat began to roll down my forehead. I looked around and one of the random people in the lobby was staring at me. I stared back and they pretended to look at their phone for a quick distraction. John scoffed at my attempt to brush him off. He wasn't easily dissuaded by my effort.

"Mike, as always, it was lovely speaking with you. Hopefully it won't be the last time we talk. Or the last time you can talk... That's the thing about a Tontine Mike... People walk around like there is some permanence to it all, let me tell you there sure isn't."

I waved John off and headed back to the elevator. As I turned away, I thought about that term. Tontine, I'd been meaning to look it up. I just didn't have time. I turned back to John for a second and whispered, "Tontine. You mentioned that last time. Why do you keep bringing it up?"

John smiled and said, "Mike you have problems now. Do you want trouble too?"

John stepped forward and closed the gap between us.

He whispered out of the side of his mouth, "It's this simple Mike. A Tontine is basically a group annuity."

"Yeah. What's so special about it?"

"Basically a bunch of people pool money together and invest it. As each member of the Tontine dies, the remaining shares split among the surviving members. In the end, the last person to live collects all the money."

"Pfff... And what? Man, I can't be having you waste my time like this."

"The Roman's used to have an old saying, it's one I think you should learn. It's Qui Bouno?"

"Qui Bouno?"

"It basically means, who benefits? Flushy has changed quite a bit in a short amount of time. People tend to be perfectly healthy one day and perfectly dead the next. But, who benefits?"

"Why don't you cut the bull? What do you want from me?"

"You're asking all the wrong questions Mike. I just sell insurance. Simply that. I sell insurance."

"Look, drop the act. What do you want?"

John handed me a manilla file folder that was about two inches thick.

"Why don't you start by looking over this insurance proposal I put together for you? I spent quite a bit of time working on this for *you*. I hope we can come to terms on this proposal, for your sake."

I snatched the folder out of his hand and shoved it in my arm pit. John smiled, put his aviators on and headed towards the exit. If I never saw that guy again, I could consider that a good life. On my way back up to my office, I was oddly escorted by a new face. A stout, very tan gentlemen accompanied me on the elevator. Apparently, where this guy came from they didn't believe in necks or dieting for that matter.

Before I knew it, he started drumming up small talk. We had several more floors to go, so I decided to chat.

"Whatcha got there?", he said and pointed to my folder.

"Oh. This? It's just market research on some of our competition."

"Ah. Is that why it's covered in sweat?"

"Hahaha! Chalk that up to poor genetics."

Just as the conversation was about to get interesting we arrived at my floor.

"Oh. Look at that, saved by the bell. Well, this is my floor. Got to go. Nice knowing you."

I leaped out of the elevator, like a skydiver jumping out of an airplane for the first time. I had to bury this folder away, or shred it. I scurried back to my office, opened my locked desk drawer and slammed the folder into it.

Gilroy knocked on my door and inquired, "Everything okay boss?"

"Oh yeah. Just *great*. Couldn't be better.", I replied sarcastically.

"I took the liberty of scheduling some meetings for you. I hope you don't mind."

"Mind? No, of course not. Wait, meetings, with who?"

"Meetings with agency owners who responded to the email blast."

Gilroy was staring at that manilla file folder, almost as if she was taking a mental note. I slammed the drawer shut and she snapped back into reality. Maybe she was just spacing out or maybe my paranoia was beginning to magnify the longer I kept this folder.

Gilroy started scribbling something down on a napkin she grabbed off my desk. As she was writing on the napkin, she kind of palmed it in her hand and walked over to my door jam.

"Boss. Whatcha' got there?"

"It's-it's just some competitive intelligence. Hush-hush kind of material."

"Competitive intel?"

"It's a proposal from another insurance carrier. Among some marketing materials."

"Uh-huh. Well, your first meeting should be in about an hour or so. Plenty of time to look over that competitive intel."

Gilroy crumpled up that napkin she was writing on and miserably attempted to toss it in my trash can.

"Oh, darn. I missed. Would you mind Mike?"

I waved her off and went over to pick up the napkin. As I bent down to pick it up, I couldn't help but wonder what she wrote down. I looked to my left and she was gone. The coast was clear, so, I started unraveling the napkin.

Gilroy didn't have some big mystery about her. She left something inconspicuous enough to be disregarded, but meant for my eyes only and easy enough to decipher. The napkin simply read, "Don't forget to look up."

Gilroy was pretty sneaky. Here I thought she might've been taking notes on me, but in reality she was trying to look out for me. I scrunched the napkin back up and tossed it in the trash can. For the next hour or so, I sat at my desk flushing out my options and rubbing my hands together. Before I knew it, my phone started ringing.

Ring... Ring... Ring...

I guess it was time to stat closing some deals. I quickly yelled across the office for help, "Gilroy! Who am I meeting with right now?"

Ring... Ring...

"Robert Farherter from the Farherter Insurance

Agency."

I shot a quick thumbs up her way and answered the line.

"Good afternoon. This is Mike Allen with..."

Just as I finished answering the phone an interminable thundering sound rang across the other line. What I could only surmise was someone placing the inward palms of their hands across their lips and imitating the all-to-familiar sound of flatulence. I held the phone away from my ear, because what followed next was a bellowing of laughter. I took it they were not interested in my proposal. The phone went silent and I gingerly placed it back on my desk.

"Gilroy, would you mind coming in here for a second?"

"Sure thing Boss."

Gilroy trotted into my office.

"Can I ask you something?"

"What's up Boss?"

"How are you screening these people?"

"Well, I'm not."

"Ah. That makes sense."

Gilroy titled her head in confusion.

"What happened with that last appointment?"

"Well, when I picked up the phone, he made a loud farting sound."

"What?!?"

"But wait, there's more. That was followed by a chorus of laughter, from what I can assume were all the people at his brokerage."

"Oh..."

"Yeah. Robert Farherter. I should've guess based on the name."

"I'm sorry."

"Try, if it's not too much trouble, to pre-screen some of these people for me."

"I'm on it, Boss!"

"That's all. Thanks."

Gilroy trudged back to her desk and went back to work. To be honest, I didn't have a good grasp what she worked on all day. I mean, she seemed to stay busy enough. For the next three hours I fielded more legitimate inquires and actually was able to sign up some agencies to join the Flushy team. The marketplace was rife with opportunity for fledging insurance agencies willing to accept offers. By in large, most people who are offered to sellout will sellout. When push comes to shove some people might resist, but by in large if you dangle money in front of someone they'll take it. That's just human nature.

I decided to take a break around 7 o'clock. For some reason that just felt like a good breaktime for me. I opened my desk drawer and delicately pulled out the file folder. The only safe place to look at this thing was in the confines of the restroom. Luckily, Flushy sprang for a private restroom on this floor. I tucked the folder into my arm pit and got up from my desk. I did one of those scouting out the room type stretches. After a quick scan of the room, it looked like the floor had cleared out. So, I headed over to the restroom for some solitude. I hid away in one of the stalls, and carefully examined the folder. The file folder itself seemed rather harmless. As I began to pull back the kimono, I found nothing. The first ten pages of the 'proposal' were completely blank. As I peeled back the onion, there was a note inside.

The note simply read, "Have you met Todd Dupree?".

It's funny. How in the world have I not met with him yet? I put my phone back in my pocket and perused the rest of the file folder. This time I inspected the folder in a more laborious fashion. There was an article in the folder about the galvanizing leadership of Dupree that counterbalanced and contrasted the egomaniacal style of cofounder David Berrigan. The more I read, the more it raised my level of concern.

Where was this going? Article after article, it was all the same. It seems that David wasn't the mastermind of Flushy, he was just along for the ride that Dupree created. The articles seized abruptly in the folder and transitioned to black and white photos. How is it that I haven't heard from this guy?

How is it that nobody talks about him? I was left with more questions than answers.

The last page of the folder had a note attached to it. The note read, "You've got the background, now focus the lens and find the foreground." To be safe, I flushed the note down the toilet and shoved the folder into the tank of toilet so no one would ever find it. It would seem I had some sleuthing to do.

Chapter 17: "Course Correction"

Today, I skipped all of my routine morning pleasantries and got to the office around 6:30 am. It was still dark outside. I wasn't in the mood for traffic, so I figured I'd just avoid it all together. As I was making my way thru the lobby I noticed a few people crowded around one of the many watering holes. We had these mini-coffee shops scattered all around the office, they had a barista and everything.

The group seemed to be chatting about something or other. Not to mention how incredibly early they reported in for work. I needed something to upset my rhythm, so I wandered on over and played the role of innocent bystander. It wouldn't be the first time I annoyingly interjected my way into a conversation.

As I approached the group, they each began to eye ball me and size me up. The group was standing off to the side of the barista, but close enough for me to ask, "Are you guys in line?"

"No... No... Go on ahead", the group said.

I stepped up to the barista and ordered.

"What're you having today?"

"I'll take a Cappuccino please."

"How would you like it?"

"Just the way I like my humor, Hot & Dry."

There is nothing in this world more thirst quenching than a nice and hot cappuccino.

"Is 2% Milk okay?"

"Do you have 3% Milk?"

The barista gave me this confused stare for a second. I could tell she was trying to process my joke as a serious statement.

"Three-three-percent? I don't think we have any of that. Do you mean whole milk?"

"That'll be fine."

The thing about dry humor is that people either get it or they don't.

"What'll be fine? The 2% or the Whole Milk?"

"Oh, the 2% milk will be fine."

In the meantime, I weaseled my way closer to the group. They were dressed too nice to be low level employees. Maybe they were some of these foreign investors I kept hearing about. As I inched closer, I made sure to keep my back to the group, as I didn't want to arouse any suspicion. I was merely interested in some pre-work-day ease dropping.

"The guy basically got down on his hands and knees and started begging me for his job. What was I supposed to do not fire him?", one of the suits blurted out.

The whole group started laughing out loud. That kind of bland corporate laughter that I was getting so very accustomed to. As I turned to see who was speaking, I made eye contact with one of the suits. That was a mistake.

"Can I help you?", one of them asked in an oddly aggressive tone.

"I don't know. Can you?", I said in a curious tone that matched his aggressive tone.

The suit smiled and stuck out his hand. We shook hands and parted with the hostilities.

"Mike Allen. *And you are?*"

The suit stood up a little straighter and said, "Oh. You're Mike Allen? Nice to meet you sir."

"Don't call me Sir, I work for a living."

"I'm Henry with Hubris Consulting Partners."

"Ah. HCP. What kind of consulting do you do, exactly?"

"Well, I handle Talent Procurement. Karin over there handles Executive transition programs. Charles over here handles performance assessment and evaluation. Linda handles offboarding, onboarding and if you pay her enough even waterboarding."

The group started laughing again, so much that coffee slightly spilled out of their cups. That annoying splash that everyone hates, where it pours over just slightly enough to get on to the top of your lid.

"Oh. So, basically you guys are the dream team of

layoffs?"

The group laughed out of loud, again spilling drips of coffee.

"Yeah, I guess you could say that."

"I just did say that. Would you say that?"

The barista interrupted and said, "Mike, your cappuccino is ready."

Before the group could respond, I said, "Well, that's my cue to exit. Good luck with your layoffs. If you need any muscle, give me a call."

I grabbed my cappuccino and Henry said, "Oh, don't worry, we'll be speaking again *very* soon."

I waved them off and headed to the elevator. For some reason I was in a feisty mood this morning. What an absolutely lovely way to start my day. As the elevator began to climb I heard a feint jingle in my pants, someone sent me a flurry of text messages. I looked down at my phone and it read, "Mike. My office in ten minutes. David Berrigan."

The light for my floor went off and the top floor

button had lit up. Before I knew it, the elevator had stopped off at the top floor. The elevator doors opened to some classical jazz music. As I exited from the elevator there was a large metal detector, multiple cameras and two gigantic security guards.

One of them motioned me through the metal detector and said, "This way sir."

The security guard led me through a tunnel, which led to a bridge that was extended over a coy pond, an infinity style pool, a private gym, a spa and a small Italian restaurant. The décor of the office was very modern, sleek, elegant and something I would expect to see in a magazine or better yet, a movie. Clearly David had done some minor renovations since our first interview.

David Berrigan had everything in its exact correct place. No detail was overlooked, and everything was put together with clear intention. I was starting to get a good picture of who he was as a person. Someone who was hyper-observant, detail oriented with a splash of neuroticism. You know the kind of person, a control freak. The kind of person who can't leave anything up to chance. A person who has to control the entire process from start to finish. The kind of person who has to have his fingerprints on everything, which means everything he touches better turn to gold.

This was all something I would've expected from a *Mafia Don*, not an insurance executive. As the doors opened the office brimmed up with light. His corner office was massive, from wall to wall I'd say that there was like 100 feet of space. On the wall adjacent to his desk there was a life-sized portrait of David. In the center of the room there was a large oak desk that was embossed with some kind of fancy stain. David Berrigan had his back turned to me and was looking down at the street from one of his many large tinted windows.

"Come on in Mike. You've kept me waiting long enough."

He turned to me and motioned me over to a side door with his hand.

"Walk with me Mike. Let's walk and talk. I mean, you can chew bubble gum and walk at the same time, right?"

"Sure can. This is quite the set up you have here.", I said as I galloped over to meet him.

There are many ways to get ahead in the business world, kissing butt is probably the fastest and easiest way to do it. David grinned and we kept walking for a bit.

"Mike, I heard you had a little conversation this morning with some of our consultants over from HCP."

"Uh. Yeah, I just did."

"Well?"

"Well, well what?"

I replied back to him a little confused. I mean the conversation really didn't have much teeth to it. I was more confused how he heard about a conversation that happened no more than 5 minutes ago in the lobby.

"Well, what did you think of them?"

"What do you mean?"

David Berrigan stopped dead in his tracks, looked at me and asked, "I imagine you sized them up. I know they sized you up. What did you think of them?"

Before I could answer the question we started walking again.

"Everyone was cordial. They all seemed like nice people."

"Nice. They're a bunch of trained killers wearing thousand-dollar suits. They'd steal money from a church collection jar if they knew they could get away with it."

"Ah."

"Here's the thing Mike. We value transparency at this company. In fact, we value it so much that it is one of our key value principles. It doesn't pay to be sheepish. It doesn't pay to guard your language. If something is on your mind, say it."

"I see."

"The thing about being transparent is that there is a price to transparency. There is a cost to transparency."

"A price? How so?"

We started walking around the Coy Pond and David Berrigan took a second to admire the many colorful fish swimming around in the pond.

"We have tens of thousands of employees here at Flushy. And thanks to your recent efforts that number has increased substantially."

David Berrigan crouched down to feed the fish. Someone walked from out of the corner of my eye, and handed me an NDA to sign. Without thinking I signed it.

"And just like these Coy Fish Mike, sometimes our employees get too fat and happy."

He looked away for a second and the security guard ran over with some food to feed the fish. He was holding a moderately sized burlap bag, presumably food for the fish.

"See the thing is Mike. No matter how much you try to help some people. There is always that one guy who wants to try and rollerblade up hill. Do you get what I'm saying?"

"I think so."

"Like I was saying. There is a cost to being transparent. Coy Fish don't have a great mystery behind them. When they're hungry, they show up to feast. When they're tired, they find a place to sleep. They are very transparent about what they want in life."

"Ah... I see. I mean, I don't really get what we're talking about here. Am I fired? Or..."

David Berrigan laughed and said, "No, of course not. Who said anything about firing anybody? We're just talking."

David began to sprinkle fish food across the pond. The irony of a billionaire taking pleasure in tossing scraps to mindless dependent fish was not lost on me.

"The Coy Fish live in a delicately balanced eco-system. One that I have to maintain. When one fish gets too big, we must lighten the load. When one fish takes too much out of the system, we must make adjustments. We have to bring balance."

"Adjustments, to the Coy Fish."

"Exactly, to the Coy Fish. It works the same way with any other eco-system. You follow?"

"Sure. Yeah."

David Berrigan got back up from feeding the fish and wiped his hands together. He started walking again, to where, I had no idea.

"You've done a really great job convincing these brokers to get on board with Flushy. I know it wasn't easy to do what you did, especially within such a truncated timeframe."

"Thanks David. I appreciate that."

What in the world is he getting at? I mean, where was this conversation going? We walked for a few more minutes without either one of us saying a word. This kind of felt like one of those conversations that wasn't going to be documented or written down anywhere for posterity. I hated those kinds of conversations, because they never ended well.

"Do you know how we maintain such competitive pricing? Do you know what the secret sauce is?"

"I thought it was the tech and the data."

"Well, yes. To a point it's the tech. To a point it's the data. Aside from that do you know how we do it all?"

"No, not really. To be honest, I have no clue."

"We maintain the eco-system Mike. It's by keeping our operating expense ratio at the lowest cost in the industry. We are a bottom-line company."

"So, basically you're saying we do the same thing other people do, but for much less?"

"Precisely. And what do you imagine the biggest part of our operating expense ratio is?"

"I don't know. The building?"

"Our people Mike. Our people make up about 70% of our operating expense ratio."

"Wow. 70%?"

"Wow is right Mike. Wow-is-right... Managing an

expense ratio is a lot like flying an airplane. Sometimes you have to make course corrections in order to get to your destination. This is one of those course corrections. What I need from you, is a favor. It's no small feat."

All I could do is clear my throat with a loud uncomfortable cough. *COUGH...*

"What I need from you and what I am tasking all departments with is a simple mandate. That each department head reduces operating costs by 50% and headcount by at least 22% across all areas of operation."

We stopped for a moment, I figured he was trying to gauge my reaction. Internally I was livid, but on the outside the only thing I could do I shake my head in agreement while trying to mask my disgust. Contempt aside, this just felt so capricious and arbitrary.

"Let me get this straight. So, there is no confusion here."

"Please, go right ahead."

"You want me to reduce my operating costs by 50%. My costs are made up 100% of people under my span of control."

"I realize that."

"I just convinced these brokers to sell their businesses to us and come join Flushy at a substantial short-term pay decrease. I sold them on the vision, the long-term growth opportunity working for Flushy. They are taking variable long-term payouts with no or minimal guarantees."

"I realize that. I know it's a lot of ask of you."

"David these aren't headcount, these are people we're talking about. Real people, with families, pets, mortgages..."

"Yes. I understand that Mike. I realize this is putting you out a bit, it's not an easy position. It's a necessary position if we want to stay competitive in the marketplace."

"Uh-huh..."

"That is why for every one-percentage point

decrease in your division's expense ratio, it will result in a one-time cash bonus of $10,000. You do for me; I do for you."

I spontaneously let out this uncomfortable little laugh.

"So... you're going to pay me up to $5,000,000 to fire half of my brand-new salesforce?"

"Don't look at it so transactionally Mike. These are people remember, not just names on a spreadsheet. There is a stipulation to that offer. There are strict conditions."

"What kind of stipulation?"

David smirked. The old me would've slapped that smirk right off his face. The old me would've done a lot of things differently.

"This all has to be wrapped up before the end of the fiscal year. Policyholder retention needs to be maintained at 95% for six-months following the headcount reduction."

"Oh, why didn't you say so. Not a problem at all.", I

said sarcastically.

"Annnd... I'll need an increase in revenue out of your business unit by at least $200,000 per month."

"...95% ...95% with half the sales force in play? How do you think that is achievable? How motivated do you think my sales team is going to be once we announce massive layoffs?"

"Mike, I said it once and I'll say it a thousand times. People don't care about their insurance policy. People don't care about their agent. People care about the price, plain and simple. To sell a Flushy policy is to sell a price."

"Yeah, but..."

"Mike, I entrust that you will find a way to make this happen."

"What happens if I don't hit the 50% goal?"

David Berrigan said, "Let's just hope it doesn't have to come to that Mike."

I hadn't realized it, but the two security guards had approached us both from behind and were hovering during the entire course of our conversation. We stood there in this awkward crescent moon half circle formation for a few minutes.

"Can I count on you to get the job done? Can I count on you to balance the eco-system?"

I plunged my hands into my pocket as a pathetic act of defiance. I stood there wafting in the ambiance of incredulity. What else could I say? What else could I do? I had one clear choice in front of me.

"You can count on me. I won't let you down David."

"I knew you wouldn't let me down Mike."

David Berrigan did an about face and started walking away.

"Well, I did have just one question David."

"What's that Mike?", he said without turning around. He did do me the curtesy of stopping in his tracks though.

"What am I supposed to tell them?"

"You're a salesman, right?"

"Yeah."

"Sell them, figure it out. Mike, just chalk it all up to being transparent about the process and that we have to do this in order to stay competitive but spice it up a bit. The consulting team from Hubris Consulting Partners will be around later to talk you through the process."

David Berrigan walked away and I was escorted back to the elevator by the two security guards. This might have been the longest elevator ride of my life. Time just slowed on down for a while. Somehow I managed to get back to my desk without having an anxiety attack. Before I had a chance to think my phone started lighting up. I tossed it in one of my desk drawers and decided to ignore everything for a while. Gilroy knocked on my door and popped her head in.

Knock... Knock... Knock...

"Uh... Boss?"

I looked up so she could acknowledge I was at least trying to listen. Given my resent assignment it was hard to not ignore her. It was hard to not block out the whole world around me.

"You have some people here from Hubris Consulting Partners."

"See them in."

One by one the consultants came marching in. Everyone promptly sat down and had eager stamped across their foreheads. They were chomping at the bit to start.

"Did David Berrigan brief you on my situation?"

Henry said, "He did. He also mentioned that you were a right-to-the-point kind of guy. You don't mince words and you don't care for fluff."

"Given the task at hand. Let's subdue the chitchat and get down to business. Did he tell you about the riff?"

"Ah. Yes. You really don't waste any time."

"You have a headcount reduction issue. We are aware.", one of the other consultants chimed in.

Henry took the lead by staring down the other

consultant, making them instantly aware that they just spoke out of turn. I thought all the subtle cues in body language were rather hysterical. I mean, we were talking about eliminating people's livelihoods here. Why not cut with the semantics?

Henry jumped back into the conversation and said, "Mike. The first thing you need to do, is remember, these aren't people you are firing. These are numbers on a spreadsheet. You're decreasing liabilities and increasing positive cash flow for the org. There is some light at the end of the tunnel."

"Right... it isn't personal, right? It's just business. No, I get it."

The utterance of those very words nearly made me vomit in my own mouth. For a moment there, I despised my subconscious for the proclamation of such corporate dribble. The thought of falling on my sword and quitting had crossed my mind.

"Exactly right", the group said in unison.

The group of consultants all nodded their heads at the same time, like a synchronized swimming team.

Clearly, this wasn't their first rodeo.

"How do you suggest I do that, exactly?"

"Simple Mike. Two words."

Henry wanted to add some weight behind his advice so he paused. He stuck out his hands and made the peace sign. He affirmed his statement and said, "Two words..."

I really wasn't in the mood for theatrics. I moved my shoulders and exaggerated my eyebrows in an attempt to get him to spit out the two words.

"Qualitative and Quantitative.", he said dramatically and magnanimously.

"Tell me more.", I said while shrugging off his comment.

"We use mostly objective assessments to determine the ongoing viability of a role. We have to ensure that the role is not redundant in nature. Sometimes we can over hire and have to right-size."

"Mostly objective? So..."

"A Role Specific Competency Correlation Assessment

to be precise."

"A competency correlation assessment. How exactly is that supposed to help?"

"Mike, how many salespeople did you bring on recently? How much did you staff up?

"I brought on nearly 100 insurance salespeople in the span of a few months."

"Perfect. One Hundred. A nice round number," he said as he softly clapped his hands together.

I could tell he was getting just a little too much enjoyment out of this whole thing.

"Here's what we can do. We create a test for each of the 100 employees. We can set the test to have an artificial 50% failure rate. Thus, 50% pass and 50% fail. The 50 people who fail the test will all lose their jobs. Nice and easy. Nice and objective."

"Uh-huh."

"I mean, objective enough to pass the smell test at least."

The group laughed out loud, like a laugh track on

those old 1950's style sitcoms.

"What do you mean objective enough?"

"We just need it to pass the smell test. That way we don't get sued. We want it to at least appear fair."

"Ah... You seem to have all this down to a science."

That statement seemed to really resonate with the consultants, because they each perked up a little bit.

"Figure it this way. You're paying most of these guys a salary, but the majority of the offer you made was for a non-vested equity position based on a variable pay-per-performance bonus structure. It was a huge gamble for these guys to come aboard, with a massive upside potential."

Henry started rubbing his hands together and almost began frothing at the mouth as he was laying down the groundwork for this mass layoff.

"The most we would calculate to pay in a wrongful termination lawsuit is one year of salary. Assuming it goes to legal action. And that's the worst-case scenario for the average Wrongful Termination lawsuit. Now you have 100 salespeople, we want to reduce that number by 50. Meaning, you have a salary total combined base of $5,000,000. Which would be our potential total exposure from a legal standpoint, assuming each lawsuit was average."

"Go on..."

"Believe it or not Mike, Attorneys are just like people. People do things for money. Let's say you have a wrongful termination lawsuit asking for $100,000. The attorney gets like 33% of that figure. The average cost of an attorney is $300 per hour, meaning they can work on that case for $33,000 divided by $300 per hour... or One Hundred and Eleven hours before they lose money. Each hour an attorney works on a case is a chomp into their profit margin. If we use an assessment it will dissuade attorneys from even taking on the case in the first place. In the event they do decide to sue, which we anticipate that figure to be about 15%, then we have the assessment as an objective measure for why we fired the person. We can dangle that assessment in front of the judge or use it as a bargaining chip to negotiate down our eventual settlement offer."

"I take it back. You have this down to an exact science."

"Look, it's not personal. It's just business."

"Just business," the other consultants chimed in together, like a church choir.

"We have to fire half of our recently acquired insurance agents two weeks before Christmas. I'd imagine it will seem rather personal to the people we fire."

"Mike. That is a great point. That's why we are going to offer a lucrative severance package to all employees who agree to an arbitration arrangement. Which will further reduce potential losses."

"Ah..."

"We're going to offer affected employees two weeks of severance pay."

"Two weeks? Two weeks per?"

"Two weeks in total. Pretty good. I know, right?"

"These people sold their agencies, quit their jobs and brought all of their clients over to Flushy. And for that..."

"And for that we are going to give them two weeks of pay. Pretty generous, I know. I mean, these are employees with less than a year with the org and they get two weeks of severance."

"Uh-huh."

"All jobs are temporary. Either you get fired, the company goes out of business, you get promoted, you get riffed, you die, etc. Every job comes with risk. The thing is Mike we need to be nimble; we need to be able to pivot and with a bloated salesforce, we are just unable to do that."

"We?"

"Well, you know what I mean. Flushy."

"Ah... Tell me more about the assessment."

"I thought you would never ask."

"Can you give me an example of some of the questions? I'm assuming they will be sales specific questions. I mean, these are salespeople we're talking about here."

"These are core competencies we are looking for in the future."

"What would those be?"

"Would you like me to give you an example?"

"I think that might help."

"If you're approached by a regulator and asked to provide information about Flushy. What should you do?"

The room became uncomfortably silent and the consultants all stared at me. I couldn't tell if they were baiting me into answering or just marinading the conversation.

"Are you asking me? Or..."

"No, no, no... Nothing like that. Your options are;

    A. provide the information,
    B. say nothing,
    C. refer them to management
    D. ignore the regulator."

I wanted to shake my head in disbelief, but made sure to keep my poker face on. What in the world does that have to do with selling insurance? The consultants began to stare at each other and gauge my reaction.

"Would you mind giving me another example?"

"Of course! We aim to please."

"A customer asks you to speak to a manager about a claim not being paid. What should you do? Pick from one of the options below:

A. tell your manager
B. don't return the call
C. tell the customer the payment is on the way without confirming
D. schedule a follow up appointment with the customer for another time hoping they will forget about it."

"Mm-hmm... Do you mind if I ask something Henry?"

"Mike, mind? I strongly encourage it."

"What exactly are the competencies of the future we are looking for with those kinds of questions?"

Henry slapped his knee and pointed at me. Henry

chuckled and looked around the room.

"That's classic Mike Allen right there."

"Classic", one of the other consultants said.

"Classic", the other consultant chimed in.

"Great question. Future state Flushy looks much different than current state Flushy. Let me put it this way. Do you like movies Mike?"

"Sure, who doesn't?"

"Do you mind if I use some hyperbole?"

"Oh, be my guest. I'm in sales not legal."

"We're looking for people to ride with us until the wheels fall off. We're looking mostly for loyalty; we're looking for people who know when to keep their mouth shut and most importantly when to do what they are told. In other words, we are looking for team players."

"You weren't joking about the hyperbole."

"Sorry to use all these colorful analogies. I find it helpful to paint a vivid picture. That way I know we're all on the same page."

"It really helps hammer home your point. So, how long is this assessment?"

"It's an 8-hour test designed to be completed in a single sitting. The test will ultimately tell the employee one of two things. If they fail, then we deem them incompetent. If they pass, then we deem them competent enough to keep their job."

"Ah. So, when do these tests get sent out to the employees?"

The consultants all started rotating their heads on a swivel looking at each other and then back at their watches.

"Today...", Henry said as he looked down at his watch.

"Today? You got to be kidding me, right?"

"In fact, right... about now. Right as we speak."

My immediate reaction was to scoff and murmur a sarcastic laugh.

"Wait. We're not giving any advanced notice?"

"Part of what we're looking for are people who can be agile, flexible and adaptable. How can we truly assess that characteristic if we give an advanced notice?"

"Well, when you put it so reasonably like that, that makes complete sense to me.", I said sarcastically.

I was being sarcastic, but I felt that was lost on the consultants. These consultants were all blunt instruments, the kind of instruments used to knock people over the head with.

"Mike, we weren't born yesterday. Clearly, you have some reservations with this whole process. Is that fair to say?"

"Am I that transparent?"

Apparently, I wasn't as slick as I thought I was.

"It's okay. Most people grapple with the process."

"Really? You *don't* say."

"Look at it this way Mike. This is simple addition through subtraction. It's really that straight forward. We're only as strong as our weakest link. It'd be a lot tougher if we had to make the decision from a position of weakness. We are making this from a position of strength."

"What do you mean?"

"I mean Flushy is about to pop an IPO and hit record profits this quarter. That means fat bonuses for everyone up stream and job security for those downstream. Imagine if we had to make these cuts if the business was struggling? The fact we are thriving now, means we shouldn't rest on our laurels."

"Uh-huh", I answered with trepidation.

"I mean, imagine what that would do to our bonuses?"

"Oh no, I couldn't even dream of that. What a shame that would be."

The consultants nodded in agreement. Again, my sarcasm fell on deaf ears.

"Now, we've automated most of the process for you at this point. Let everyone take the test today. If they have questions give them this email address."

It read,

HRAssessmentSolutionsQuestions@Flushy.com

"Okay, who monitors that email box?"

"What do you mean Mike?"

"I mean, who is on the other end of that email address?"

"What do you mean Mike?"

"I mean, if I send an email to that email address, who responds to it?"

"Well, that's the beauty of it Mike."

I looked at each of the consultants and waited for some kind of answer.

"No one."

"No one, what?"

"No one looks at that email address. It goes nowhere."

"So, you're telling me that you set up an email address for people to submit questions, but no one responds to, or even looks at the questions?"

"Correct."

"Okay. Well, let me ask you one more question."

"Shoot away."

"What if the employee refuses to or for some reason doesn't take the test?"

"That's a great question. A person who doesn't take the test gets a score of Zero."

"So... they fail?"

"They fail. I mean, that would be ideal, because it would sure make our job a lot easier. If they refuse, they lose."

My stomach started ripping out these loud inaudible gargling noises. For some reason, when I got super nervous I felt the urge to eat.

Grrrrrr... Blarggg...

"Well, I'm starving. How about we all head out and grab some lunch?"

And that's how the fate of half the employees at Flushy were decided. Three consultants decided the fate of thousands of employees. What could I say? Sometimes in life you do the chopping and sometimes in life you get chopped.

"Hahaha. Uh. Mike, that all sounds like a pretty wild ride, man."

"Robert, you don't know the half of it..."

Ultimately, I found myself right back where I started, slinging policies in the San Fernando Valley. Sitting in a moderately sized office strip mall, on the corner of first and nowhere. Don't worry, the irony was not lost on me. I started back at the bottom rungs of the insurance industry. Maybe that's precisely where I belonged. Robert hadn't changed a bit from the last time we spoke. Thinking about it, I really missed conceiving our random back and forth banter sessions.

Robert scoffed and said, "I knew you had the '*look*'. It was stamped across your forehead the second your strolled through those doors."

"The *look*?"

"Yeah, the *look*. You know, the look of unbridled ambition. Hey everybody, I'm too cool for school.

The look", Robert said with a patronizing tone.

"*Ah*, yes. The look."

Robert was captivated by the whole story. I mean, if it didn't sound so absurd, it might even make a great book. Robert leaned forward with both hands clasped around his coffee mug, he was hanging on my every word.

"Did you end up laying off all the Brokers?", he inquired with the similitude of a news reporter hot on a story.

"Robert, that's more of a second cup of coffee kind of conversation. Speaking of which, why don't we reload our mugs?"

Without uttering a word Robert downed what was left of his coffee and sprung up from his chair. As we got up from our chairs a large crackling sound rang off. Apparently, we'd been drenching the pleather in sweat for the last two hours. As we began to walk back to the breakroom Robert continued his inquisition.

"C'mon tell me what happened. Did you layoff

everyone or what?"

"It played out more or less like the consultants predicted."

"More or less?"

"I mean, you can't make an omelet without breaking a few eggs. After we initiated the headcount reductions, about ten-or-twenty of the employees turned state's evidence."

"Turned? What do you mean?"

"Well, John wasn't lying when he said the house of cards would come tumbling down quickly. They ratted on Flushy and on the way out took proprietary data with them to the FED, the District Attorney, well to anybody that would listen."

"Yeah, like what?"

"Well, just ticky-tack stuff. But, enough to get the ball of yarn to unravel."

"So, did you ever get in contact with the FBI guy... uh... John... John Daily?"

I couldn't help but react with a terse laugh.

"Ha! John Daily, it turns out that wasn't even his real name."

"Sneaky F-B-I Agents."

"Boy isn't that the understatement of the century."

Robert and I refilled our beverages then headed back to the salesfloor. I decided to take the sweetener back with me. Robert hadn't noticed at first. I started pouring the Irish crème sweetener into my mug. Robert looked at me with this disfigured expression.

"What did they do to you over there?"

"Robert, I'm now a man of refined tastes."

"Clearly. Did you want coffee with your creamer? Ha!"

As I finished pouring the sweetener it dawned on me that might make a perfect embarkation to continue with my earlier thought.

"What were we talking about again?"

"John Daily!", Robert eagerly said.

"Oh yes. John Daily. Something they kept out of the

headlines and financial gossip columns was what happened to John Daily. John put his orbit too close to the sun and got burned."

Robert began to drink his coffee slowly and methodically. This gave me plenty of room to hype up the story even more.

"Turns out his real name was Ralph Mancento. The kind of person, under better circumstances that I might actually consider being friends with."

"Well, spit it out. What happened to him?"

I didn't peep a word. Instead, I decided to stir the sweetener in my cup. I grabbed a spoon off my desk and started swirling it around in my mug. As it swirled the spoon occasionally made this annoying ding sound as it hit the edge of the cup.

"Ralph was caught by Flushy security snooping around after hours. He was poking his nose around where it didn't belong."

"So... How'd you find out?"

After stirring the cup for several seconds, I abruptly

and intentionally stopped. I held the mug close to my nose to appreciate the warm wafting aroma of the freshly brewed coffee.

"Who do you think called security on him?"

"You snitched on an FBI agent?"

"Well, in all fairness to me, it was dark and I saw someone rummaging around after hours. I didn't know who it was."

I took a big sip of that overly sweetened coffee. Man did it taste bad, but better than jail house coffee.

"Our security converged on him like a highly trained SWAT team and, well, did what they do best."

"What happened?"

"That night, I have no idea. The next day however...", I said trailing off.

I took a deep breath and gulped down the rest of my coffee.

"All I know is that the next day, someone found his body in a dumpster somewhere in East Los Angeles."

Robert was a loss for words, his jaw was practically on the floor.

"Yeah... that's not the worst of it."

"How could it possibly get any worse?", Robert pleaded.

"Oh... I was just about to find out."

I shook my head and took a deep breath.

"Todd Dupree..."

"Yeah. What happened to Todd Dupree?"

"That's, that's not an easy question to answer. I'm sure you read about it all in the papers. It was plastered all over the news for weeks."

"I did."

"Well, what'd you read in the papers?", I asked Robert with some trepidation and mystique.

"Todd was the mastermind behind the entire scheme. He fled to some non-extradition European country with all the money and left Flushy holding the bag."

"Uh-huh. That's what the papers said. Did they?"

Robert looked at me with an inquisitive grin. I could tell he was hooked, the feeling of having someone hang on your every word was quite intoxicating.

"Here's what you didn't read in the papers. Let me ask you something Robert. Are you familiar with the concept of a Tontine?"

"Nope. What is it?"

"Let's say you and me pool our resources together and put One-Hundred dollars a week in a bank account for fifty years."

"Okay..."

"What's going to happen if we combine funds for that many years?"

"Well, it's going to earn interest."

"A lot of interest. Gobs of money. Ding! Give that man prize," I said as I pointed to Robert.

"So..."

"So, the idea is that if one of the people in the

Tontine dies, the money is split among the surviving members of the Tontine."

"That sounds pretty great."

"Does it? Let me ask you something else."

"Shoot.", he said with fleeting interest.

"What if you're the one that dies? Better yet, what if the other members of the Tontine decided to eliminate you?"

"Eliminate me? Like, kick me out of the Tontine?"

"Eliminate you, as in Six-Feet under eliminate you."

"Oh..."

"Oh is right. The reason why Tontines are illegal, is that it creates a financial motivation for murdering the other members of the Tontine."

"So... what're you saying? What happened to Todd?"

"Todd was the one of the two founding members and majority interest holder in Flushy. Todd was an innovator. Todd was a victim of his own success. Todd was an unknowing participant in the world's largest Tontine."

Robert was speechless, at least until he finished off his cup of coffee.

"Tell me you at least got some of that sweet startup money out of this whole thing? What about the IPO? What about your equity in the company?"

"When we completed our second round of funding the valuation was anticipated to be in the ballpark of One Hundred billion dollars."

Robert nearly had a heart-attack. He grabbed his chest to exaggerate his excitement and surprise.

"So what happened when you guys went public? Mike, spill the beans man. C'mon!"

"What happened? As part of my contract, I had the option to purchase up to 50,000 shares of the IPO. The IPO had an initial price per stock of $1,000."

"Mike. You made $500,000,000? Are you telling me you walked away with Five Hundred Million dollars? And you ended right back up here, how?"

"No. Not exactly Robert."

"C'mon man. What happened?"

"As part of my plea deal, the government forced me to pay restitution to our victims. They froze my assets before I could even see the zeros hit my bank account."

Robert started laughing so hard his coffee nearly ran down his nose. In fact, we both laughed at my expense for a little bit. Robert covered his eyes rubbing his entire face with his two hands.

"I walked away with a bunch of goose-eggs and the pleasure of being a star witness in the world's largest Ponzi-scheme trial."

"Yeah, I read what happened to David."

I shook myself, "Hung himself in his prison cell, allegedly."

"Allegedly...", Robert replied in skeptical agreement.

We both shook our heads for a second, given the morbid nature of the conversation.

"You know the craziest part about that?", I asked Robert.

"What?"

"Turns out he didn't even have a life insurance policy.", I explained.

"Blah! What? Unreal.. How?"

"Yeah, what are the odds? Guess David was right, he wasn't a life insurance guy after all."

"The sixty-four-thousand-dollar question is Mike, how in the world did you end up working back here?"

I swirled my coffee around in my mug, making these long slow concentric circles. Admitting defeat wasn't something I was accustomed to.

"Well…"

"He came back to work here, because of common sense…"

Bill stepped into the foreground, cup of coffee in hand and a big fat grin on his face.

"He came back because he knew how good he had it here in the first place. That should be a the lesson for the lot of you. The grass ain't always greener on the other side."

"Good morning Bill", I responded as I turned around to greet my new boss. It turns out he was the same as my old boss.

He raised his mug up, it was a classic Bill way to greet someone. Something so simple, yet at the very same time something so gracious. Bill didn't have to say it, but he had I-told-you-so written all over his face. Ultimately, some of us float to the top and some sink to the bottom, but in the end we all get Flushed.

The End.

Made in the USA
Middletown, DE
21 April 2021